More praise for the N
Cats and Curios Mysteries

"Written with verve and panache."

—Carolyn Hart, national bestselling author of *What the Cat Saw*

"Quirky characters, an enjoyable mystery with plenty of twists, and cats, too! A fun read."

—Linda O. Johnston, author of the Pet Rescue Mysteries

"[A] wild, refreshing over-the-top-of-Nob-Hill thriller."

—*The Best Reviews*

"This exciting road trip goes from danger to humor and back as the adorable cats are brilliant tacticians who amusingly but cleverly maneuver the niece somewhat for treats but often to keep her safe. Fast-paced cozy readers who enjoy something different will relish the charming Cats and Curios Mysteries (see *Nine Lives Last Forever* and *How to Wash a Cat*) as Oscar's niece continues her dangerous adventures into the weird, whimsical world of her late uncle."

—*Genre Go Round Reviews*

"Whimsical . . . Contains a stunning clever twist . . . Cozy readers who enjoy something amusingly, satirically different will relish this."

—*Gumshoe Review*

"Full of quirky, yet credibly described characters . . . Intriguing . . . Doubly fun for those familiar with this beautiful city . . . This is a PURR-fect treat for feline and mystery fans alike! Warning: Like cat treats, this series may prove to be addictive!"

—*Fresh Fiction*

"[A] neatly constructed mystery . . . Cat fanciers will find plenty to love in these personified felines . . . The setting is very well drawn, old town San Francisco is well detailed, neatly blending into the more modern city."

—*The Mystery Reader*

Titles by Rebecca M. Hale

Cats and Curios Mysteries

HOW TO WASH A CAT
NINE LIVES LAST FOREVER
HOW TO MOON A CAT
HOW TO TAIL A CAT
HOW TO PAINT A CAT

Mysteries in the Islands

ADRIFT ON ST. JOHN
AFOOT ON ST. CROIX

HOW TO PAINT A CAT

REBECCA M. HALE

BERKLEY PRIME CRIME, NEW YORK

THE BERKLEY PUBLISHING GROUP
Published by the Penguin Group
Penguin Group (USA) LLC
375 Hudson Street, New York, New York 10014

USA • Canada • UK • Ireland • Australia • New Zealand • India • South Africa • China

penguin.com

A Penguin Random House Company

HOW TO PAINT A CAT

A Berkley Prime Crime Book / published by arrangement with the author

For information, address: The Berkley Publishing Group,
a division of Penguin Group (USA) LLC,
375 Hudson Street, New York, New York 10014.

ISBN: 978-0-425-25886-6

PUBLISHING HISTORY
Berkley Prime Crime mass-market edition / March 2014

PRINTED IN THE UNITED STATES OF AMERICA

10 9 8 7 6 5 4 3 2 1

Cover illustration by Mary Ann Lasher.
Cover design by Diana Kolsky.
Interior text design by Kristin del Rosario.

For Helen Hale, my grandmother

Introduction

IN A REMOTE corner of the Sonoma woods, far from the nearest public road, a man's humming floated up through the branches of an ancient redwood grove.

It was the only sound in the otherwise quiet forest. A damp winter mist hung in the air, an acoustic insulator that soaked up all but the most vigorously transmitted noise.

The source of the happy humming knelt by a fire pit in the middle of a small clearing. Built like a lumberjack, Sam Eckles sported a thick overgrown beard and a mass of tangled red hair, both of which threatened to ignite as he paused his singing to puff on the embers in the bottom of the pit.

The rest of the rustic campsite featured a tiny tin-roofed cabin, a few fallen logs used as benches, and a hammock strung between the gnarled trunks of two redwoods.

"Ah, there she is," Sam whispered as a flame flickered in the charred remains of the fire he'd stoked earlier that morning. Leaning back on the heels of his thick-soled hiking boots, he placed a metal rack over the pit and positioned its foldout legs so that the grated surface would be centered over the heat.

Two bright green frogs sat on a log a few feet away, watching as Sam nursed the flame, slowly feeding in kindling. They had observed the procedure countless times since the group's arrival at the campsite last November, but the amphibian pair never seemed to tire of staring at the fire's dancing orange light.

Before long, Sam had built a blaze suitable for cooking. He slid a cast-iron skillet filled with cooking grease onto the grate and waited for its temperature to rise. Once the grease melted and began to pop in the pan, he reached for a paper bag containing two dozen raw chicken legs mixed with a specially formulated flour coating. Folding over the bag's top edges to secure the contents inside, he gave the bag a vigorous shake. Despite the sealing precaution, a cloud of flour filled the air, leaving a white dusting on his red beard.

After a few choking coughs, Sam picked up a pair of metal tongs, slid the pointed ends into the sack, and began fishing out the legs. It was a tricky procedure, but he missed only once as he dropped each piece of battered meat into the hot skillet. Then he covered the meal with a metal lid and sat back to wait.

As the legs began to simmer, the scent of crisping chicken wafted toward the cabin, drifting through its open doors and windows.

Inside, an elderly man with thinning white hair and short rounded shoulders stood in front of a two-by-six canvas propped onto an easel. Holding a pencil-thin paintbrush in his hand, he leaned toward the painting, squinting at the densely populated street scene spread across much of its surface.

A weariness tinged the man's graying blue eyes, and there was a tired slump to his already bent posture. He felt as if he had aged more in the past two months than in the previous two years combined.

Painting was strenuous work, even for someone with his skills, but it was critical that he get each brushstroke right. The finished product was destined for a public location in downtown San Francisco, where it would have an important message to convey.

The piece was a re-creation of a much larger mural, one composed during the Great Depression for the interior of a well-known San Francisco landmark. It was an exact replica—with a few subtle differences.

The painter checked the emerging image against a color photocopy of the original; then he dabbed his brush into a palette of paints.

His arthritic hands ached from the hours of tension, but he ignored the pain, spurred on by the knowledge that this project might be his life's last significant contribution.

"Hey, Oscar. You ready for a break?" Sam called out from his cooking station by the fire. "Lunch will be ready soon."

The old man set down his brush and stepped to the cabin door. Massaging a stitch in his lower back, he looked out over the campsite. As he breathed in the welcome aroma smoking up from the fire pit, he glanced into the woods.

A white cargo van was parked in the brush beyond the clearing. He and Sam had covered the roof with camouflage-colored netting to ensure that the vehicle wouldn't be spotted from the air.

He stroked his chin, pondering the rash of fresh dents along the van's metal sides and front bumper.

The vehicle had taken a beating during their off-road journey through the woods to the campsite, but it had managed the task admirably. Whether the van would survive the return trip, however, was still an open question.

Putting those concerns aside, Oscar joined Sam by the fire. For the time being, all that mattered was that they were safely hidden.

An owl hooted down from the dizzying heights above the camp, and the old man craned his neck to look up, marveling at the site's concealed location. He and Sam were but two dots of flesh in a vast wilderness of green.

Their campsite was situated on a private parcel of land, which was, in turn, surrounded by acres of public forest.

For the last century, the property had been owned by a secretive group of artists, businessmen, and politicians, formally known as the Bohemian Club. The members valued seclusion over ease of access, and the camp was located in one of the property's most remote locations.

It was the perfect hiding spot for a pair of fugitives.

The duo had fled San Francisco in November following the gruesome murder of a City Hall intern. So far, the police had been unable to definitively link them to the young man's slaying, but as they had last been seen fleeing the crime scene, they were now the primary suspects.

In the eyes of the investigators, the pair's sudden disappearance had only confirmed their guilt.

The humans', that is—the frogs were just along for the ride.

The Portrait Sketch

Chapter 1

THE ARTISTIC ADVISER

"STOP FIDGETING!"

A cold drizzle soaked San Francisco, trickling down steep sidewalks and funneling through gutters and drains. The moisture had settled into every crack and crevice, sending a shiver through the hardiest of the city's weatherworn residents.

But the owner of the Green Vase antique shop would rather have been anywhere else other than inside her nice warm store. She'd been trapped there for more than two hours, posing for her neighbor, Montgomery Carmichael, as he worked on a sketch that he intended to use as the basis of a painted portrait.

An area had been cleared in the center of the showroom, providing space for the artist and his equipment. He'd set up a full-sized easel on the wooden floor and propped a large sketchpad on its frame. A toolbox filled with an assortment of charcoal pencils and replacement leads lay open at his feet.

Monty's busy hands rotated a flat-sided charcoal pencil as he scraped the stylus across the textured paper, adding depth and shading to the sketch. Every so often he looked up from the drawing and compared it to the real-life model seated just a few feet away.

The woman sat on the cushions of a leather recliner once used by the patients of a Gold Rush–era dentist. A display of gold teeth, rusty pliers, and other rudimentary dental equipment had been positioned to her left. Additional antiques were arrayed to her right and behind the chair, providing further background material for the painting.

The artist's brow furrowed with concentration, reflecting a level of intensity far out of proportion to the simple sketch he'd initially described, and the woman wondered, not for the first time, what was really being drawn on the opposite side of the easel.

Monty had already blackened and rejected several pieces of paper over the course of the lengthy posing session, and she was quickly losing patience with the process.

This would be his final attempt—if for no other reason than to avert a mutiny.

A frustrated sigh weighed in over the pencil's etching.

"Couldn't you just take a photo and work from that?"

Monty snorted a rebuke. He tapped the pointed toe of his dress shoe against the floor; his thin lips tensed into a stern expression.

"As if I could use a two-dimensional image," he muttered with a dismissive *pfft*. "I'm not scribbling on the side of a cereal box, you know."

He pointed the charcoal pencil at the recliner and repeated his order.

"Stop fidgeting!"

RESIGNING HERSELF TO a few more minutes of picture-posing torture, the woman took in a deep breath and straightened her shoulders. She shifted her weight ever so slightly, trying not to disturb the fluffy orange and white cat sprawled across her lap.

Rupert let out a wheezing snore as he burrowed his furry

face into his person's knees. The plump feline didn't mind the extended sitting session. He could pose for hours—so long as it was in a sleeping position.

He rolled sideways, exposing the round bulge of his stomach. His mouth opened into a wide yawn as he stretched his front legs up and over his orange-tipped ears.

Groggily smacking his lips together, he raised himself into a sitting position. After a quizzical gaze at the back side of the easel, he threw his head and shoulders into a vibrating shake. Then he collapsed back onto the lap and immediately returned to a state of peaceful slumber.

As Rupert exhaled a wheezing snore, a tuft of white cat hair floated up from his body, slowly traveling toward his person's face.

Puckering her lips, the woman blew out a steady stream of air, trying to divert the downy clump's course, to no avail. As it rose higher and higher, drifting ever closer to her nose, the first hallmarks of a sneeze tickled her sinuses.

Her eyes began to water. Her nasal passages started to twitch.

"Ah . . . Ah . . . Ah-*choo*!"

The high-pitched sneeze brought a second reproachful glare from the artist. As Monty tutted his disapproval, a second cat of similar coloring but far sleeker physique peeked around the edge of the easel.

The cat perched on a round stool that typically resided behind the cashier counter. It had been moved to the center workspace to provide an elevated ledge where she could monitor Monty's progress.

Isabella gazed keenly at the leather recliner. Her blue eyes swept from her brother's snoozing heap to her person's watering eyes. She made a series of sharp clicking sounds with her mouth; then she disappeared once more behind the wooden frame and tapped a padded paw against the paper.

"I agree, Issy," Monty said as he resumed his sketching. "We need a little more detail in that quadrant over there."

"How much longer is this going to take?" the woman asked wearily. "My feet are falling asleep."

"It would go a lot faster if you would stop jiggling around," Monty replied, his focus still trained on the sketchpad.

"I haven't moved," she protested indignantly.

A quick rebuttal came from the feline artistic supervisor hidden behind the easel.

"Mrao."

Chapter 2

THE TROUBLE WITH NEIGHBORS

MONTY POPPED HIS head up over the easel and stared at his subject. His thin mouth twitched in critical assessment as he tapped the blunt end of the charcoal pencil against his chin.

"Try tilting your head up and a little to the right," he instructed, skewing his face to squint with one eye.

"Why did I let you talk me into this?" the woman muttered before reluctantly complying.

Staring up at the ceiling of the Green Vase antique shop, she thought back to the conversation earlier that morning that had led to the portrait-posing marathon.

"A few minutes of your time," Monty had falsely assured her. "That's all I'm asking. Just a quick sketch. I'll do the rest in my studio. You can sit comfortably on the recliner while I work. You won't even notice I'm here."

I should have known better, the woman thought ruefully. Monty's schemes rarely concluded without some form of nuisance or bother.

She paused, reflecting on their previous misadventures.

By Monty's standards, this latest intrusion was only a minor inconvenience.

"I guess I should consider myself lucky," she mused as she listened to him converse with Isabella on the opposite side of the easel.

"It could have been worse."

THE DARK-HAIRED WOMAN had plenty of experience dealing with the neurotic man sketching her portrait. For the last two years, Montgomery Carmichael had been a constant, pestering presence in her life—like a persistent weed that continually regrew despite all attempts to remove it.

From the moment she inherited the Green Vase antique shop from her uncle Oscar and moved into the apartment that occupied the two floors above its showroom, Monty had managed to insert himself into almost every aspect of her daily routine. His art studio on the opposite side of the street provided an excellent vantage point from which to observe her building, and he made frequent trips across the twenty-foot distance to chat, pry, or otherwise meddle in her affairs.

No wonder Oscar faked his own death to get out of this place, she thought with a grin.

Her wry expression quickly faded to a frown.

Even after all this time, it was difficult for her to reconcile the man she'd once known as her curmudgeonly uncle with the shadowy figure he had morphed into following his artfully crafted—and artificial—demise.

A gust of wind swept through Jackson Square's misty tree-lined streets, smattering raindrops against the shop's front windows. Rivulets ran down the glass, blurring the images on the opposite side—a match to the confused and conflicted emotions swirling through the niece's head.

Her uncle's many transformations and myriad disguises had allowed him to do more than just escape an irritating neighbor.

Using his talents, Oscar had delved deep into San Francisco's colorful past, unearthing information about lives lived long ago—along with many valuable treasures the deceased had left behind. He had snooped through dusty attics, warehouses, bank vaults, and refuse heaps—anyplace where forgotten artifacts might lay hidden.

The niece glanced down at the shop's wooden floor, thinking of the boxes and crates stashed in the basement below, a holding that represented the bulk of her uncle's collection. There were books, photos, and newspaper clippings as well as broken dishes and rusty lamps. Hulking pieces of furniture stood draped in dusty drop cloths, their drawers filled with an array of tiny trinkets, knickknacks, and dime-store souvenirs.

To the untrained eye, it looked like a room filled with junk. Indeed, most of the items had been discarded by their previous owners, who were apparently unaware of the pieces' underlying value.

The niece grimaced as she pictured the disorganized scene below. Her first instinct had been to rent a moving truck, load up all of the boxes and crates, and haul the mess to the dump. Two years later, the rationale behind much of her uncle's vast collection was still a mystery to her. He meted out clues and guidance in discrete, often coded, morsels.

Oscar's secretive methods—while frustrating to his niece—reflected more than just eccentricity.

In addition to the physical objects stored in the basement, her uncle had uncovered countless intangible secrets, many of them related to people in powerful positions of politics and industry.

Her uncle might still be running the Green Vase, the woman reflected, if not for this second aspect of his work.

The insights he had gained into the city's inner workings had been an enticing lure for mischief. The temptation to tinker and manipulate had been too great. Few areas were off limits to the intrigues of Oscar and his crew of like-minded Bohemians. They had influenced the outcome of city referendums, controversial ordinances, and, of course, the selection of the pending interim mayor.

The niece felt a knot of worry tighten in the pit of her stomach.

It had been two months since she'd last heard from Oscar, and she was growing more and more concerned. She would gladly take one of his cryptic messages over this long stretch of silence.

She feared her uncle's latest scheme might have landed him in more trouble than even he could outmaneuver.

Chapter 3

THE IMPROBABLE SELECTION

"PULL YOUR SHOULDERS back," Monty barked, returning the niece's attention to the showroom. "Your posture's gone soft. You're all slumped over."

Isabella peeked around the easel to warble her concurrence.

The woman directed her glare at the artist.

"That's enough, Monty. I don't care what high-and-mighty position you've been appointed to. You've got five more minutes. Then I'm kicking you out."

THE PORTRAIT—IF indeed Monty ever finished it—was intended to be a memento of his humble Jackson Square beginnings, the unlikely launching pad for his now burgeoning political career.

Monty planned to hang the painting in his new office suite at City Hall, where, in a few days' time, he would be inaugurated as San Francisco's next mayor.

Like most residents, Oscar's niece still found it hard to

believe that her wacky neighbor had been appointed to the city's top governmental position. While the town had a long tradition of colorful, often eccentric leaders, Monty's inexplicable rise to power represented one of the most bizarre episodes in recent memory.

It all began last November after the city's sitting mayor was elected to the state office of lieutenant governor. The task of selecting his replacement fell to the San Francisco board of supervisors, a legislative body made up of representatives from each of the city's eleven districts. The interim mayor would fill the vacancy for an abbreviated term until the next election cycle.

The board meeting had opened with no clear contenders. While many of the supervisors would have preferred to fill the mayoral position themselves, few were willing to support the nomination of a fellow board member for the slot. The contentious meeting dragged on for hours with no end in sight as numerous candidates were proposed and multiple votes taken. Not one of the nominees could garner the necessary six-vote majority.

The board members had reached a state of sheer exhaustion when Monty's name was put forward.

The suggestion drew chuckles from the packed audience. Most thought it was a joke, a much-needed amusement to relieve the tension that had built up over the course of the lengthy meeting.

To the surprise of most observers, including the local political punditry, Monty was unanimously approved as the interim mayor.

THE LANKY ART dealer with curly brown hair and an extensive collection of whimsical cuff links appeared to have few qualifications for the job. His only work experience entailed running his Jackson Square art studio and serving as the outgoing mayor's personal life coach—a position that had been serially mocked in the editorial pages of the San Francisco newspaper.

The supervisors had declined to explain the rationale behind their peculiar mayoral choice. Most had immediately embarked on extended holiday vacations, effectively avoiding public questioning. The local news media, along with their assorted political consultants, were left scratching their heads.

How could a Machiavellian maneuver of this magnitude have slipped past their collective radar? How could they have been so effectively duped? Surely there must have been signs that they missed, some indication that the board members were secretly leaning toward this ridiculous selection?

A guilty blush reddened the faces of the city's press corps, reflecting their inner shame at having failed to warn the citizenry of the supervisors' impending decision.

Publically, of course, there were no apologies. The media pinned the blame squarely on the board members.

The day-after headlines predicted a future of gloom and doom. The following morning, a line of bold black print ran across the top of the newspaper's front page:

**SUPS SHOCK THE CITY—
PREPARE FOR MONTY-GEDDON!**

TO BE FAIR, in the days leading up to the vote, the city's cadre of esteemed reporters had been distracted by a competing storyline, one far more compelling than the mundane selection of an interim mayor.

Like everyone else in the Bay Area, the media had been fixated on the theft of Clive, San Francisco's celebrity albino alligator.

Less than a week before the supervisors' historic meeting, the prized gator had been stolen from the aquarium at the California Academy of Sciences, an esteemed science museum in Golden Gate Park. Nefarious persons, as yet unknown, had removed Clive from his Swamp Exhibit in the middle of the night, leaving behind only a trail of dehydrated fish biscuits, the gator's favorite snack, which had been used to lure him from his enclosure.

With no leads or letters for ransom, the situation seemed dire. Just when authorities began to fear that Clive had been chopped into albino-themed sushi and his rare hide tooled for designer leather handbags, the police received a tip. The alligator had been sighted in an unusual location—among the shoppers at San Francisco's Union Square.

Clive was soon making appearances at random spots across the city: strolling along the sidewalk outside the South of Market ballpark, ambling among the buskers at Fisherman's Wharf, and lounging on the bench seat of a Powell Street cable car.

There was something odd about the rogue alligator's wanderings, other than the crowded places he chose to pop up. In addition to his apparent fondness for sightseeing, the renegade swamp creature began accessorizing his scaly white body with an assortment of scarves, hats, and false beards. The costumes grew more elaborate at each stop.

With the public captivated by the alligator's shenanigans, the city's news professionals found themselves in a heated competition to provide the best and most recent footage. As reporters ran themselves ragged trying to keep up with the elusive Clive, the comparatively mundane developments at City Hall fell by the wayside.

The alligator prank eventually culminated in Clive's discovery at Mountain Lake, a small body of water on the south side of the Presidio. Other than yearning for his heated rock at the aquarium's Swamp Exhibit, Clive was unharmed and in good spirits. He was found a mere forty-five minutes after the completion of the board of supervisors' marathon mayoral selection meeting.

The coincidence of the two seemingly unrelated events—Monty's appointment and Clive's recapture—prompted numerous conspiracy theories.

Some thought the alligator chase might have been a ruse designed to divert attention away from the supervisors' scurrilous behind-the-scenes negotiations. Or maybe the supervisors had been blackmailed into making their Monty decision, with Clive being held as alligator ransom to ensure their compliance.

Rumors that the interim mayor himself was complicit in an alligator-related plot began to circulate—speculations that were fueled by the publication of a cell phone video showing soon-to-be Mayor Carmichael in a wet suit and snorkel mask tromping through the reeds of Mountain Lake, tossing his flippers into the air as he fled the gator's glowing white jaws.

THE NIECE EASED herself forward in the leather recliner, causing the worn seat cushions to creak.

She had her own theories about the mysteries surrounding Monty's improbable mayoral endorsement, but she kept them to herself. As for his involvement in the alligator antics, that much was a given. Monty had driven the niece and her two cats to Mountain Lake to assist him in the operation. She had witnessed the snorkel incident firsthand—although in the commotion surrounding Monty's near alligator-annihilation, she'd failed to notice the hidden observer who had filmed the infamous cell phone footage.

Regardless, the niece reflected as she rotated her head sideways to ease a stiffness in her neck, once Monty was ensconced at City Hall, he would be spending a lot less time in his Jackson Square art studio. Likely, he would have to shutter his shop while he pursued his daily mayoral duties.

A mirage of Monty-free months stretched out across her future horizon. The prospect was almost too good to be true.

She might even start to miss her crazy neighbor, she concluded with a blissful smile—at least until the next election.

Suddenly, Monty slammed his charcoal pencil onto the easel's bottom ledge, snapping the lead. Ripping off the top sheet from the sketchpad, he wadded it into a ball and threw it to the floor in disgust.

Then again, the niece thought with a sigh—probably not.

Isabella peered around the side of the easel. Twitching her whiskers, she gave her person a knowing look.

"Mrao."

Chapter 4
THE FACE

MONTY SCOOPED UP what was left of the charcoal pencil and tossed it into the air. He watched the slender stick tumble end over end. Then with a well-timed swipe, he caught it in his hand.

Clutching the pencil in his fist, he set off on a frustrated circle through the showroom.

"Every time I try to sketch this scene, it falls apart when I get to the face." He blew air through his lips, causing them to vibrate. "I just can't get it to come together properly. Something's not right." He gave the pencil another toss. "I've never had such difficulty capturing an image."

The niece gently dropped Rupert to the floor and stood from the recliner.

"Which face?" she asked warily. "Rupert's or mine?"

Blinking sleepily, Rupert yawned himself awake. After a deep lunging stretch, he waddled beneath the easel to where Monty had thrown the crumpled piece of paper. His feather duster tail swished back and forth as he inspected the discarded drawing.

Dropping his chin to the ground, Rupert slid a front paw

forward, turned it sideways, and swatted at the balled-up paper, sending the wad skidding across the floor and under a display table.

"Rupert isn't the problem," Monty said as he once more lobbed the pencil into the air. "I've got a perfect feline model."

He gazed warmly down at Rupert—or, at least, his fluffy rear end. The cat's front half was wedged beneath the display table, where he was trying to reach the crumpled paper ball.

Distracted by Rupert's antics, Monty missed the pencil's downward arc. It clattered onto the floor, instantly transforming into a new cat toy, one that was far easier to reach.

As Rupert scooted after the pencil, Monty plopped onto the vacant leather chair and pulled the recline lever. With a creaking *whomp*, the seat shifted into its flattest horizontal position.

"I think it's the nose that's bothering me," Monty said, throwing his arms back and cupping his hands behind his head. "The shape is off."

The woman folded her arms in front of her chest. "What's wrong with my nose?" she demanded testily.

Rupert captured the wayward pencil. Holding it trapped beneath his paw, he gave it an investigative sniff. After tentatively mouthing the distasteful charcoal lead, he spat out the pencil and returned his attention to the crumpled paper.

Sliding like a dust mop across the slick wood flooring, he reached once more beneath the display table. This time, he managed to tap the wad of paper with the tip of an extended front claw, sending it flying toward the recliner.

The pudgy cat continued the chase, bumping into table legs and the bottom facing of a bookcase during an increasingly wild pursuit.

Fully extended across the recliner, Monty crossed his legs at the ankles and squinted up at the ceiling.

"Then there's the chin," he murmured thoughtfully. His face contorted into a sour expression as he envisioned the sketched image. "I just can't get the dimple right."

"I don't have a dimple on my chin!" the niece sputtered indignantly.

Despite the temptations of the clattering pencil and the skittering clump of paper, Isabella had maintained a dignified stance on her seat by the easel. But as Rupert once more careened past on the floor beneath her, she couldn't help joining in the play.

With a flying leap, she bounded after her brother. A rolling ball of cat fur ensued, leaving the crumpled paper abandoned in a corner.

Stepping gingerly around the wrestling feline pair, the woman bent to pick up the abandoned drawing.

"Painter's block," Monty muttered at the ceiling. "That's what I have. Instead of being stymied on a word, I'm struggling with an image."

In typical fashion, he had ignored the niece's previous comments. It wasn't an unusual response, just one of many in his repertoire of annoying mannerisms.

His stance swiftly changed, however, when he noticed the woman's movement toward the crumpled sketch.

"Oh no," he gasped, lunging off the recliner. "No, no, no. You can't look at that. It's not ready."

The niece paused, her eyes slanting suspiciously.

It was only a short hesitation. Before Monty could reach her, she scooped up the paper and sprinted toward the front of the showroom. Monty followed, his long arms flailing as he tried to grab the wad of paper.

Reaching the cashier counter, the niece tugged at the edges of the sheet, spreading it across the counter's flat surface. Her brow furrowed in confusion.

"This doesn't look anything like me!" she exclaimed as Monty clambered up behind her. She jabbed her finger at the human figure in the drawing. "This person is wearing a baseball cap and high-top sneakers . . ."

Monty snatched the paper from her grasp, but she had already seen the entire sketch.

"And it's a *man*," she finished, perplexed. "Monty," she said, placing her hands on her hips, "what's going on?"

Her chatty neighbor suddenly lost his voice. Inexplicably mute, his freckled face blanched to a shade of pasty pale.

Shaking his head, Monty shoved the paper into his pocket. He returned to the center of the room, collapsed the easel to its folded position, and headed for the exit.

The woman watched as he squeezed the easel and the sketch pad through the doorway and hurried across the rainy street to his studio.

Pondering, she bent to pick up the charcoal pencil from the floor. Slowly rotating it in her hands, she reflected on the sketched picture.

Try as she might, she couldn't think why Monty would have replaced her position in the drawing with the image of Spider Jones—the young intern who was murdered in City Hall the same night the board of supervisors met to select the interim mayor.

Chapter 5

THE DISAPPEARANCE

"WHAT IS WRONG with that man?" the niece murmured as she slipped the charcoal pencil into a drawer behind the cash register.

Isabella gave her person a blank stare, the feline version of a shrug. The woman's question required far too long and complicated of an answer for the cat to attempt a verbal response. And besides, she reasoned, it was unlikely her human would have understood the explanation.

Still puzzling over the image of the dead intern in Monty's sketch, the niece walked around the counter to the front door and propped it open so that she could get a clearer view of the art studio across the street. The rain streaked down the studio's front windows, but a light had been turned on in the main room. While still blurry, it was possible for her to see inside.

Isabella joined her person in the doorway, and the two of them watched Monty's slim figure pace around a row of easels. He appeared to be engaged in an animated conversation, agitatedly throwing his hands in the air as he stormed back and forth.

The niece shook her head, relieved not to be on the receiving end of this overwrought display of emotion.

The rant reached a fever pitch as Monty stopped and grabbed a picture frame from a stack near his desk. His narrow face howled in a silent scream as he raised the frame over his head, waved it threateningly at the ceiling, and slammed it onto the ground. Then he proceeded to stomp on the frame's wooden boards, jumping up and down until he slipped and fell backward onto the floor.

The woman frowned. The behavior was odd, even for Monty. She squinted through the window, her eyes searching the corners of the art studio, but as far as she could tell, Monty was alone in the room.

THE NIECE CLOSED the door, turning away from the scene across the street, but she continued to ponder her neighbor's strange actions. Who was he talking to over there in his art studio and why had he thrown such a tantrum?

Her earlier questions remained just as puzzling. Why had he superimposed the image of the murdered intern into her spot on the recliner?

"And why did he make me sit there all that time if I wasn't even in the picture?" she demanded aloud in frustration. She felt like stomping on a picture frame herself. "The nerve of that man."

Isabella looked up at the niece, her furry brow crinkling as she contemplated a response.

The cat kept close surveillance on the Green Vase and its surroundings. As usual, she knew far more about the goings on in Jackson Square than her person.

Deciding it was worth a try, Isabella emitted a series of sharp clicking sounds, an eloquent attempt to describe what was tormenting their neighbor, but at the sight of the woman's confused expression, the cat cut short her commentary and reverted to the blank stare.

"Spider Jones," the niece said softly, setting Monty's problems aside as she returned to the topic that had started the day's trouble. "What's all this got to do with the murdered intern?"

Stroking Isabella's soft fur, the woman reviewed what she knew about the horrific crime. The story had been widely reported in the press, and the niece, like the rest of San Francisco, had read all the gory details.

The grisly scene had played out on the second floor of City Hall, inside a specially designated area called the ceremonial rotunda.

Located at the top of the building's central marble staircase, the elevated platform provided one of the best views of the building's soaring dome and ornate interior. A circular third-floor balcony directly above the small round space conveyed an extra element of fairy-tale mystique. It had been a favorite spot for wedding ceremonies—at least, until last November's murder.

The crime took place less than an hour after the completion of the supervisors' interim mayor meeting. City Hall had emptied out as soon as the marathon session finished. The intern was one of the few people still left inside the building when the interior lighting dimmed to its nighttime security setting.

The assailant had apparently approached Spider from behind, reaching around the young man's torso to stab him in the chest. Multiple blows followed in quick succession, an act of both strength and dexterity. Forensic experts estimated that the entire event, from start to finish, spanned less than a minute.

By the time anyone realized what had happened, it was too late to save the young intern. His body was found in a pool of blood in the middle of the ceremonial rotunda—just a few feet away from the memorial bust of Supervisor Harvey Milk, who, along with Mayor Moscone, was slain in City Hall more than thirty years earlier.

TWO MONTHS AFTER the tragic death, interest in the victim continued to surge. Spider Jones had become a macabre celebrity. Posthumously, his grinning face was one of the most well known in the Bay Area.

Family pictures of the cheerful dark-skinned lad in a baseball cap and high-top canvas sneakers had been widely circulated by the media. Every aspect of his short life had been extensively investigated and reported.

Just a year out of high school, Spider was a local boy, born and raised in the East Bay suburb of Walnut Creek. He still lived at home with his mother and younger siblings. For the last several months, he had been taking the BART train into the city for an unpaid intern position with the outgoing mayor.

In the days following his death, Spider's tearful mother had given a heart-rending interview, praising her son as a good-natured young man who had enjoyed being outdoors, eating spicy takeout food, and riding his bike. He had recently retaken his SATs and had hoped to be admitted to UC Berkeley for its upcoming fall semester. Sadly, his college acceptance letter had arrived days after his death.

Like everyone else with an interest in local politics, Spider had been hanging out at City Hall the night of the supervisors' meeting, eagerly awaiting the results of the interim mayor selection.

Once the meeting concluded, he had worked for a short while in his basement cubicle. Later, he had planned to meet a friend in North Beach for a bite to eat. Police speculated that he was preparing to leave the building when the murder occurred, although they were at a loss to explain why his body was found in the second floor's ceremonial rotunda.

Spider's mother hadn't been concerned about his absence that night. Her son was a night owl, she explained, and he routinely worked late into the evening. The night of his murder, she had gone to bed without worry, expecting to feed him breakfast the next morning.

It wasn't until she received the middle-of-the-night phone call from the police that she learned the terrible news.

THE NIECE RUBBED her temples, once more envisioning the sketch Monty had drawn on the textured art paper. After weeks of saturated news footage, the face of the murdered intern was permanently inked on the subconscious of most San Franciscans, but that didn't explain why Monty had inserted the man into the drawing.

Of course, in the two years since she'd first met Montgomery Carmichael, she'd failed to understand the motivations behind most of his actions.

With a sigh, she wandered through the showroom to the dentist recliner, the spot where she had posed for the ill-fated sketch. Isabella followed closely behind, her dainty feet soundless on the wooden floorboards.

The woman circled the leather chair, thinking of the distinctive image of Spider Jones on the crumpled paper. The insertion of the dead man—and her omission—were the only aspects of the drawing that departed from the posed setting. The surrounding Gold Rush relics had been replicated with meticulous precision; the fluffy round cat lazily stretched across the young man's lap had been an exact duplicate.

The real-life Rupert lay sprawled across the recliner's leather cushions. His brief burst of frenetic energy had quickly dissipated following the earlier race around the room, and he had retaken his spot on the chair for a midmorning nap.

The chair was still reclined into its flat, horizontal position, the setting in which Monty had left it when he leaped up to chase after the niece and the discarded sketch.

Gently rolling Rupert to one side, the niece slid onto the seat beside him. As the cat wheezed out a peaceful snore, the niece's thoughts returned to Spider's murder.

DESPITE THE INTENSE public interest in the crime, the police had yet to make any arrests. Given the height and direction of the knife wounds, the perpetrator was believed to be of short to medium build, but despite the vast amount of blood spilled, no other substantive clues had been left in the ceremonial rotunda. Even the murder weapon remained as yet unaccounted for.

In the days following the incident, several people known

to have been at or near the scene that night were interviewed and, one by one, dismissed from consideration—leaving as the main suspects two men seen fleeing the building in the minutes after the murder.

The first was a tall burly man with flaming-red hair, quickly identified as former City Hall janitor turned amphibian specialist Sam Eckles. The day after the murder, Sam failed to turn up for his current consulting position with the California Academy of Sciences. His name and photo had been widely distributed, but his whereabouts were still unknown.

The second fugitive's description was more nebulous in nature. An older gentleman with a balding head and short rounded shoulders, his identity was at first a mystery.

Soon after, however, the police issued a bulletin seeking information on fried chicken entrepreneur James Lick, the front man for a North Beach fried chicken restaurant—and Uncle Oscar's most recent alias.

THE NIECE THREADED her fingers into Rupert's fur, anxiously running them through his fuzzy coat. Despite the suspicious circumstances, she refused to believe that Sam and her uncle were responsible for the intern's gruesome slaying.

Sam was a gentle soul, intimidating in size and frequently off-putting in odor and personal hygiene. But the frog whisperer's large hands had held the tiniest and most delicate of tree frogs. His mannerisms struck some as strange, but he was fundamentally incapable of harming another living being.

The niece felt similar confidence in her uncle's innocence. Even after his last two years of clandestine activity, it was impossible for her to imagine him taking such a violent, malicious action.

And yet, she thought pensively, the day of the murder, Lick's fried chicken shop had been emptied out and shuttered. All of the pots, pans, and cooking implements had vanished—along with her uncle.

Rupert let out a sleepy grunt of protest at the woman's nervous tug on his fur. She couldn't convince herself that the intern's death was totally unrelated to Oscar's disappearance.

Reaching for the lever at the base of the chair, she pulled herself into an upright position. The chair back clicked into its vertical slot, but her fingers remained tightly wrapped around the metal handle.

There was one more troubling fact she couldn't dismiss.

Her uncle's short-statured height fit the only description thus far known about Spider's assailant.

Chapter 6

A CLAIRVOYANT CAT

ISABELLA PERCHED ON the edge of a display table, staring curiously at the leather recliner where the niece sat. The tip end of the cat's orange and white striped tail strummed the table surface as she tilted her head inquisitively.

Isabella and her person had been living together for several years now, and the cat was adept at reading the woman's thoughts. She knew the murder at City Hall and the possible connection to Oscar's disappearance had been weighing heavily on the niece's mind.

It was too bad that humans had such limited means of communication, Isabella reflected with a superior twitch of her whiskers. If only the niece spoke the cat's more sophisticated language, Isabella could have given her a great deal of useful information—about more than just Oscar and the murdered intern.

To start with, there were a number of minor everyday events that her person's less advanced faculties simply missed or glossed over.

For instance, Isabella knew that a brightly colored cat toy had recently fallen into the dirty clothes hamper. The catnip-filled packet was likely to cause the niece great consternation after the next wash cycle. Isabella had tried every possible means to alert the niece to this hazard, to no avail. The woman was destined to find the toy's disintegrated remains in the dryer vent and strewn throughout the washed clothing.

Then there was the large hairball that Rupert had coughed up beneath the couch in the second-floor living quarters. Isabella had been monitoring the cylindrical-shaped lump for several days. It had almost cured to the optimal weight and soft, spongy texture.

Late one night when her unsuspecting person was on her way to the bathroom, the barefoot woman would step on the strategically placed lump and emit a terrified shriek—one that indicated she thought she'd accidentally smushed the body of a dead mouse.

Isabella paused, reconsidering. Even if the niece were suddenly capable of understanding the complicated feline vocabulary, the cat probably wouldn't share this tidbit with her. The fake mouse–hairball trick was far too much fun to spoil with a warning.

Speaking of mice, Isabella mused, continuing the list of items her person failed to pick up on, a small family of rodents had taken up residence in the crawlspace beneath the stairs. After chasing a few members through the showroom, Isabella and the mice had reached a temporary truce. She would tolerate the mice's presence in the Green Vase so long as they stayed clear of her food bowl in the second-floor kitchen.

The cat lifted her head, proudly preening. She was nothing if not accommodating.

LEAVING THE NIECE still pensively gripping the recliner lever, Isabella hopped off the display table and meandered slowly toward the front of the showroom, pausing every so often to sniff at a floorboard or to rub the side of her face against a sharp corner. After a long course weaving in and around table legs and bookcases, she arrived at her favorite spot on the cashier counter and resumed her surveillance of the wet, wispy morning outside the store's front windows.

Isabella's thoughts shifted from the mundane happenings inside the Green Vase to the far more nuanced machinations of Uncle Oscar and his crew. This was another area where the cat's vast knowledge and expertise exceeded that of her human.

She, for one, had always known that Oscar spent his days doing more than just cooking great chicken.

The cat's gaze dropped to the floor as she pondered the basement that lay below, stuffed to the rafters with Oscar's eclectic antique collection. It also held the entrance to a secret underground tunnel that ran beneath downtown San Francisco.

The tunnel was first formed during San Francisco's Gold Rush era; its origins went back to the landfill expansion of the city's downtown area and the coinciding construction of the Green Vase's redbrick building. Over the years, countless individuals had used the passageway to slip in and out of Jackson Square undetected.

It had been a busy thoroughfare of late. The most recent users included an intrepid antique shop owner, her two cats, an art dealer with lofty political aspirations, a burly amphibian expert, and a remote controlled mechanical alligator—in addition, of course, to Uncle Oscar.

Isabella blinked, focusing her finely tuned senses. Her sonarlike ears closely monitored the foot traffic both above and below the showroom.

Just a few months back, she had detected a pair of rubber-soled sneakers sliding through the second-floor kitchen window overlooking the alley behind the store. The intruder had made a daring leap from the roof of the alley Dumpster, giving him a precarious finger-hold grip on the window's exterior ledge. Dangling down the side of the building, the young City Hall intern had managed to push open the unlocked windowpane and pull himself inside.

Isabella's shoulders stiffened with disapproval. The

antique shop wasn't the only target of the intern's extracurricular investigations.

It was this persistent snooping, she suspected, that had led to Spider's downfall. Somewhere along the way, he had unearthed a secret that was meant to stay hidden.

CONTEMPLATIVE, ISABELLA RETURNED her attention to the art studio across the street.

Monty's lanky silhouette could still be seen storming about the open room. With the picture frame now thoroughly demolished from his frenzied stomping, he threw his hands up and clasped them over his head.

As Isabella studied the scene, her extraordinary vision honed in on an item that her human had, predictably, missed.

A vaporous being, not discernible to human eyes, trailed two steps behind the tormented artist, energetically keeping pace with Monty's agitated gait.

It was the spiritual presence of the young man who had been viciously slain two months earlier. He was dressed in the same style of clothes he'd worn during his break-in to the Green Vase: a long-sleeved T-shirt, a pair of worn blue jeans, a baseball cap pulled down over his dark-skinned forehead, and high-top canvas sneakers.

The bridge of Isabella's nose crinkled and her ears turned sideways, an outward expression of her inner bafflement. Some answers eluded even her cunning insight.

After much thought and analysis, she couldn't figure out what Spider's ghost was doing in Jackson Square—or why he had chosen to haunt the city's soon-to-be inaugurated interim mayor.

The Reporter

Chapter 7

YESTERDAY'S NEWS

SAN FRANCISCO'S DAILY newspaper occupied an Art Deco–style building at the corner of Fifth and Mission. A square tower ridged with streamlined piping rose from the grimy front entrance. Just above street level, a series of small reliefs depicted vintage scenes of printing and reporting.

Decades of pollution and rain had grayed the stone facade. The aging structure was as much of a relic as the Linotype presses it had once housed.

The faded retro design seemed to fit right in with the surrounding neighborhood's mix of auto body shops, secondhand thrift stores, seedy hotels, and industrial warehouses. The bus stop shelter across the street was scarred with countless spray paint markings. Makeshift cardboard tents had been pushed up against the back side of the shelter's plastic sheeting, the temporary home to a rotating pool of vagrants. Scattered trash littered the sidewalk, and a stale stench of sweat and cannabis hung in the air.

A less discerning eye might have recoiled from this grim setting. But for Hoxton Finn, one of the city's veteran reporters, the newspaper's offices couldn't have been situated in a better location.

The building was eminently functional, blessedly lacking the so-called improvements that often came with modern-day infrastructure. Automatic lighting systems that flicked on and off as a person entered and exited a room annoyed him to no end.

As for temperature controls, the heat that emanated from the building's network of ancient water pipes was more than sufficient. He would rather work from a cardboard box by the bus stop than behind a sealed window in a room pumped with central air.

In terms of convenience, the spot was unmatched. One block south of Market, the paper's offices were only a short walk to both City Hall and an underground station for the BART and Muni lines. Multiple cabstands were within a few minutes' reach. Hox could easily get anywhere he needed to go with minimal cost and hassle.

The gritty scene that played out each day near the building's front steps was, in his opinion, one of the office's highlighting features.

There was no risk the place would ever be described as pretty.

AFTER MORE THAN twenty-five years of reporting, Hoxton Finn's broad shoulders and chiseled chin were recognized throughout the city. Taxi drivers, policemen, street vendors, and bankers knew him on sight—and everyone called him Hox. He was a fixture, an eccentric in a town that venerated caricature.

The reporter brushed all notion of celebrity aside. Divorced with no children, he preferred his own company to that of others. Gruffly succinct, he was direct in his questioning and sparing in his follow-up, a no-nonsense man living in a nonsense-filled world.

The juxtaposition was often jarring—for both sides.

For the last several weeks, however, the community had

been spared the brunt of Hox's caustic jabs. He'd spent every waking hour sequestered inside the newspaper's offices, barricaded behind the locked door of a third-floor conference room.

Piles of news clippings, Internet printouts, files, and handwritten notes were spread across the room's wooden table. A ceramic mug emblazoned with the logo of the local baseball team occupied one of the table's few open spaces. The residue from several pots of coffee stained the cup's interior.

Insulated from phone calls, drop-bys, and the other distracting nuisances that typically occurred at his assigned desk in the newsroom, Hox had devoted his full attention to the table's accumulated papers and files, stopping only for the occasional takeout delivery or a nap on the floor.

The reporter's clothes bore the wrinkled fatigue of the most recent all-night session. A tweed jacket had been tossed over a nearby chair, and the sleeves of his collared shirt were rolled up to his wrists. His denim blue jeans sagged around his waist, the fabric tired and loosened from lengthy wear.

Rubbing his temples, Hox shut his eyes and groaned. It had been far too long since his last shower. A lawn of peppered gray stubble had sprouted across the lower half of his face, and he smelled almost as fragrant as the homeless men camped outside.

A migraine pounded inside his forehead, knots of tension strafed the muscles in his neck and lower back, and his left foot throbbed with pain.

The last ache emanated from the amputated stub of his big toe. It was an old injury, the result of an inadvertent mishap with a Komodo dragon during a visit to the Los Angeles zoo a few years back.

He'd been accompanied by his now ex-wife, a famous movie star best known for her role in a box office thriller set in San Francisco. They'd been fighting nonstop for months, and the relationship was on the verge of a breaking point.

Nevertheless, the star had used her celebrity to finagle a behind-the-scenes visit with the showcase lizard. It was a special anniversary present for her worldly reporter husband, a man for whom it was impossible to select gifts. The toe-chomping melee that followed had resulted in an emergency room visit, an unsuccessful toe reattachment surgery, several weeks of sensational tabloid stories, and the eventual filing of divorce papers.

Hox had never blamed the movie star for the injury, but whenever he felt a shot of pain in his foot, his already dour disposition tended to darken.

It reminded him of what he had lost—far more than just a portion of his toe.

WITH A YAWN, Hox opened his eyes and stared bitterly at the piles scattered across the table, a clutter that represented the collective intel on the Spider Jones murder.

He'd started with the newspaper's findings and added on from there. Copies of the police reports took up one corner of the table. The files he'd bullied out of reporters from competing news agencies had landed on another. Internet printouts on any number of random queries that had struck him as potentially useful filled in the rest.

Hox had reviewed each item multiple times. He had considered the evidence from every possible angle and drawn out endlessly varying scenarios. But the anticipated insight had yet to appear. He was no closer to finding an answer than when he had started this exercise.

There was still something missing.

Throughout his long career, the veteran reporter had covered the entire range of issues related to state and local politics. A couple of overseas sabbaticals had taken him through war zones, political unrest, and countries wracked with famine. He had seen it all: the whimsical, the bizarre, and the totally outlandish. He'd experienced up close the worst greed, corruption, murder, and brutality had to offer.

But never had a story gripped him with such an intense fervor.

He was immersed in an unsolved murder—one in which he was personally involved.

Chapter 8

THE SPIDER FILES

HIS MIND INTENSELY focused, Hox leaned back in his chair. Turning away from the table, he propped his sock-covered feet on the nearest heating pipe and stretched his arms up over his head.

The horrifying murder of the young intern had shaken everyone who worked at City Hall. For Hox, who spent several hours each week inside the building covering the city's political beat, the incident had been particularly disturbing.

The night of the young man's death, mere minutes before the attack, Hox had passed the doomed intern on the central marble staircase. The reporter was on the descent, preparing to head home, while the intern was climbing up toward the ceremonial rotunda.

He was likely the last person, other than the murderer, to have seen Spider Jones alive.

HOX QUICKLY BECAME obsessed with the crime, its troubling anomalies, and the related reams of unanswered questions.

First off, why Spider? Why had such a nonthreatening, seemingly unimportant person been targeted for such a violent stabbing? What had the intern done to attract that level of vicious rage?

By all accounts, Spider was an affable young man, good looking and with an easy sense of humor. There was no indication he had any enemies. He was enthusiastic about his work, but not in competition with anyone else at City Hall. His position in the mayor's office was so far down the totem pole, few people even knew who he was—that is, until after his murder.

What had triggered the killer's attack? Had Spider simply been in the wrong place at the wrong time?

Hox stared at the conference room ceiling, his mind rehashing the same outline of issues and concerns that he had reasoned through countless times before.

Shifting from motive to the matter of the two primary suspects, Hox reached for his file on Sam Eckles.

"The frog guy," he muttered as he riffled through the pages to a photocopy of Sam's driver's license. A ruddy-faced man with tousled hair, ragged beard, and a slightly dazed expression peered out from the paper.

Sam's ten-year stint as a City Hall janitor had been relatively uneventful. Despite the overlap in their locations, Hox had never engaged with the man. He had only a vague recollection of the hulking red-haired brute in coveralls pushing a refuse cart.

The building's infamous frog invasion that had led to Sam's termination, however, was a far more vivid memory.

Hox *thunked* his thumb against a newspaper clipping covering the story.

"The slimy critters were all over the place," the reporter groaned, remembering the scene.

A *ribbiting*, croaking mass of several thousand amphibians had surged into City Hall from an improvised tadpole farm in the basement, covering the marble floor beneath the main rotunda. During the height of the occupation, frogs could be seen lounging on the central marble staircase, meandering down hallways, and loitering in the rest rooms. It had taken weeks to get them cleared out.

Hox shook his head, cringing at the recollection. He didn't share the frog phobia that had caused the current lieutenant governor, then San Francisco's sitting mayor, to suffer a state of near mental collapse, but after the City Hall invasion, Hox had seen enough amphibians to last him a lifetime.

"Sam Eckles," Hox summed up, slapping the file shut. "Clearly an odd bird."

But was he a knife-wielding killer? Grimacing, Hox found himself circling back to the same tired conclusion.

"I just don't see it."

"NEXT UP, JAMES Lick," Hox grunted as he switched to the slim folder containing the few details known about the second murder suspect. If Sam had gotten into trouble, Hox was willing to bet James Lick was the instigator.

The only picture in the file was a black-and-white image of a man who had died in 1876.

"Not the current Lick." Hox frowned. "Obviously."

The lean face and strong hawkish nose belonged to a San Francisco millionaire who had made his fortune in real estate during the Gold Rush boom. An eccentric, notoriously miserly gent, Lick never forgot the penniless years he endured before landing his windfall. Even after becoming one of the wealthiest men in California, Lick continued to wear cheap threadbare suits and to shun luxuries like expensive restaurants, which he deemed frivolous and unnecessary.

Lick's name was still prominent throughout the Bay Area, commemorated on freeways, high schools, the San Jose observatory that his estate endowed, and, most recently, as the namesake for a North Beach fried chicken joint.

Hox held up the photo, staring at the man's steely eyes. For his money, the original James Lick would have made a good murder suspect. Surely the man who hid behind this mask was just as menacing.

"I can only guess," Hox mused grouchily. "No one knows who you are."

Even though the Lick restaurant had been wildly popular during its short North Beach run, the proprietor had kept his real identity a secret. A grungy fellow in ripped-up overalls had handled the counter operations. The man behind the famous fried chicken recipe, the one responsible for obtaining the diner's requisite licenses and lease, remained an enigma.

Hox glanced down at the open file in his lap. The only other paper in the folder was a green-colored flyer that had accompanied the restaurant's takeout packages. The flyer provided a brief historical background on the millionaire miser James Lick. There was no reference to the man behind the alias.

Hox tossed the second sheet back into the file with disgust.

"I never liked fried chicken," he groused bitterly.

Once more resting his head against the back of the chair, Hox reflected on a last Lick-related item. In the police report, which he could now recite by memory, there was no mention of how the fried chicken Lick had been matched with the description of the second fugitive, an elderly man with thinning white hair and short rounded shoulders.

Hox blew out a frustrated sigh. "Yet another missing piece of information."

THE REPORTER GAZED silently at the ceiling, the somber lines deepening in his weary face as he reached a last question, one that bothered him more than all the others.

After leaving the empty supervisors' chambers, Hox must have passed within feet of the murderer. The villain would have been lurking in the shadows, knife in hand, as Hox crossed through the ceremonial rotunda and started down the staircase. He could have easily been caught up in the attack.

The face of the grinning intern flashed through Hox's head.

Why had he been spared Spider's fate?

Chapter 9

THE MINUTES BEFORE THE MURDER

AS HAPPENED EVERY time Hox reviewed the details of the Spider Jones case, the analysis inevitably led him to revisit his own firsthand account of the minutes before the murder.

The reporter had been extensively debriefed by the police both on the night of the crime and in the days that followed. He had repeated his story on multiple occasions for the investigating detectives. In his mind, he had played the sequence over and over again.

No matter how many times he ran through the short scene, he couldn't shake the sense that he'd forgotten something from his brief, but now crucial, interaction with the young intern.

As Hox sat in the makeshift war room, sleep-deprived, over-caffeinated, and disheveled, he envisioned the episode once more, letting each step of the memory unfold in slow motion.

FOR ALMOST A half hour following the conclusion of the supervisors' meeting, Hox had sat in the empty chambers, staring down at the vacant podium as he pondered the board's mayoral selection. He'd remained in the public arena–style seating long after everyone else had left, alone—or so he thought—with his thoughts.

"Montgomery Carmichael," he'd groaned in disbelief. "How could they have picked Montgomery Carmichael?"

Finally, he got up from his chair and began a brooding march out of the building. He'd spent much of the day chasing the renegade alligator all over town, and the stub of his left toe felt as if it were on fire. That, combined with the appointment of the most ill-qualified mayor in the history of San Francisco, had put the reporter in a particularly foul mood.

Still muttering under his breath, Hox turned from a second-floor hallway and stepped into the ceremonial rotunda. A glint of light reflected off the Harvey Milk bust, and Hox paused to look at the slain supervisor's smiling bronze face. He could almost hear the sculpted metal figure laughing at the ridiculous situation that had unfolded in the supervisors' chambers.

Grumbling bitterly, Hox started the descent down the marble stairs. Lurching from one slick step to the next, he looked out across the dimly lit interior.

The huge crowd that had attended the supervisors' meeting had dispersed, quickly emptying out of the building, and the lighting system had been switched to its reduced nighttime setting.

Despite the vast windows along the upper portions of the north and south walls, the night's dense fog masked the moon and stars, leaving only the eerie glow from a few scattered lamps inside the darkened structure.

Hox paused as a slim figure entered the main rotunda, crossed to the bottom of the stairs, and began to jog effortlessly up the steep steps. It was a young man in blue jeans, high-top sneakers, and a T-shirt. He wore a baseball cap pulled down over his brow.

Spider Jones was making his final ascent.

The intern looked up, and his eyes met the reporter's grim

gaze. For a second or two, the young man appeared startled, as if Hox had somehow spooked him. But as they neared one another at the staircase's midpoint, Spider's dark-skinned face broke into a broad smile of recognition.

Accustomed to false familiarity from strangers, Hox had merely grunted his acknowledgment. The momentary distraction caused him to stub his left toe on the next step, and a shooting stab of pain coursed through his body.

Cursing, the reporter hurried down the rest of the stairs and rapidly exited the building, eager to get home to a hot soaking bath.

As the memory concluded, Hox heard Spider's fading footsteps continue up toward the ceremonial rotunda where, only moments later, he would meet his gruesome end.

THE FRONT LEGS of the chair slammed against the floor as Hox returned to the dog-eared papers and files.

He whacked his hand against the table, still haunted by the nagging intuition that he was missing something, some detail or nuance that could be critical to solving the case. He reached for his mug and drained the last gulp of stale coffee.

His face skewed up, the response more from the next image that flashed into his head than the bitter taste of the brew.

The crime scene was far more vivid in Hox's memory than the brief passing on the stairway.

HOX WAS HALFWAY home when the newspaper's dispatch operator reached him on his cell phone and relayed the news of the City Hall murder. (The reporter had ignored the operator's call minutes earlier about the albino alligator being found at Mountain Lake.) Immediately reversing course, Hox had tuned into the police scanner for more details.

Upon his return to City Hall, Hox gave his initial statement. He then convinced the lead detective to let him view the crime scene at the top of the marble staircase. It was against department regulations, but he was accustomed to navigating around such barriers. Reluctantly, the detective escorted him up the steps and past the yellow and black police tape.

The technicians had just finished processing the evidence. The body had been zippered up into a plastic bag and carried off to the morgue for autopsy.

What remained, however, conveyed a gruesome tale.

A pool of blood had dried to the marble surface, the sticky red coating marred by the imprint of the body and the handprints where the young man had struggled to drag himself across the slick floor.

Red spurts were spattered across the surrounding infrastructure. Hox turned a slow circle, surveying the carnage on the stone walls, the rounded columns, and the brass light fixtures. A few drops dotted the base of the third-story balcony overlooking the rotunda.

Grimly, Hox returned his gaze to floor level. Another spray had hit the Harvey Milk bust, leaving a gory graffiti across the statue's wide grin.

"SPIDER JONES," HOX said, leaning over the conference room table, his eyes desperately scanning the piles of papers and files. "Who did this to you? And why?"

A loud banging thumped against the door. With a testy sigh, the reporter swiveled in his chair. The harried producer from the newspaper's sister television network glared through the glass window mounted into the door's upper half.

Apparently he had blown off one too many of the woman's calls, and she had appeared in person to drag him out of the conference room.

Reluctantly, he scooted his chair away from the table. He couldn't keep ignoring his regular reporting duties.

Spider Jones would have to wait a little while longer for his murder to be solved.

Chapter 10

A WHISPER IN THE RAIN

AS THE DOOR swung shut behind Hoxton Finn, the latch to a window overlooking the street began to rattle ever so gently in its fittings. A few short jerks released the handle, and the pane cracked open.

Something less than substance, a whisper through the rain, entered through the two-inch gap and floated into the room.

The spirit circled the conference table, stopping at the far end to poke curiously through the trash can filled with discarded takeout containers.

A loud sniffing could be heard, accompanied by a strong intake of air. The moist vapors funneled together, as if pouring into an empty vessel, gradually tracing the faint outline of a young man wearing a baseball cap, blue jeans, and high-top canvas sneakers.

Spider Jones—or, at least, a spectral version of the former intern—bent wistfully over the half-empty food containers, slowly moving from one carton to the next. He lingered the longest over a square paper box holding the remnants of a spicy kung pao chicken dish that had been seasoned with extra garlic.

After an extensive smelling session, the spirit exhaled, breathing out a sigh of disappointment as the thin edges of his form faded to a blur.

Leaving the trash can, Spider turned his attention to the piles of documents spread across the table. He bent over the collected materials, shifting stacks of paper and fluttering loose pages as he perused the information.

His manner was one of diligent but pragmatic interest—until he reached a file labeled "Crime Scene Photos."

Spider fiddled nervously with the brim of his cap; then his hand reached out for the file. His fingers wavered in the air, hesitating, before he flipped open the cover and began skimming through the contents.

There were numerous close-up shots of blood spatter and wide-angle views of the ceremonial rotunda taken from almost every possible vantage point. The pictures were shocking, both viewed individually and as a group; the exhaustive folio conveyed the carnage of the scene.

But it was the pictures of the victim that caused Spider to draw in a sharp breath, once more crystallizing the outline of his ghostly figure.

The body splayed across the marble floor was almost unrecognizable. His dark skin had turned an ashy gray; his glassy eyes stared out from a stiff, frozen face.

Subconsciously, Spider reached for his stomach as he studied the gaping knife wounds that had drained the life from his body. He recalled the force of the first stunning blow, ripping into his chest, and a shiver ran across his narrow shoulders.

As if energized by a renewed sense of urgency, he turned to a notepad containing the reporter's handwritten notes. He focused intently on the scribbling, reading through page after page. But as he digested the material, the expression on his face grew increasingly dissatisfied.

There was something missing from the reporter's notes, an important piece of critical information, an image that had been resonating at the forefront of Spider's mind from the moment he appeared in Jackson Square earlier that morning.

Picking up the reporter's pencil, Spider drew out a symbol on the notepaper—a scrawling letter *O*.

Then his translucent figure slowly dissipated, vanishing from sight.

There was a slight *woosh* of air as his spirit slipped through the open window and back into the rainy streets of San Francisco.

The Nose

Chapter 11

A NOSE IS A NOSE . . .

OSCAR'S NIECE STOOD inside the third-floor bathroom of the apartment above the Green Vase, staring at her reflection in the mirror mounted over the sink.

In preparation for her daily jog, she had put on warm leggings and a long-sleeved mesh shirt. Her tangled brown hair was tied back in a ponytail, and she had just completed several lunging stretches, loosening her leg muscles.

Ever since the aborted portrait session, she had tried to resist the urge to look at her nose. She had purposely avoided making eye contact with any reflected image. No good could come of it, she'd told herself forcefully.

But as she'd passed the bathroom on her way downstairs, she'd caught a glimpse of her face in the glass. Despite her firm resolve, she couldn't help stopping inside.

That was twenty minutes ago.

Rationally, she knew Monty's earlier statements about facial features had nothing to do with her. The comments had been in reference to the murdered intern who had inexplicably taken her place in the picture.

Likely, Monty had never even noticed the bump on the

middle of her nose. He tended to be rather self-absorbed. And despite his constant prying, he always seemed more interested in the cats than their owner.

That was fine with the niece. She would have been disturbed, she thought with a shudder, if he suddenly shifted his focus solely onto her.

Nevertheless, the comment had struck a nerve.

She tilted her head first one way, and then another, self-consciously examining her face. The connecting bridge of her eyeglass frames did a decent job of masking the lump in the cartilage. It was barely discernible from this angle.

Apprehensively, she removed the glasses and leaned closer toward the mirror.

It was a regular enough shape, she assured herself . . . perhaps a little off center. Not the ideal nose, but not grotesquely out of whack.

Pushing herself away from the sink, she slid her glasses back on, trying not to notice the upward lift as the frames settled on the bump.

So what if she had an odd-shaped nose, she thought indignantly. What did she care? And who was Monty to criticize—with that narrow chin and those goofy green eyes? She could tell *him* a thing or two about funny-looking facial features.

She paused and once more leaned toward the mirror, squinting at the reflected image.

"Hmm . . ."

ISABELLA SAT ON the edge of the bathroom sink, watching the niece's self-conscious nose analysis with curious fascination.

The cat had never experienced such insecurities. She had always been supremely confident in her appearance. After all, it was only fitting that the royal head of the household possessed a splendid beauty.

Isabella turned her gaze to the short fuzzy reflection in the mirror. She noted with approval the moist pink pad in the center of her pixielike face. The soft cushion was perfectly aligned, midway between her ice-blue eyes.

It must be difficult to be a human, she thought sympathetically, what with all that exposed skin. And those flattened ears, squashed up against the side of her head—no wonder the woman had a hard time understanding the cat's complicated language. How could the niece hear anything with such malformed structures?

As for the nose . . . well, there was no getting around it. In the cat's view, that was an inherently awkward appendage.

Isabella looked up at her person and prepared to issue her advice. Allowing for the fact that the niece was human and, consequently, would never be as beautiful as a cat, the guidance was tempered with a dose of practical realism.

The tone of the comment wasn't nearly as comforting as the niece would have liked. In fact, it sounded somewhat dubious.

"Mrao."

WITH A WIDE yawn, Rupert took a seat on the bathroom floor beside his igloo-shaped litter box. His wobbly eyes crossed as he contemplated the intricacies of human versus feline nasal function and design, but he came up with nothing to contribute to the discussion. Being an experienced male member of the animal species, he wisely offered no opinion on the relative attractiveness of either nose shape.

All of this talk about noses was, however, making him hungry. Of course, the discussion of any topic was likely to make him hungry at ten thirty in the morning.

It had been more than three hours since breakfast, and he'd burned a lot of calories in the intervening period, what with his extensive picture posing, the long cuddling session in his person's lap, and lastly, the activity that had consumed the greatest amount of energy, sleeping.

He poked his fluffy tail up into the air, kinking the tip slightly to the left, and began hopping down the stairs toward the kitchen.

It was a clear signal that he assumed his person would understand. At this point in their relationship, he reasoned, she should be well versed in the routine.

It was time for his morning snack.

MOMENTS LATER, RUPERT reached the second floor and bounded into the kitchen, his stomach rumbling as he neared his food bowl.

His was a tempered enthusiasm, as he was only expecting dry cat food. For the last two months, he had tried to be accommodating and to not complain too much about the quality of the provisions. After all, it was impossible for his person to obtain the good stuff, what with Oscar gone and Lick's fried chicken joint closed.

Fried chicken, Rupert thought, swooning at the passing mention of his favorite dish. He paused, one paw hovering in the air, overwhelmed by the memory.

Those delectable pieces of meat were still the focal point of his dreams. He often woke to find drool dribbling down his chin. It had been a very disappointing Thanksgiving and Christmas for the poultry-obsessed cat.

Nevertheless, Rupert remained hopeful that the chicken chef and his collection of cast-iron skillets would soon reappear. Until then, he would have to make do with his regular gruel.

NOW EVEN HUNGRIER than before, Rupert plopped in front of his empty food bowl and waited for his person to appear.

He cocked his head, listening for the sound of human footsteps following him down the stairs.

Nothing. The apartment was unusually quiet.

The niece must not have noticed him leaving the bathroom, Rupert thought. She had been awfully obsessed with her nose. Perhaps she'd missed his signal.

Or maybe she'd forgotten what time it was. He shook his

head, a gesture of utter incomprehension. How could she not remember something as important as his morning snack?

Rupert opened his mouth and let loose a plaintive howl, one that sounded as if he hadn't eaten for days and was rapidly nearing the end of his sad, pitiful life.

Then he paused and listened again.

Still nothing.

He peered up at the ceiling, perplexed. Summoning his vocal reserves, he took in a deep breath and repeated the request at an amplified volume, a call that clearly communicated he was a cat on the very edge of starvation.

There, he thought with relieved satisfaction as he heard the woman begin her descent. Finally, she got the message.

He looked up with anticipation as the niece entered the kitchen.

Her face bore an apologetic expression—appropriate, he reasoned, for someone who had been so derelict in her cat-attending duties.

"So, uh, Rupert," the niece said as she approached the pantry where she kept the cat food. "I noticed you've put on some extra weight lately."

Extra weight, Rupert thought, looking frantically down at his plump stomach. *What extra weight? I don't see any extra weight.*

The niece opened the pantry door and took out a plastic container, different than the one that held his regular dry food.

"You just finished off a bag of your old stuff, so I thought we might try some of this new brand to see if it helps you out . . ."

"*We* might try." Rupert puzzled at the phrase as he switched his gaze back to his person. *What do you mean* we*? Since when have you been eating my cat food?*

"It's a low-fat formulation," she said informatively. "To help you with your diet."

Diet? The dreaded word echoed inside Rupert's head. In the entire human vocabulary, there were few words more foul.

He watched suspiciously as the niece carried the plastic container to his bowl. Bending, she dribbled a small amount of the new food into the bottom of the dish.

Rupert dropped his head for a tentative sniff.

The brown particles carried a strange, off-putting smell.

Cautiously, he picked up a single kibble and gummed it in his mouth. After a brief taste, he spit it out onto the tile floor. Then he looked up at his person with disgust.

Skewing his face into a disdainful expression, he concentrated his contempt into a single retaliatory thought.

You really should do something about that nose of yours.

TRYING NOT TO worry about Rupert's negative reaction to the diet cat food, the niece laced up her running shoes, zipped her rain jacket, and headed to the first floor.

Isabella joined her person by the front door, supervising the last clothing preparations. From her perch on the cashier counter, she watched as the niece secured the lock and set off on her route.

The cat was about to return upstairs to investigate Rupert's new cat food when she noticed a movement across the street.

She stared through the rainy window, thoughtfully contemplating as Spider Jones's ghostly presence floated out of the art studio and jogged after the niece.

The Previous Mayor

Chapter 12

REGRETS

A BLUE AND black taxi pulled up outside San Francisco's City Hall, disgorging a dark-skinned man in a trench coat, tailored suit, and two-toned leather wing tips. As the city's Previous Mayor climbed out onto the curb, he placed a gloved hand over the felt bowler balanced on his head, anchoring the hat from a sudden gust of rain.

Out of elected office for almost a decade, the Previous Mayor still exerted powerful leverage within local political circles. He was an obligatory invite to any public ceremonies, a sought-after guest for dinner parties, and a must-have attendee at new restaurant openings.

Standing on the sidewalk, he glanced up at the second-floor balcony to the mayor's office suite. In a few days' time, he would officially become the *previous* Previous Mayor. He thought of the monogram-based code language used by Oscar and his underground Bohemians, who referred to him as the PM.

They would have to give him another *P*, he thought wryly.

THE PM SHIFTED his grip from his hat to the handrail as he mounted the short flight of steps leading to City Hall's front entrance.

The passing years had taken their toll, and the regular assortment of aches and pains had begun to accumulate. His gait wasn't as spry as it once was, and there was a slight shake in his right hand that he noticed—and tried to ignore—when he buttoned his jacket or lifted a cocktail glass.

None of these physical frailties, however, had impeded his daily life as much as the murder of the young City Hall intern.

In the months since the tragic event, the Previous Mayor had dramatically curtailed his public appearances. He had been noticeably absent at December's raft of holiday festivities. Even the city's glamorous New Year's Eve celebrations had failed to draw him out.

He had put his weekly op-ed column for the local newspaper on temporary hiatus, and it had been weeks since he'd dined at his honorary table in his favorite French restaurant.

The current trip to City Hall was a rare outing. As he topped the stairs, raindrops streaked down a face stained with sadness. His suit and overcoat were a mix of muted browns and blacks, matched by a similarly drab tie. The only color contrast could be found in his closely cropped mustache, which was growing whiter by the day.

For a man once known for his stylish panache and perpetually cheerful smile, it was a remarkable change.

The death of Spider Jones had left a sorrowful mark on the seasoned politician.

THE PREVIOUS MAYOR walked through City Hall's gilded iron-and-glass doors, trying to suppress an involuntary shudder. It was the first time he had ventured into the building since the night of the fateful supervisors' meeting.

A flood of emotions swept over him as he navigated through the security station and approached the rotunda. He paused on the pink marble floor to reach inside his jacket for a handkerchief. Dabbing his eyes, he stared up at the domed ceiling.

Spider had been the perfect protégé, the likes of which the PM feared he might never see again.

The young man had exhibited innate skill, keen perception, and sharp political wits. The PM had quickly taken him under his wing. How could he not? The intern had reminded him of an earlier version of himself.

The PM's biological children were all grown and married, with their own careers and hobbies to keep them busy. Despite his best efforts, none of them had shown any interest in the family business—that is, running the city.

He had begun to despair for the future of San Francisco, which seemed devoid of suitable leadership candidates, particularly of late.

But then he'd met Spider.

The PM soon began to regard the intern as his heir apparent. He'd sent the lad on training missions designed to hone his natural talents. Spider had succeeded at every task. Be it sneaking around City Hall's many corridors to pick up information, tailing soon-to-be-mayor Montgomery Carmichael, or even breaking into the building that housed the Green Vase antique shop, Spider had exceeded all expectations.

The PM had even started to work on Spider's social etiquette, grooming him for the many power lunches, dinners, and cocktail parties ahead. To his view, the first requirement for any successful Bay Area politician—other than a proficiency in espionage—was the development of a fine palate.

He smiled, remembering Spider's initiation to French cuisine and the intern's valiant attempt to finish off platters of both oysters and snails.

With a sigh, he shook his head.

"Such a waste," the PM muttered under his breath. He turned away from the rotunda and headed for one of the narrow staircases leading to the basement.

"I had so many more dishes for him to try."

As he started down the steps, he grinned, despite his grim mood.

"I think Spider would have liked calamari."

THERE HAD ALWAYS been a danger, the Previous Mayor reflected, his somber mood returning as he descended into the building's basement. The young man was just the sort to get in over his head—and not realize the risks he was taking.

The engrossing research project Spider had taken up the last weeks of his life had set off alarm bells from the get-go. The PM had puzzled at all of the late hours the intern had spent digging around unsupervised in the City Hall archives. He had puzzled at the air of secretiveness and the covert nature of the intern's investigations.

It was one thing for Spider to sneak around the building and report his findings to the PM, quite another for him to keep the spoils to himself.

The PM had followed up on his suspicions. Using his extensive information network, he had quickly managed to determine what Spider's secret project was not.

It was not, for example, part of the intern's regular duties. Nor did it involve any of the currently pending or contemplated legislation being discussed by the board members.

Given the archives Spider had been accessing, the project likely related to something much older, some aspect of San Francisco's long-forgotten history.

Unfortunately, that guidance only served to widen the inquiry—and to increase the PM's concern.

The city had more than its fair share of dark secrets, and a number of them were hidden in the dusty files in the basement where the intern was searching.

THE PREVIOUS MAYOR had finally confronted Spider, gently but firmly insisting that he share the details of his special project. It hadn't taken much persuasion; after a minimal resistance, the intern appeared relieved to share the burden of his secret.

Spider was set to reveal everything to the PM the night of the lengthy board of supervisors meeting to select the interim mayor. They had planned a late dinner at a garlic-themed restaurant in North Beach. The venue was the young man's choosing, a payback for the earlier oyster and snail torture he'd endured.

The PM remembered sitting at a booth inside the Columbus Street eatery, checking his watch as trays filled with plates of grotesquely over-garlicked dishes floated past his booth. His eyes had begun to water from the aromatic stench, and he sensed an anticipatory heartburn building in his stomach.

But Spider never showed. The garlic mashed potatoes the PM had ordered for the intern went cold. He was about to give up and leave when his cell phone rang.

The PM had puzzled at the number. It was Mabel, the outgoing mayor's administrative assistant. He recalled her voice as she politely conveyed the news: informative, but, true to her reserved personality, emotionally detached.

Afterward, he'd hung up the phone and sat in stunned silence.

He'd been so shocked, he'd eaten the entire plate of stinky potatoes.

"IF ONLY I'D stepped in sooner," the PM lamented. It was a thought he had repeated over and over in the weeks since the staffer's death.

"I might have prevented this tragedy."

Chapter 13

BENEATH THE VENTILATION SHAFT

THE PREVIOUS MAYOR entered the basement level of San Francisco's City Hall and started down a side corridor, pausing every few feet in front of open office doorways to peek inside.

He was in a lesser-used corner of the building's basement, away from the public administrative activity that took place on the opposite end. It was a quiet, remote location, with only the occasional low-level staffer or intern passing through its windowless depths.

After about five minutes of wandering, the PM stopped, turned his head sideways, and listened. He thought he'd heard a familiar noise.

He held up a hand, raising a finger toward the ceiling. There it was again—the squeaking of wheels.

His somber face broke into a broad smile. A moment later, a grungy man clad in faded overalls rounded the corner. He used a mop to push a plastic bucket filled with dingy gray water.

"My friend," the PM said, stretching out his hand to clasp that of the janitor. "So good to see you."

The PM knew everyone who worked in City Hall—from the most powerful professional advisers to the lowest-level staffers. He worked hard to maintain these relationships. They were his primary means of keeping tabs on the ins and outs of San Francisco politics.

While many high-profile figures liked to think they knew everything that went on inside the building, they tended to limit their information to sources of equivalent stature.

The PM had learned to seek as many inputs as possible. He would stop and listen to anyone who had something to say, no matter the person's station. The lower the social standing, he'd found, the more reliable the insight. In his experience, no confidant was more valuable than those working in janitorial services.

The cleaning corps circulated virtually unseen throughout every inch of the vast domed structure. They were the first to detect when a scandal was about to break, and they were sometimes the only ones to suspect the private alliances that subtly dictated voting patterns and back-room favoritism.

So when the PM received an urgent message from his trusted network of cleaning professionals, he broke his self-imposed isolation and proceeded immediately to City Hall.

Lowering his voice to a whisper, he bent toward the janitor's shoulder. "Now, what did you have to show me?"

THE JANITOR ROLLED his bucket along a dimly lit hallway, motioning for the PM to follow. After checking to see that no one was watching, the man pushed open a doorway leading into a long narrow room holding several rows of pre-fab office cubicles. He bumped the bucket over the threshold and then waved the PM inside.

The PM stood in the outer hallway, hesitating. He had been to this location several times before. Spider's old desk was located at the far end of the rows of cubicles.

"This way, sir," the janitor urged in a hushed voice.

Sucking in a deep breath, the PM pushed his feet forward.

The janitor steered the mop bucket down an open space between the wall and the cubicles. As he passed each workstation, he leaned over the partition wall to ensure it was unoccupied.

The place was deserted. Most of the interns were still on their holiday vacation.

The PM clenched his hat, nervously bending the brim as the janitor reached Spider's cubicle at the end of the aisle.

The desk had been cleared of the many folders and files that Spider had accumulated. Presumably, they had been taken into evidence by the police. Only a few stacks remained on a nearby bookshelf, mostly copies of proposed legislation from last fall's session of the board of supervisors.

On the empty desk space, a makeshift memorial had sprung up. Friends and well-wishers had dropped off notes, cards, and various trinkets symbolizing the intern's life.

Spider's bike, painted the same burnt-red color as the Golden Gate Bridge, leaned against the side of the desk. A plastic helmet, purchased by Spider's mother, but rarely worn by her daredevil son, hung from the handlebars by its chin strap.

The PM turned away, unable to look any longer.

The janitor propped his mop handle against the cubicle wall. Stepping around the desk, he crouched in front of a ventilation shaft on the rear wall. With a last glance over his shoulder, he ran his fingers along the edge of the metal grate cover and prized it from its fittings.

"I was cleaning down here this morning when I noticed the cover was a little loose." The janitor grunted as he set the grate on the ground. "I thought it just needed to be tamped back into place." He moved away from the opening so that the PM could see inside. "But then I saw this."

Holding his bowler against his chest, the PM edged toward the shaft. The janitor fished a small flashlight from one of his many pockets, switched on the light, and aimed the beam into the hole.

There was an extra space inside the wall, beneath the opening for the metal funnel connecting the vent to the rest of the building's heating system. Inside the cubbyhole rested a cardboard box stuffed with papers, binders, and several expandable file pockets.

"And this is how you found it?" the PM asked, turning from the vent to look at the janitor. "Are you sure it was Spider's?"

At the man's shrugged response, the PM took the light and returned his attention to the cardboard box. With a gloved hand, he pulled out a sheath of loose papers and aimed the beam at the top sheet. The unique scrawling, a cramped print style, provided the confirmation he was seeking.

"Have the police seen this yet?" he asked, still skimming the handwritten words.

"No," the janitor replied, sheepishly staring at the ground. "They were all over this place the day after . . ." He sighed ruefully and shook his head. "The day after Spider's death, but I guess no one thought to check the vent. I thought I'd give you a look before I called it in."

The PM replaced the sheath of papers and began thumbing through the rest of the box's contents. It was pretty tame stuff, he mused. He noted the personnel files of previous interns who had worked for the outgoing mayor over the years. They were a transient bunch, typically staying no longer than a month or two. He couldn't imagine any of them having information that needed to be hidden in a secret box.

After a few minutes' review, he cleared his throat as if he had seen nothing of interest. Then his eyes narrowed on a name printed on the edge of one of the file pockets—this man was not a previous City Hall intern.

"You did the right thing," he said tensely as he lifted the expandable file from the box. He walked around the partition wall to Spider's desk, took a seat in the chair, and switched on a nearby lamp.

Flipping through the pages, he pulled out a long A4-sized sheet of paper that had been folded in half. He opened the sheet and held it under the light.

It was a picture of two elderly men standing in front of a brightly colored mural. The men wore loose-fitting coveralls, which appeared to be stained with splatters of paint. Buckets and brushes of various types were spread out across a drop cloth protecting the floor.

The mural covered the wall's entire length. It depicted an earlier San Francisco street scene, populated with dozens of citizens captured in poses reflecting their daily life and activities. An accident attended by a squad of policemen and a bright red fire truck took up one section, while a number of recognizable landmarks spread across the painted horizon.

The PM examined the details and then refolded the sheet. The janitor watched, eyes widening with curiosity.

The PM stroked his chin for a moment before he spoke. "Let's keep this between us for now."

Refolding the paper, he slipped it back inside the file. With a conspiring nod to the janitor, he tucked the file under his jacket and strode briskly out of the cubicle area.

The Mural

Chapter 14

THE EXERCISE REGIMEN

RUPERT HUDDLED BENEATH the living room couch, where he'd retreated following the earlier diet cat food fiasco. Dark and filled with dust bunnies, the furniture bunker was the perfect place to brood.

The aftertaste from the sample bite of diet cat food still lingered in his mouth. He smacked his lips, trying to rid his taste buds of the displeasing residue.

Oh yes, Rupert thought bitterly. *I will have my revenge.* Wickedness went against his typically sweet nature, but there would be retribution for this dastardly deed.

His furry brain spun as he considered his options. There were many potential avenues for attack, but he had to plot his course carefully. Patience and cunning would certainly be required.

He spread himself into a full-length arc across the floor, his favorite thinking position. The distance from the tip of his fluffy tail to the paws of his outstretched front legs spanned almost four feet. His furry eyelids squeezed shut for a moment of intense concentration, as he imagined all sorts of maniacal schemes.

But he soon tired from the effort.

It was difficult to be devious on an empty stomach.

WADDLING FROM UNDER the couch, Rupert blinked in the main room's brighter light. As he took a seat next to the coffee table, he turned his gaze to the bulge of white fluff that poked out from his round middle.

Where did that come from? he wondered with concern. There seemed to be a lot more of him than he remembered.

Maybe he *had* put on an ounce or two. Perhaps he could use a little exercise . . .

Slowly, he slid his body into an alert lion's stance. The ruff of fur around his neck puffed out as he flexed his muscles and extended his nails. His orange ears swiveled mischievously. His tail began to swing back and forth, thumping loudly against the floor with each rotation.

He glanced furtively around the room, tracking the movements of an imaginary prey. He hunched forward, every fiber in his being ready for the attack.

Suddenly, he was off, scooting across the living room in a fuzzy white blur. Rugs slid out of place, lamps rocked in their fittings, and picture frames rattled against the walls.

After a kamikaze tour of the second-floor living quarters, he aimed his trajectory toward the stairwell at the corner of the kitchen. His rear legs powering him forward in leaps and bounds, he flew down the steps like a short-legged, pot-bellied gazelle.

Skidding through the turn at the bottom of the stairs, he continued his breakneck pace into the showroom. Claws scraping in spastic frenzy, he zoomed into and around obstacles, crashing into several table legs and the base of the recliner.

Isabella froze in an arched-back hiss, every hair extended in alarm as Rupert blitzed past her. But there was no slowing his crazed, chaotic sprint—until he reached a meager beam of sunlight that had broken through the clouds, casting its faint warmth on the showroom floor.

Screeching to a stop, his feet curled beneath him. He rolled sideways, perfectly positioning his body within the narrow beam, and fell instantly asleep.

Fighting off a snore, one eye popped open to admire his reflection in the window. In his opinion, his fluffy round figure looked perfectly svelte.

There, Rupert thought proudly. *That should do it.*

Diet cat food. He sniffed derisively as he drifted off into his favorite fried chicken dream.

• • •

UNAWARE OF THE feline exercise routine that had just taken place inside the Green Vase, the niece continued her morning jog. She rounded the corner of Jackson and Montgomery, picking up speed as she turned toward the Italian neighborhood of North Beach.

It was a regular busy day on Columbus Avenue. A steady stream of Muni buses rumbled through traffic, their brakes squeaking at every intersection and passenger stop.

The niece powered through the packed sidewalk, threading between a pair of well-dressed women in fitted jackets and knee-high boots. Her ponytail swinging, she dodged around an elderly Asian couple bundled up in heavy parka jackets.

The winter's wet air captured the scents of the coffee shops and bakeries that lined the street. The decadent aroma of chocolate-stuffed croissants just out of the oven mixed with the hissing steam of brewing espresso beans and cinnamon-sweet cider.

As the niece passed one of the many pasta joints preparing for the day's meal service, a pulse of roasted garlic flooded the sidewalk.

Maybe I'll stop for lunch on my way back, she thought wistfully.

She turned her head toward the storefront—and stopped short at the sight of her reflection in the window.

This time, it wasn't her nose that caught her attention.

A feathery gray glow in the shape of a man appeared to be running along behind her.

A nearby bus blasted its horn, and the niece jumped, instinctively turning her gaze toward the street. When she looked back at her reflection, the vaporous figure had vanished.

Shaking her head, she resumed her jog.

"Probably just the glare from the bus's white siding," she murmured, trying to reassure herself.

And yet, as she jogged past the empty diner that had once housed Lick's Homestyle Chicken, she couldn't shake the feeling that she was being followed.

Chapter 15
THE DOCENT

THE DRIPPING MIST thickened to a light rain as the niece reached the end of the Columbus Avenue restaurants. She turned into Washington Square and circled the park's lower perimeter, a spray of droplets quickly coating her eyeglasses.

"I would have been better off leaving these at home," she said, whipping the frames from her face and tucking them in her shirt pocket.

Without the specs, her nose felt naked—the bump particularly so. Beyond that, her vision was severely compromised. The second issue was of little concern. She knew the scene by heart.

A Catholic church framed the park's upper half; its cream and gold facade of delicate dual spires pointed emphatically at the sky. Down below, the playful shrieks of several uniformed schoolchildren could be heard inside a gated courtyard, evidence that the students were enjoying their recess break.

Beneath the protection of the trees that lined the park's outer edges, several Asian women practiced their morning tai chi. Oblivious to the increasing rain, or perhaps calmed by its rhythm, they swung their arms in slow synchronized motions, their palms pushing against invisible barriers of resistance.

Near the park's grassy center, a damp dog walker stood holding the leash of a pokey pug. The dog nosed the ground, curiously sniffing as its owner checked his watch, looked skyward at the darkening clouds, and pleaded for his pet to hurry.

Above it all, Coit Tower's nozzle-shaped cylinder rose like a beacon. Perched at the peak of Telegraph Hill, the quirky landmark was one of San Francisco's most beloved fixtures—and the turnaround point for the niece's run.

LEAVING WASHINGTON SQUARE, the niece veered into the quiet residential neighborhood surrounding Coit Tower and its encircling green space, Pioneer Park.

There were a dozen or more ways to climb Telegraph Hill. Street signs marked a route for vehicular traffic that gradually wound up the steep incline, first in turns at square-cornered intersections, then, within the grounds of Pioneer Park, in a curling spiral to the peak.

With only a limited number of parking spaces at the overlook, the line of cars often stretched all the way around the circular road. Tourists would sit for hours, waiting for one of the cherished parking spots to open up.

It was far easier to hike up the hill.

The niece left Washington Square, still jogging, albeit at a slower pace, and began the climb. As the streets steepened, the curbside parking switched from parallel to perpendicular alignment. The sidewalk itself transitioned to a pitched groove and, eventually, graded steps.

Pastel-colored apartment buildings made up most of the residential housing. Like much of San Francisco, the architecture ranged from Mission-style stucco to Edwardian stick, and pretty much everything in between—the unifying factor being the adapted use of bulging bay windows to draw in as much natural light as possible.

Few modern day residents could afford the luxury of a Telegraph Hill apartment. What had started out in the Gold Rush era as undesirable squatters' land (due to the landscape's extreme slope) was now one of the most sought-after locations in the city. On a midweek day such as this, the rent-paying apartment dwellers were all at work, earning their keep.

As the niece chugged up the sidewalk, she glanced at the fog that had begun to drop down over the hill, graying the sky and blurring the edges of the nearby buildings.

The place was eerily silent.

There was no one around . . . no one except for an unseen presence, which constantly caused her to look over her shoulder.

TRYING TO SHAKE off the creepiness, the niece cut around to the bay side of the hill and started up one of the many sets of wooden stairs that scaled its near-vertical face. Her feet pumped from one step to the next as she hit the steepest portion of the climb.

Every inch in elevation increased the span of the view, a sweeping panorama of the waterfront, the bay, and the isolated fortress of Alcatraz. But the vista was lost in the haze that had seeped over the city, and the niece kept her limited vision focused on the slickening steps.

Flight after flight of stairs passed through the exclusive neighborhood. Spared the fire sparked by the 1906 earthquake that engulfed much of San Francisco, the hillside contained several tiny wooden cottages that were built in the mid-1800s. The homey structures, with their shaker siding and overgrown gardens, stood side by side with contemporary town house–style mansions. Both properties were valued in the multimillions—and both clung precariously to the side of the cliff, as if the slightest quake might send them tumbling all the way to the Embarcadero.

Panting and nearly out of breath, the niece reached the summit of the last set of stairs and stepped over the curb onto the asphalt path leading to Coit Tower's front drive. A chattering swarm of green parrots swooped through the mist as she walked the remaining hundred yards to the monument's entrance.

The center of the small parking lot was manned by a bronze statue of Christopher Columbus. Depicted with an (unlikely) tall, brawny physique, the tarnished green figure looked across the bay toward the Golden Gate, a place the explorer might possibly have heard of, but certainly never ventured.

Despite being soaked from the rain, the niece was ready for a drink. She reached beneath her rain jacket for a zippered pocket sewn into the waistband of her leggings, pulled out a dollar, and headed for the tower's front lobby to buy a bottle of water from the convenience store inside.

A series of stone steps led up to the tower's square base and an entrance marked by a concrete casting of a phoenix. The bird's symbol of rebirth through flames had been enthusiastically adopted by fire-prone San Francisco, a city accustomed in its early days to the constant threat of flame-born disaster.

The niece passed beneath the phoenix as she weaved through a small crowd gathered around the main door, waiting for a docent tour to begin.

Slipping past the throng, she proceeded into the convenience store, a round room centered at the tower's core. Bypassing the souvenirs and trinkets packed into the shop's minimal square footage, the niece grabbed a bottle from a tiny refrigeration unit. After a quick stop at the cashier stand, she carried her purchase out of the store's rear door and into a hallway that ringed the inner edge of the tower's ground level.

Behind her, a window of plated glass opened up the east-facing wall. The rest of the hallway's vertical space was completely covered with painted murals.

With an apologetic glance at a sign forbidding food and beverage in the mural area, the niece discreetly unscrewed the lid and took a long sip.

Given the noise in the front foyer, it appeared that the docent for the morning tour had arrived. A woman's voice echoed through the hallway.

"Crowd around, ladies and gentlemen, and we'll get this thing started. Congratulations are in order for everyone who made the trek up Telegraph Hill. As some of you may already know, the hill is named for the signal station positioned here back in the Gold Rush days. This was, in fact, the site of the first West Coast telegraph."

The niece nearly choked on a gulp of water. She recognized the voice at once. It belonged to one of her uncle's comrades, the first of his crew to surface in over two months.

After a difficult swallow, her eyes widened with intrigue. She tiptoed toward the edge of the group and whispered softly, "What's Dilla doing here?"

• • •

A SHORT DISTANCE away, Spider's soggy spirit staggered over the top step of a Telegraph Hill staircase and onto Coit Tower's asphalt drive. His barely visible disturbance in the pattern of raindrops bent over, gasping for breath—or whatever substance it was that energized his supernatural being.

With unaccustomed fatigue, Spider shook his head. The brown-haired woman had smoked him on the steep steps. Before his untimely demise, he routinely rode his bike straight up San Francisco's most daunting hills, but his ghostly persona wasn't in nearly as good a shape as his human form had been.

Righting himself, he lifted his baseball cap to wipe his forehead. He then focused on the concrete structure at the end of the drive.

Coit Tower.

He suspected he knew what Oscar's niece was doing there.

The run, he reasoned, was just a ruse. She was taking the same path he had followed during his research in the weeks before his death.

Chapter 16
A FEATHERED LADY

INSIDE COIT TOWER, the niece pulled out her glasses, wiped off the lenses with her shirttail, and tried to see over the heads of the tour group gathered by the front entrance. Still lacking a direct line of sight, she pushed herself up onto her tiptoes as the docent launched into a brief discussion of the landmark's history.

"Now, you've all observed the tower's overall shape. It's visible from a good many vantage points throughout the city. If you were to ask the casual observer, 'What shape is Coit Tower?' nine out of ten would tell you, without hesitation, that it looks like a fire hose."

The niece spied a clump of peacock feathers bobbing back and forth in the middle of the crowd. The blue and green plumes stuck straight into the air, part of an elaborate arrangement affixed to the docent's hat.

She couldn't see the face beneath the elaborate headgear, but Dilla Eckles was the only person she knew who would wear such an eccentric accessory.

The niece edged closer to the tour group as the docent continued her monologue. Dilla was also one of the few people who might be able to tell her where her uncle had been hiding out and when he might plan to reappear.

"The fire hose shape seems like a logical conclusion," Dilla continued. "After all, the tower was built with funds from the estate of Lillie Hitchcock Coit, a woman who had a great fondness for firefighters. When Lillie was a young child, she was saved from a raging house fire by one of the city's volunteer fire departments. From that day forward, she became an enthusiastic supporter of the local firefighting heroes. She cheered their units whenever she saw them go by, and she eventually became the official mascot for fire truck number five."

The niece shuffled to one side, finally gaining a view of the woman beneath the heavily plumed hat. Her ears hadn't led her astray. It was definitely one of her uncle's coconspirators.

What was Dilla doing working as a park service docent, the niece wondered.

And then a second thought crossed her mind: she'd been taking the same running route for the last several weeks.

Was their meeting here at the tower a coincidence or was this one of her secretive uncle's attempts to communicate?

THE NIECE WATCHED Dilla corral the tour group in the foyer, gathering them around her so that they didn't miss any of her spiel.

A bubbly woman with a wild flair for fashion, Dilla was easily the most unusual character in any given room. She put the *e* in eccentric.

In addition to the feathered hat, today Dilla's plump, pear-shaped figure was clad in a bright blue sweater, green velvet skirt, and matching horizontal-striped stockings—a relatively tame outfit, by her standards. In the two years since they'd first met, the niece had seen Dilla in far more elaborate get-ups.

A lifelong resident of San Francisco, Dilla's family tree was as colorful and varied as her wardrobe. She'd been married multiples times—the niece had never managed to obtain an accurate count on the total number of ex-husbands. And she had married on both sides of the law: one of her exes was locked up at San Quentin, while her current spouse was a retired policeman.

Dilla's offspring, too, tended to polar opposites.

Her daughter, Miranda Richards, was a high-powered San Francisco attorney, whom Oscar had appointed as the executor of his estate.

The mere thought of Miranda's prickly personality and acrid perfume made the niece cringe. She was unsure whether Miranda knew that Oscar wasn't really dead, but the niece wasn't about to voluntarily relay that information.

Dilla's son, on the other hand, was a far gentler if often misunderstood soul, who had inherited more of his mother's quirky nature. Sam Eckles had worked for many years as a janitor at City Hall before finding his true calling as an amphibian consultant to the California Academy of Sciences. Known in biologists' circles as the Frog Whisperer, Sam had disappeared along with Oscar the night the missing albino alligator was discovered at Mountain Lake—the same night the intern was slain at City Hall.

The niece's hand tightened around the water bottle as she recalled that both Sam and Oscar (or at least, the James Lick version of Oscar) were wanted for questioning in the Spider Jones murder.

Straightening her shoulders with resolve, she took another step toward the docent.

If anyone could shed light on the situation, it was Dilla.

DILLA TRAINED HER attention on the assortment of locals and out-of-town visitors who made up the tour group. She appeared not to notice the newcomer peeking around the far side of the crowd.

"Given Lillie Coit's love of firefighters and the tower's obvious nozzle shape, you might think the tower design was intended to emulate a fire hose. But you'd be wrong."

A spectator standing next to Dilla took a feather to the face as she turned and motioned for the group to move into the entranceway.

"Arthur Brown Jr., the architect of this and many other famous buildings and landmarks across San Francisco, swore to his dying breath that any resemblance between Coit Tower and a fire hose was pure coincidence. He insisted the fluted shape was, instead, a well-recognized Art Deco motif, and that it had absolutely nothing to do with firemen, fire hoses, or . . ."

Dilla took a wide step out the door. Cocking one eye, she looked pointedly up at the phoenix mounted over the tower entrance. "Or any other fire-related symbols."

Returning to the foyer, Dilla's gaze met that of the niece.

The feather-topped woman gave the sweaty jogger a broad wink, as if she'd been expecting her arrival all along.

Chapter 17
MISMATCHED MONUMENTS

THE NIECE FOLLOWED Dilla's tour group through the hallway that circled Coit Tower's base, puzzling over the fortuitousness of having stumbled across one of her uncle's close colleagues during her daily run. She was growing more and more convinced that the meeting was not a coincidence.

But if Dilla's role as docent was an improvised performance, she showed no signs of it. She resumed her monologue with ease. Other than the conspiring wink, she made no indication that she'd recognized the niece or had expected to run into her during the day's tour.

"All of the fresco murals here in Coit Tower were painted under the New Deal Public Works program enacted during the Great Depression. The program was designed to provide short-term employment for out-of-work artists. Twenty-seven primary artists were given wall space within the tower, and each one brought several assistants. You can imagine that this hallway got a little cramped when they were all packed in here. No one believed that so many artists could work together productively and without conflict."

She swept her hands through the air, gesturing at the murals. "Not only did they manage to get along, but they painted in such harmony that most visitors believe that all these pieces were done by the same person."

Mingling with the rest of the tour group, the niece scanned the colorful images plastered across the walls.

The murals depicted panoramic scenes from the 1930s, capturing Californians in various aspects of their regular life. There were agricultural landscapes featuring farmers tending their livestock, picking oranges, drying apricots, and processing grapes into wine. Industrial settings focused on engineers supervising the construction of dams and railroads, workers manning assembly lines, and welders forging metal. In the Sierra Mountains, prospectors panned for gold, and in laboratories, scientists pursued intellectual breakthroughs. Lastly, there were city scenes, showcasing examples of San Franciscans going about their daily routines.

Dilla gave the tour group a few minutes to study the murals before moving on with her dialogue.

"The Works program proved so successful that it was expanded to public buildings across the country. Additional New Deal murals were contracted in San Francisco, the most prominent being in the Rincon Post Office down by the Embarcadero and the Beach Chalet in Golden Gate Park."

With her overview of the murals completed, Dilla began highlighting some of the paintings' specific features.

"Now, I said that the artists all worked in harmony. That's true. But these were creative, independent types, so as you might expect, there was plenty of back-and-forth, good-natured pranking."

She drew the crowd to a farm scene painted adjacent to one of the hallway corners. "The painters needed models for the figures they depicted in the murals, so they took inspiration from what was readily available: themselves and the other artists."

She pointed at a farmer standing in a barn next to a cow.

"You see on the wall here, the man who's been tasked with cleaning the animals? That's one of the artists—not the one who painted this mural. Note that he's shown hosing down the cow's rear end." She grinned at the crowd. "The painter thought that was funny."

After highlighting a few more mural jokes, Dilla shifted to a different type of visual allusion.

"Some of the subtextual meanings were far more serious or controversial in nature. If you look at this library scene, you'll see an example. A number of the artists apprenticed under Diego Rivera—a famous Mexican muralist who was also a well-known Communist. The painters were influenced by Diego's political views as well as his artistic techniques. Now, focus on the bookshelf there on the left. One of the artists is depicted reaching for a book. It's *Das Capital* by Karl Marx."

After everyone had a chance to inspect the various books painted into the library scene, Dilla guided the tour group toward a painted wall across from one of the plate glass windows. A bench anchored to the tile floor in the middle of the hallway provided a comfortable viewing spot out the window to the Bay Bridge and, on the inward-facing angle, the colorful mural, which depicted a San Francisco street scene.

"There were other messages conveyed through the murals . . ." Dilla began, when a member of the tour group piped up with a question.

"Excuse me, ma'am. How did you get interested in these murals, if you don't mind me asking?"

Dilla acknowledged the speaker. "I worked on a renovation project here a few years back. The interior is exposed to a great deal of moisture from the air, and the paintings need constant attention. They're always looking for volunteers."

Her gray eyes twinkled mischievously. "A close friend got me involved. He brought me in and showed me around. He knew everything about the history of the place and the artists who worked here."

She nodded at the San Francisco street scene and then turned to look directly at the niece.

"He was particularly fascinated with this mural."

DILLA RAISED HER hand above her feathered hat and dangled a key ring in the air.

"I've got a treat for you," she said, ushering the tour group toward the tower's front entrance. "I have special permission to let you into the stairwell today. There are several additional murals inside that are closed off to the general public. Step along right this way."

As the group filtered around the corner and up the staircase, the niece stayed behind to inspect the cityscape that Dilla had so adroitly referenced.

Brass railings had been posted throughout the hallway to keep the viewing public a safe distance from the walls. Small plaques affixed to the rail gave the title of each mural and the principal artist.

The cityscape was titled *City Life* by Victor Arnautoff.

The niece took a seat on the bench and stared at the brightly colored painting. Spanning two huge quadrants on either side of the rear entrance to the trinket shop, it was one of the largest murals in the Coit Tower collection. The mesmerizing tableau was filled with dozens of busy San Franciscans, countless moving pieces frozen mid-action.

According to the information on the railing placard, Arnautoff had painted himself into the piece. Using the placard's description, the niece was able to spot the artist near the center of the mural, next to the trinket shop door.

Arnautoff's self-portrait depicted a man with broad imposing shoulders, a strong jaw, and closely cropped hair. He wore a thick camel jacket and a jauntily tilted fedora hat. While his figure stood facing toward the left, his head was turned to look straight out into the hallway. He had a crafty, cagy stare that was almost unsettling to the viewer.

"It feels like he's trying to tell me something," the niece said. "I just wish I knew what it was."

Sliding her gaze to the left, she picked out a signpost marking the intersection of Washington and Montgomery.

That would put the mural's viewpoint at the lower end of Columbus Avenue, she reasoned, mapping the location in her head. She'd passed by the intersection at the beginning of her run.

The niece frowned, perplexed. Something was off.

She broadened her view, seeking additional markers.

On the mural's right-hand span, a second street sign pointed toward the Oakland auto ferry. That service had been rendered obsolete by the construction of the Bay Bridge, and she wasn't sure where in downtown San Francisco the car ferry had originally docked.

Puzzled, she returned her gaze to the mural's left-hand panel. Across the upper horizon, she recognized the square shape of the national bank building and the sculpted pillars that fronted the Pacific Stock Exchange. Toward the center, in the space over the convenience store entrance, she found City Hall's ornate dome and the Asian Art Museum. On the mural's upper right, another museum, the Legion of Honor, resided on a hilltop.

"That's not right," the niece murmured, shaking her head. "There's no way you could see this view from that intersection."

She shifted her focus to the many human figures spread across the wide scene.

In the upper middle, policemen and firefighters attended to the victim of a traffic accident, while a fire truck, marked engine number five, raced down what appeared to be Columbus's diagonal roadway.

Closer to the front of the mural, a postman removed letters from the storage cabinet of a US Mail drop box. In another mini-scene, a suited man was held up by a robber who had slipped in behind his back and pulled a gun. A few feet away, a policeman stood at a call box, apparently unaware of the nearby crime. Dockworkers unloaded boxes of produce, and businessmen milled about a newspaper stand perusing the latest headlines.

And there, in the middle of it all, was Arnautoff, overtly eying her.

The niece rotated her head one way, and then the other. The details were myriad and incredibly distracting. She stood from the bench, leaning forward and back, her brow furrowed as she studied the full sweep of the scene. Then she blocked out the people at the front of the mural and concentrated on the landmarks across the top.

"City Hall, the Legion of Honor, the Pacific Stock Exchange, they're not in the right orientation," she finally concluded, placing her hands on her hips.

"They're in the wrong place."

AS THE NIECE stood in the empty hallway, pondering the mural's geographic anomalies, an eerie sensation swept over her. It was similar to her earlier experience during the start of her hike up Telegraph Hill.

She was not alone.

Someone—other than the painted Arnautoff—was watching her.

She spun around, quickly scanning the curved corridor. She peeked into the souvenir shop, but even the attendant manning the cash register had left his post. Turning, she looked out the window, craning to see around the side of the building, certain that someone must be hiding in the bushes.

Nothing.

Anxious, she eased back down onto the bench, trying to calm her nerves.

Then she watched, stunned, as a set of wet footprints—in the distinctive tread of rubber-soled high-top sneakers—appeared across the tile floor and tracked toward the tower's exit.

The Painted Words

Chapter 18

YOU ONLY DIE ONCE

LEAVING THE BEFUDDLED niece inside the mural hallway, Spider hurried out of Coit Tower and down the asphalt drive.

Since his sudden ghostly appearance earlier that morning, he'd been waiting for direction, some indication of his intended purpose.

What he was doing here and how long would his supernatural visit last? Why had he been brought back to the land of the living? To avenge his death or to help identify his killer?

But after observing the niece in front of the *City Life* mural—and her obvious confusion at its mismatched monuments—he was infused with a new sense of motivation and resolve.

The brown-haired woman clearly hadn't appreciated the significance of what she'd seen in the mural. She must not have known about the trail of hidden markers her uncle had discovered in San Francisco's New Deal artwork.

It was his task, he intuited, to steer her in the right direction—along the same path her uncle had followed—and toward the scrawling letter *O*.

Spider grinned with confidence.

He had an idea of how to prod her along.

JOGGING THROUGH THE rain, Spider reached the edge of Pioneer Park and started down a sidewalk that would take him toward Columbus Avenue.

He had at least a five-minute lead on the niece. That should give him enough time to get into the Green Vase and leave his clue before she returned.

If only he had his old bike, he thought longingly. He could have quickly ridden it down to Jackson Square. He felt lost in the city without his trusty wheels.

Then his eyes lit upon an object propped against the front porch of a second-story walk-up—a plastic plank with rollers attached to its bottom side. The skateboard was scuffed and missing several chips of paint, a sign that it saw regular use.

"That might do the trick," Spider whispered eagerly.

He glanced surreptitiously up and down the street, checking for bystanders. Not yet adjusted to his new ephemeral existence, he completely forgot that he held the advantage of invisibility.

Seeing no potential objectors, he edged casually toward the building's front stairs. After one last look around, he sprinted up the steps and snatched the board. Carrying it in his arms, he raced back to the street.

A MOMENT LATER, Spider was flying down the hill. His sneakered feet balanced with ease on the board's contoured surface. He knees bent to a deep forty-five-degree angle, skillfully absorbing every bump and rut in the road.

He was a picture of perfect coordination—that no one could see to appreciate. To the few pedestrians who noticed the seemingly self-propelled skateboard rocketing along the pavement, it was just another odd occurrence on the streets of San Francisco.

For Spider, the skateboard provided the fun of an amusement park ride combined with the challenge a video game, all rolled into one fantastic thrill. A rush of freedom coursed through his phantom body. He was a vibrant memory of his former self, brazenly whipping around corners, splashing through puddles, and skidding across slick spots. The wet wind slapped his face, and a laugh bubbled up through his chest, casting a shimmering disturbance in the rain.

He rounded a sharp turn, tilting the board to lean into the curve. It was a tight hook, and he narrowly avoided a catastrophic wipeout on an unexpected pothole cover.

Spider looked back at the turn, admiring his feat. Still celebrating the successful maneuver, he returned his gaze to the road ahead—and spied a small delivery truck parked outside of a corner grocery, blocking the road as the truck's driver unloaded supplies.

The barrier was located directly in front of him. There was no way to stop or even jump off the board.

He winced, anticipating the collision, as the speeding skateboard closed in on the side of the truck. A second before impact, he let out an involuntary yelp, and threw his hands up in front of his face.

But the crash never came.

Spider's body passed through the outer metal flashing and into the truck's cramped cargo hold.

His eyes popped open to a whipping view of shrink-wrapped packaging, boxes of fruit, and crates of bagged potato chips.

"What?" he managed to peep out before sliding through the flat blank of the truck's opposite wall and out the other side.

Dazed, Spider looked down at his feet. They were still planted on the skateboard, which had rolled through beneath the truck without hindrance.

PUZZLING AT SPIDER'S voice, the driver looked up from his loaded dolly, which he'd just hefted over the curb.

He spied the apparently unmanned skateboard rolling down the hill. Concerned, he parked the dolly and bent to look under the truck's carriage. Seeing nothing, he shrugged his shoulders and resumed his delivery.

SPIDER ROLLED SLOWLY toward Washington Square, keeping the skateboard under much greater control. Despite having streamed through the truck without harm, the experience had left him momentarily dazed.

A drizzling mist shrouded the park. The church's courtyard had fallen silent; the students had returned inside for their next round of lessons.

Chattering groups of Asian women peeled off for the bus stop, their morning tai chi session having just finished. One of the practitioners looked at Spider as he surfed past, and for a moment, he thought he saw his reflection in her eyes.

Then she pointed at the skateboard and laughed at its apparent self-propulsion.

She was looking right through him, Spider suddenly realized. He was invisible, a spirit released from his human form.

The magnitude of the situation finally hit him. The joy of the day's adventure deflated like a popped balloon. He was nothing more than an empty shell, an illusion of life, missing all of its essential elements.

There was no threat or danger that could touch him. The adrenaline from his near-collision faded with the negation of the risk. Without the possibility of pain or fear, the emotions on the opposite end of the spectrum were impossible to achieve. These were sensations reserved for the living.

His turn was over.

You only die once.

Chapter 19
COLLEAGUES

A SOMBER, SUBDUED Spider returned to Jackson Square a few minutes later.

"Time to get down to business," he said firmly.

The skateboard rounded the corner just as Montgomery Carmichael stepped out of his art studio and into a waiting taxi. The interim mayor looked the part, dressed in a dark suit and shiny leather shoes.

Spider watched the taxi pull away. Then he steered to a stop on the exact spot where he'd begun the day. Leaning the board against the studio's front entrance, he approached the nearest glass window. He slipped seamlessly through and began searching for supplies.

After circling the many easels set up around the room, he reached a desk positioned in the center. He dug around in the desk's drawers before shifting to an adjacent plastic shelving unit.

"Aha," he exclaimed upon finding Monty's collection of paints. The bin was packed with tubes, tins, cans, and glass jars of every imaginable size, color, and formulation.

Spider sat back on his heels, pondering the vast array of options.

Then he made his selection.

He picked up a small can of water-based paint labeled with a sticker colored dark brick red, the shade of spilled blood.

ARMED WITH THE paint can and a medium-sized brush, Spider returned to the sidewalk, this time by unlocking the front door and passing through its opening.

The rain had begun yet another cycle of lessening, and the wet street sparkled as the sun once more broke through the clouds.

Spider crossed to the Green Vase antique shop, striding up to its redbrick storefront. He stopped in front of the scrolling iron-framed door and stared down at the brass handle, whose surface was shaped in the form of a three-petaled tulip.

He'd been stymied by this locked door the last time he'd tried to gain access to the store. In that instance, he'd circled to the alley around back, climbed on top of a metal Dumpster, and leaped toward the ledge of the building's second-floor window.

"That was an adventure," he said, allowing himself a triumphant smile. He had hung from the ledge for several seconds before finally forcing open the window and crawling inside.

"No need for such antics now," he added, grimly observing his reflection in the door's glass panes—no more than a paint can and a brush hovering in the air.

With a sigh, Spider kicked his left foot forward, expecting to flow smoothly through to the other side. Mid-stride, however, his motion was abruptly stopped.

Clink.

The brush fell to the ground as the paint can, still gripped in his hand, smacked against the door's outer surface.

"Right."

Muttering under his breath, Spider jumped back outside, set the can on the sidewalk next to the brush, and slid through the doorway, this time unimpeded. Once inside, he unlocked the door, swung it open, and retrieved his supplies.

"I'll never get the hang of this ghost business."

It wasn't until he shut the door and turned back toward the showroom that he realized he was not alone.

An orange and white cat sat on the floor looking up at him.

A line of hackles rose along Isabella's back as she stared suspiciously at the intruder.

"She can't see me," Spider assured himself. "She's just looking at the brush and paint can."

He waved his free hand to the left, expecting no reaction. But he watched in amazement as Isabella's ice blue eyes tracked the movement. Then she returned her gaze to his chest.

"Can you see me?" he whispered excitedly. He paused, tamping down his enthusiasm. She was probably just tracking his voice.

Spider decided to test the cat with a different action. Setting the supplies on the cashier counter, he silently jogged around to the opposite side of where Isabella was sitting. He waited, expecting her to remain stationary.

He watched with elation as she warily turned to face him.

"You don't know how happy you just made me," he said gleefully. Taking a step forward, he reached down to pet her.

At Isabella's stern *"Mrao,"* he jumped back, holding his hands, palms out, in front of his chest.

"Okay, okay. We don't have to be friends." The mere possibility of animal interaction greatly improved his mood. He felt far less isolated and alone. "We can be associates. Colleagues, if you like."

Spider walked around the showroom, inspecting the display area. It was almost exactly the same as when he had last visited, except that the hatch to the basement was now closed.

As he stood by the leather recliner, reflecting, he heard the elegant saunter of paws padding across the wooden floor.

Isabella circled his feet, sniffing ever so delicately. She seemed to have relented, if only just a little. She sat on her haunches and waved a front paw in the air.

"Oh, so now you want me to pet you," Spider said with a grin.

Isabella lifted her head in a regal gesture that clearly conveyed her response: I have decided to allow you the privilege of petting me.

Tentatively, Spider bent again.

Isabella held her head perfectly still as the ghostly hand reached out and dropped onto the silky white crown between her orange-tipped ears.

Spider felt a tingling beneath his fingertips—the slight vibration of a rumbling purr.

Chapter 20

THE PANTRY

WHILE ISABELLA COMMUNED with Spider's ghost, Rupert returned to the feeding station in the upstairs kitchen, in the hope that his old food might have magically reappeared.

Rupert cautiously approached his bowl and took a short whiff of the offensive material that had been left there. As he stared in disgust at the off-putting brown tidbit of diet cat food, his earlier anger returned.

Here he was, wasting away, a mere shadow of his former fluffy self, while his person was out running around San Francisco. How could she have left him here for—he glanced up the clock on the wall—for forty-five minutes with nothing but a bowl of diet cat food? It was the ultimate betrayal.

Disgruntled, Rupert paced a circle through the kitchen, his furry feet stomping in indignation.

As he passed the pantry door, however, a faint scent, smothered by packaging, triggered an alarm in his sensitive nose.

It was coming from inside the pantry.

Sniffing loudly at the half-inch space along the door's

bottom threshold, Rupert sucked in the closet's full array of odors, creating an aroma inventory of the interior contents.

It took him a moment to process the data. Mentally, he sifted through the identified objects, filtering out a box of cereal, several cans of soup, various cleaning supplies and dry goods, and, of course, the container holding the new diet cat food.

Then he sat upright, straightening his shoulders. He had reached his conclusion. He was certain of his results.

His person had not been altogether truthful earlier when she told him he'd finished off the last bag of his old cat food. There was an unopened bag trapped on the other side of this door.

Traitorous scoundrel of a woman.

Rupert focused his feline brain waves on the flat wooden surface. His wobbly blue eyes crossed with concentration. His whiskers quivered with intensity.

Open sesame, he commanded, but the door didn't budge.

Trying a different approach, Rupert raised himself up on his back legs, propped his front paws against the door's lower panel, and pushed with all his might.

The door rocked in its hinges, but remained solidly shut.

Dropping back to all fours, Rupert trotted into the center of the room, about five feet away. Puffing out his chest like a raging bull, he charged at the door, slamming into it with the full force of his furry body.

Still nothing—other than a dull ache in his shoulder.

He was about to despair when he heard a noise on the stairs. Turning, he spied his sister and a faintly glowing figure in the shape of a young man.

Rupert trotted amicably over, his tail popped up in a friendly gesture.

Perhaps their newfound friend had better taste in cat food than Oscar's niece.

IT DIDN'T TAKE much effort for Isabella to guide Spider to the pantry door and convince him to open the bag of regular cat food. Under her supervision—and Rupert's delighted gaze—the diet formulation was tossed into the trash, the bowls rinsed out in the sink, and a generous amount of the old concoction poured in.

As a loud munching commenced beneath the kitchen table, Spider popped open the paint can and dipped his brush inside. Crouched on the tile floor, he held the red tip in the air for several seconds, contemplating the right words.

Then he began to paint his message.

"Follow the Murals."

Beneath this slogan, he drew a large looping *O.*

The Newsroom

Chapter 21

SWEET CAKES

HOXTON FINN SAT in a barber chair with a vinyl cape strapped around his neck, his peppery-gray hair wet and combed back.

The newsroom had been converted into a makeshift salon, with the barber chair at its center and the stylist who worked for the newspaper's television affiliate standing on a short stool behind it, snipping away with his shears. The same stool had assisted a few minutes earlier when, accompanied by a considerable amount of grumbling, the stylist had washed Hox's hair by dunking his head in one of the bathroom sinks.

The wispy little man had been assigned by the news station to revamp Hox's image. The reporter could no longer hide behind his black-and-white byline; modern media demanded a much more visual presence. The increasing number of television appearances had dictated a makeover—of his upper half, at least, the portion that was routinely captured on film.

It was not a process that Hoxton Finn had readily embraced.

Several months into the project, neither the reporter nor the stylist was satisfied with the results—but the pair had developed a lively rapport.

"Humphrey," the reporter sniped, "I've got cold water running down the back of my neck."

"There, there, dear," the stylist replied soothingly, dabbing the drips with a clean towel.

Hox rolled his eyes in annoyance.

"I told you, don't call me 'dear.' "

Humphrey nodded agreeably.

"Yes, yes, of course," he replied impishly. "I wouldn't dream of it . . . *sweet cakes*."

HOX CLOSED HIS eyes as Humphrey continued his work. The whirring scissors provided a calming background noise, and the reporter's thoughts returned to the unresolved questions surrounding the murdered City Hall staffer.

His jaw clenched as he mulled over the case. He still couldn't shake the unsettled feeling that he had overlooked an important piece of evidence.

Humphrey finished the day's clipping and switched out the shears for a hair dryer. As he aimed the hot air gun at the reporter's scalp, he noticed Hox's tense expression.

He was starting to worry about his prickly friend. This was the third all-night session after which he'd been called in to revive Hox for a television shoot. The Spider Jones murder was becoming an unhealthy obsession.

The stylist pumped his thin eyebrows as an idea popped into his head. He knew just how to distract the moody reporter. Shutting off the dryer, he picked up a comb.

"Guess who's on the front cover of the gossip magazines this week?" he asked slyly.

Hox groaned his response. He knew where this was going. He'd seen the horrifying spread on a Market Street newsstand when he'd slipped out to grab breakfast a few hours earlier.

"Your ex, the movie star," Humphrey supplied with a cheeky grin. "And her fiancé."

Ever since her New Year's Eve engagement, the celebrity news had been full of stories about Hox's ex-wife and her impending marriage—to a much younger male model.

Hox sighed testily. "Why'd it have to be the model?"

IT WASN'T A matter of jealousy—or, at least, that wasn't the primary cause of Hox's angst. Long ago, he had accepted the fact that his ex-wife would eventually remarry.

Since their divorce, she had dated a slew of powerful and distinguished men. There'd been politicians, business moguls, and movie producers, any one of which Hox would have been relatively content for her to choose as her next husband. He felt he could measure up to the representatives she'd chosen from those categories.

Not so, the male model.

The comparison wasn't solely one of Hox's making.

Every entertainment news report featuring his ex-wife included an obligatory dating biography, starting of course, with her failed marriage to Hox. He was forever lumped together with the men who came after.

Since the movie star's engagement, however, the coverage had been intensely focused on the comparison between the first husband and the new fiancé. Each article included a picture of Hox—not the distinguished headshot from his official newspaper bio, but a paparazzi snap taken as he was being wheeled out of the hospital after having the tip of his left toe amputated.

It was, quite possibly, the worst photo ever taken of him. His face was pale from the recent blood loss. The administration of numerous vaccine shots and an IV drip of Komodo dragon anti-venom had sickened his stomach. His hair was rumpled and sticking up all over the place from having slept the previous night in a hospital bed.

The miserable post-operation photo was now being juxtaposed with that of the model fiancé, who, by all accounts, was an athletic Adonis.

The situation was bound to get worse before it got better. The wedding wasn't scheduled to take place until late spring.

As Hox brooded over the unfair celebrity news coverage, Humphrey squeezed a dollop of hair gel into the palm of his hand and tutted sympathetically.

"Don't you fret, Hoxy. That gorgeous man's got nothing on you . . . *dear*."

IGNORING HUMPHREY'S MOCKING endearment, Hox refocused his thoughts on the Spider Jones case. Once more, he began mentally reviewing the information he'd collected in the spare conference room.

After a moment he sat bolt upright in the barber chair, his rugged face registering a sudden insight. Blinking, he rubbed his eyes.

"Humphrey, I need a file from the workroom. Second pile to the left, third one down."

"You can get it yourself," Humphrey replied with a flourish. "We're all done here."

He unsnapped the vinyl cover he'd secured around the reporter's neck.

Hox grimaced as Humphrey gave him a reassuring pat on the shoulder and blew a kiss into the air.

"*Mmm-wa.* You look fabulous."

Chapter 22

FRIED CHICKEN FANATIC

TWENTY MINUTES LATER, Humphrey knocked on the closed door to the newspaper's conference room. He could see Hox inside, bent over the table, examining one of the many file folders relating to the Spider Jones murder.

The reporter strummed his chin, pondering a line item in the police evidence report. If he'd heard the stylist's knock, he showed no indication of it.

Humphrey opened the door and stuck his head inside.

"Uh, Hox?" he said, tapping the designer watch strapped to his wrist. "We've got to head over to City Hall for your interview with the interim mayor."

Slowly, Hox rotated toward the door.

"Tell me this, Humphrey," he said as he scooped up the file. "What's your favorite place to eat here in San Francisco?"

The stylist pumped his eyebrows. "Why? Are you asking me out on a date?"

Humphrey laughed at his own joke, but after Hox's reprimanding stare he straightened his mouth into a serious expression.

"Let me see. It changes by the week. There's that Vietnamese joint in the Mission—that's high on everyone's list right now. Long lines to get in though. And, of course, there's the fusion spot on Polk Street, one of my all-time favorites. It's hard to pick just one. There are so many good restaurants . . ."

"Exactly," Hox cut in. "You're a foodie. And pretentious." He smacked the file against his left thigh. "The kid was neither."

Grabbing his notepad, he shoved it into his coat pocket. Then he pushed past Humphrey and strode briskly down the hallway. At the corner, he paused to look back at the confused stylist.

"Come on, let's go. We're making a quick stop along the way."

Humphrey grabbed his jacket from a hook on the wall and jogged down the corridor.

"Where?" Humphrey panted. "We don't have much time, you know."

Hox started down the stairs leading to the building's street level. "North Beach."

"That's not on the way," Humphrey called out as he chugged after Hox. "That's on the other side of town. The producer lady made me promise I'd get you to the mayor's office at one P.M. sharp."

Hox waved his hand dismissively. "Montgomery Carmichael can wait. He's not going anywhere."

As he pushed open the building's front door, he added a sarcastic aside. "Unfortunately."

AFTER A SHORT cab ride up and over the city's hilly center, Hox and Humphrey hopped out at Columbus Avenue. The reporter set off briskly along the sidewalk, *thwacking* the file against his left leg, his broad shoulders deftly parting the lunchtime crowds.

A number of waiters stood outside the street's row of Italian restaurants, catcalling to passersby and waving menus in the face of anyone who slowed or showed the slightest interest. Hox fended each one off with his steely-eyed stare and a menacing *pop* of the file folder.

Humphrey trailed several feet behind. Detained by every entreating waiter, he politely declined the offers as he fought his way past.

It was all the stylist could do to keep sight of Hox's peppered gray head and the perfectly coiffed hair that was quickly deteriorating in the day's misty air.

A FEW BLOCKS up the street, Hox stopped at a corner to consult the information in his file, allowing Humphrey time to catch up.

Licking his thumb, Hox pulled out a photocopy of a recent newspaper article.

The article was from the newspaper's dining section. It wasn't a typical review entry but an obituary-styled posting, mourning the closing of a North Beach diner whose signature dish had become an overnight sensation.

> *Fried chicken gourmands throughout the city have suffered a terrible loss with the impromptu closing of Lick's Homestyle Chicken . . .*

Hox noted the address listed at the end of the article and compared it against that of the empty storefront about five yards from where he stood.

"Hox," Humphrey panted between breaths as he gripped his side. "We're going to be late."

"It's up here," Hox replied, motioning for the stylist to follow.

"But, but . . ." Humphrey protested, before throwing his hands up and trotting after the reporter.

CUPPING HIS HAND across his forehead, Hox peered through the vacated diner's grimy storefront glass. The interior was empty, devoid of any tables, chairs, or wall hangings, but a dim light appeared to be turned on in the rear of the building.

Sliding over to the entrance, Hox pushed in on its flat handle. The door swung open, creaking on its hinges.

Humphrey peeked nervously over the reporter's shoulder as together they looked inside. They were greeted by a puff of musty air. The abandoned diner smelled of mold and the faint whiff of stale chicken grease.

Hox leaned forward, listening intently. Hearing nothing, he glanced back at the stylist.

"Cover me."

Humphrey's face registered alarm.

"Oh, no. No, no," he sputtered in protest. "That's not in my job description."

"Sure it is, *honey muffin*," Hox replied caustically as he crept into the diner. "Don't you think my hair is going to need a touchup after this?"

HUMPHREY HOVERED IN the doorway as Hox circled what had once been the diner's front seating area and then passed through an opening to the kitchen. A bare bulb screwed into a ceiling socket had been left burning, the source of the light he'd seen from the street. Other than a worn stool, the area had been cleaned out of all skillets, pans, or other cooking utensils.

But on the floor behind the counter, Hox noticed a discarded takeout box. Lifting it up to the bulb, he examined the gold writing on the green paper exterior.

Mumbling to himself, he once more consulted the article from the file, scanning to the last line of the text.

And so, we resign ourselves to the end of the precious little green and gold takeout boxes. So long to Lick's fabulous fried chicken.

Setting aside the article, Hox flipped to a page that he'd copied from the police evidence report. It listed everything that had been found within a ten-foot radius of Spider's desk in the basement of City Hall. He thumped his finger against a line item at the bottom of the list.

The nearest trash bin to the intern's desk had contained several greasy green takeout boxes.

"It's a match," Hox mused as Humphrey scampered up behind him. "Spider was a fried chicken fanatic."

"What's that got to do with anything?" Humphrey asked.

With a grunt, Hox slapped the file shut. He pondered the eyewitness statement that James Lick had been seen fleeing the crime scene. "It may well have gotten him killed."

The stylist looked at the reporter as if he'd lost his mind.

"Okay, Columbo," he said, threading his arm around Hox's elbow. "Let's get you to your interview."

The Interim Mayor

Chapter 23

THE ALLIGATOR WRESTLER

FROM THE BACKSEAT of his taxi, Montgomery Carmichael watched the sun break through the clouds, shining bright rays across San Francisco's sodden hills.

Like the weather, his mood had dramatically improved since the temper tantrum he'd thrown a few hours earlier.

His artistic frustration at the difficult sketch had lifted, seemingly mid-stomp. He'd swept up the shards of broken wood from the destroyed picture frame, tidied the studio, and retreated to the upstairs apartment to change for his afternoon interview at City Hall—his first since receiving the interim mayor appointment.

Checking his look in the car's rearview mirror, Monty tugged at the corners of the emerald green bowtie secured around his neck. Then he gently pulled back the sleeves of his jacket so he could straighten his gold cuff links. Forged in the shape of leaping frogs, they were his favorite pair—a bona fide good luck charm.

On the car seat next to him lay a new sketchpad, still wrapped in its protective shrink-wrap, and a small toolbox of art supplies that he'd scooped up on his way out the studio door.

A broad grin beamed across his narrow face.

Tapping the sketchpad's flat surface, he made a confident announcement.

"I'm ready to give that drawing another go."

The driver glanced quizzically over his shoulder and then grunted a noncommittal response. Monty's next statement, however, drew a more concerned look.

"I've wiped the image of that dead kid completely from my mind."

MINUTES LATER, MONTY marched cheerfully up City Hall's front steps. Even carrying the two-by-four-foot sketchpad and the artist's toolbox, he still managed to greet every person he passed—whether they recognized him as the interim mayor or not.

"Good morning, folks," he called out to a group of Japanese tourists exiting an enormous tour bus. "Welcome to San Francisco."

Passing a couple in wedding gear headed inside for their civil ceremony, he sang out another enthusiastic, "Good morning!" Nodding at the woman's dress, he added, "And congratulations!"

Inside the main doors, Monty approached the security checkpoint and lined up behind the president of the board of supervisors. After handing his packages over to one of the guards for inspection, he tapped the supervisor on the shoulder and said gleefully, "Supervisor Hernandez, it's great to see you."

The supervisor jumped as if he'd been zapped by an electric shock. He glanced warily around, hoping that no one had seen him in such close proximity to the controversial new mayor.

"Mornin', sir," he whispered with a limp finger wave before hurrying off.

Unfazed, Monty swaggered through the security scanner, retrieved his packages from a donut-munching guard on the opposite side, and proceeded through the front foyer to the bank of elevators.

Cocking his arm, he used his elbow to push the elevator call button. As he waited for one of the doors to open, he tapped out a tune with the toes of his dress shoes, grooving his hips back and forth in time with his self-made music.

He was living the dream, and no one could convince him otherwise.

Mayor Monty—the phrase still sent chills down his spine.

The foot tapping slowly subsided as he thought back to the night it all happened, the magical evening when he became the interim mayor.

He remembered the scene like it was yesterday. If he closed his eyes, he could bring it all back: the foggy chill of Mountain Lake, the mud seeping up between his toes, the full-body wet suit chafing at his thighs—and the hungry *chomp* of an albino alligator snapping at his rubber-coated posterior.

Yes, Monty thought with another blissful smile, it was a fabulous night.

MONTY HAD NOT been among the crowds watching the board of supervisors deliberate the interim mayor selection. He had avoided City Hall altogether that evening.

He was, instead, several miles away, hard at work on the people's business—that is, returning Clive the albino alligator to his rightful place at the California Academy of Sciences. Acting on a tip he'd received from the proprietor of James Lick's Homestyle Chicken, Monty had driven with his neighbor and her two cats to Mountain Lake, intent on implementing an alligator rescue.

He had just parked his van in the secluded lot beside the lake when news of the board's decision was broadcast over the radio. The announcement was met with supportive cheers and congratulations from his colleagues, both female and feline alike—or at least, that's how he remembered it.

Flush with the triumph of his mayoral success, Monty jumped from the driver's seat and, protecting his modesty by hiding behind the van's back door, changed into a wet suit, snorkel mask, and flippers. Suited up, he charged valiantly into the murky water, splashing fearlessly through the marshy reeds, intent on wrestling the cagy beast out of the lake and into the van's rear cargo space.

It was a hard-fought battle, one that severely tested his mettle. Bravely, he faced the creature's vicious jaws, swiping claws, and wild swinging tail. There were moments when death or mortal injury appeared imminent, but the man who would be mayor would not give up.

In the end, he was victorious. He was about to load the pesky gator into the van when the police arrived on the scene.

Monty blinked his eyes, returning his vision to the flat facing of the elevator door.

At least, that's how he remembered it.

DING.

The elevator door opened, revealing a well-dressed man in a trench coat, tailored suit, and two-toned leather wing tips.

"Good morning, Mayor," the Previous Mayor intoned, placing a gloved hand on Monty's slim shoulder as he walked past.

The gesture represented, quite possibly, one of the most magical moments of Monty's life.

He nearly fell over himself trying to return the greeting.

"Hello, Mr. Mayor . . . Mr. Honorable Mayor . . . Mr. Honorable . . . Sir!"

Chapter 24

ASK THE ALLIGATOR

STILL BEAMING OVER the brotherhood he now shared with the Previous Mayor, Monty squeezed into the elevator carrying his sketchpad and toolbox.

"Two, please," he said to the woman who joined him inside.

As the carriage rumbled its way toward City Hall's second floor, he reflected on the excitement—and drama—of the two months since his miraculous appointment.

Even he had to admit it hadn't been all smooth sailing.

The morning after the board meeting, cell phone video surfaced showing the wet suit–clad interim mayor being chased out of Mountain Lake by the city's missing albino alligator.

In Monty's opinion, the video footage had been unfairly edited. The clip highlighted an unfortunate moment in his battle with the gator where the beast had temporarily gained the upper hand. It failed to include his brave march into the water. Moreover, the harsh light of the cell phone's flash feature had cast an unflattering glow on his already gaunt figure.

The video quickly went viral across the city. In coffee shops and Internet cafes, top-floor boardrooms and basement cubicles, it seemed everyone was streaming the thirty-second spot.

But the worst was yet to come.

The press quickly gathered outside Monty's art studio, demanding an explanation for the events depicted in the video. Quiet Jackson Square hadn't seen such a ruckus since the Barbary Coast days. News vans lined the street, their antennas extended in every direction. Reporters and their crews, armed with lighting equipment, microphones, and massive shoulder-held cameras crammed onto every available inch of sidewalk outside Monty's glass-walled studio.

When he finally emerged to give his carefully prepared statement, he was greeted with a barrage of rapid-fire questions.

Who had tipped him off to the location of the stolen alligator?

Was he involved in the gator's theft from its Swamp Exhibit in Golden Gate Park?

Had he leveraged Clive's hidden location to gain votes from the board of supervisors?

What was he doing running around at night in a wet suit and flippers?

Monty had finally hollered out over the crowd, "You'll have to ask the alligator!"

Then he stepped back inside the studio and locked the door.

WITH A SHUDDER, Monty shelved the memory. The elevator creaked to a stop on the second floor. He stepped out into the lobby and crossed to the entrance of the mayor's office suite.

Thankfully, the intrigue involving the murdered City Hall staffer had quickly swamped the coverage of both the cell phone video and Monty's panicked response to the reporters outside his studio.

He expected that the issue might be raised during today's interview with Hoxton Finn, but he felt that this time, he was better prepared. He planned to attribute the Mountain Lake episode to his previous life-coaching duties for the outgoing mayor. Any follow-up questions as to what life coaching could possibly have to do with wet suit alligator wrangling he would deflect with an assertion of executive privilege.

If that didn't work, he'd send a signal to Dilla. She had agreed to fill in as his administrative assistant for the afternoon. Should the interview become too confrontational, she was prepared to trigger the building's fire alarm.

Feeling confident and self-assured, Monty strode briskly into the mayoral office suite. Except for a massive wooden desk and a few armchairs, the area had been emptied of the previous occupant's belongings. Monty wouldn't officially move in until the day of his inauguration, but he had obtained clearance to use the facilities for the afternoon's interview.

He had about fifteen minutes to kill before the news crew was scheduled to arrive, so he unwrapped the sketchpad and laid it on the wide surface of the office's wooden desk. Opening the toolbox, he selected a charcoal pencil.

Then he began, once more, to draw the scene from the Green Vase antique shop, starting with Rupert's fluffy orange and white heap asleep on the dentist's recliner.

As his pencil scraped across the textured paper, he forced all thoughts of wily alligators and the murdered Spider Jones from his mind.

The Green Vase

Chapter 25

MESSAGE RECEIVED

THE NIECE JOGGED around the last corner of her return route, slowing to a walk as she approached the entrance to the Green Vase antique shop.

She unzipped her rain jacket and wiped her sweaty brow. Once the rain stopped and the sun came out, she had quickly overheated.

With a few deep lunges, she stretched her legs, carefully pulling on the muscles in her calves.

She had all but convinced herself that she'd imagined the footprints in the mural hallway at Coit Tower. Probably some sort of endorphin-induced delusion, she told herself, preferring to make up a condition rather than consider the alternatives.

The "Closed" sign hanging from the inner doorknob fluttered as she pushed open the door and stepped inside.

"Hello, kitty-cats," she hollered, loud enough to be heard in the upstairs apartment. She bent to remove her soggy running shoes and socks. "I'm back."

It wasn't until she straightened and began wiping her glasses on a tissue from the cashier counter that she noticed the set of red paw prints dotted across the wooden floor.

"What happened?" she gasped, fearing the paint was blood. "Rupert! Issy!"

As the niece scrambled to follow the prints across the showroom, two healthy, uninjured cats raced down the stairs, both of them covered in globs of red paint. The pair had paint on their paws and splotches across their backs. Isabella sported a perfect Q-tip of paint on the tip end of her tail, while Rupert bore a red stripe down his forehead.

"What did you two get into?" the niece demanded, although her immense relief drowned out any sternness in her voice. "Where did all this paint come from?" She suppressed a laugh at Rupert's comical facial expression. "And how did you get it all over yourselves?"

Isabella looked informatively up at her person. She made a series of vigorous chirps and clicking sounds, an apparent explanation of the circumstances that led to her paint-spotted condition. The lengthy commentary finally terminated in an opinionated *"Mrao, mrao."*

Rupert sat on the floor next to his sister, listening to her story. He tilted his head sideways, as if confirming Isabella's version of events.

The niece put her hands on her hips.

"I'm not understanding any of this."

Rolling over, Rupert sprawled his plump body across the floor at his person's feet. After a wide yawn, he let out a cat food–smelling burp.

ON THE HUNT for the source of the red paint, the niece tracked the red paw prints to the rear of the showroom. The trail clearly led up the stairs to the second floor.

"Stay here," the niece ordered firmly. She bent down toward Isabella, who had followed her to the edge of the steps.

"And don't try to lick off any of that paint."

Isabella gave her person a disgruntled look.

"Merrao-a-wao," she warbled.

From the center of the showroom, Rupert wheezed out a loud snore.

"Enjoy the nap," the niece muttered under her breath. "You're headed for a bath, mister."

THE NIECE SOON reached the kitchen, the epicenter of the cats' painting activity. The place was a mess, with spatters of red paint slung throughout the room.

A near-empty can of water-based latex lay upended on the tile floor amid a pool of its previous contents. Curious cats had obviously skidded through the dumped liquid, creating paw-shaped streaks. With paint coating their paws, they had then made the rounds of the kitchen table, the counters, and even the stovetop.

She sighed, envisioning the upcoming cleanup task.

Gingerly, she stepped through the maze of wet paint blots to the empty can, hoping its label might contain instructions on how to remove the sticky substance. She didn't have long before the stuff would start to dry.

As she made her way across the room, she glanced beneath the table at the cats' food bowls. The containers were empty except for a few giblets of cat food—the regular formulation, not the diet replacement she'd put out before she left for her run.

"How did the cats get into the pantry?" she murmured, before posing an even more troubling question. "And how did they get the bag down from the top shelf and pour the food into their bowls?"

She was halfway to the pantry when she noticed red lettering on the far side of the floor.

The paint here seemed dryer than the rest, and the markings had been left with a paintbrush. Human hands, not feline paws, had created these images.

With a wary look over her shoulder, she knelt to examine the writing. The cat-related chaos had blurred some of the words, but she could still make out the message.

Follow the murals, she pondered. Then she studied the letter *O* scrawled beneath. "Uncle Oscar?" she called out, before catching her breath.

Among the paw prints at the far corner of the room, she spied smudges from a pair of rubber-soled sneakers—the same imprint she'd seen earlier at Coit Tower.

Someone else was in the kitchen with her, and it wasn't her uncle. She couldn't see the intruder, but she could sense his presence.

"Who's there?" she whispered hoarsely.

Jumping to her feet, she spun around, her eyes searching the room, but there was no one to be seen.

"You must be invisible," she said, incredulous at the idea.

Grabbing a broom, she began waving it through the air. Before she could flush out the mysterious painter, a knock thumped against the downstairs door.

The niece watched, awestruck, as sneaker-sized footprints scampered across the kitchen and down the steps to the first floor.

Chapter 26

MORE THAN A MURAL

TWICE, THE NIECE nearly slipped and fell on her way down the stairs to the Green Vase showroom. Loose gobs of paint from the kitchen floor stuck to the soles of her feet, and at this point, the steps themselves were covered with plenty of red splotches. The combination made for slick going.

Staggering around the corner at the bottom of the stairwell, the niece righted herself to see the shadow of a pedestrian on the sidewalk outside the store. A man in a trench coat and fedora hat peeked in through the window—not Victor Arnuatoff, despite the similarity in headgear.

"We're not open," she yelled, even as she scanned the showroom for signs of the sneaker-wearing intruder.

The man knocked again, politely persistent.

"We're closed," she repeated, squinting toward the window. But then she got a better look at the visitor.

"I'll be right there," she said, skipping over the painted paw prints to the front of the store.

SECONDS LATER, THE niece unlocked the door and cracked it open for the Previous Mayor. She had never met the famous politician, but his was one of the most well-known faces in San Francisco. His influence in local politics—long after the completion of his mayoral tenure—was legendary.

It was turning into quite an eventful day for the demure antique shop owner.

The morning had started with Monty's portrait session. That unproductive effort had culminated with a sketched image of the murdered City Hall intern sitting in her showroom—and left her feeling horribly self-conscious about her nose.

Then, during her daily jog up to Coit Tower, the niece had run into Dilla, one of her uncle's closest coconspirators. The overlap of her regular bottled water purchase with Dilla's tour guide shift seemed an unlikely coincidence—particularly after Dilla's thinly veiled suggestion that the niece study a particular New Deal mural inside the tower's base.

It was while staring at the mismatched monuments on the Victor Arnautoff mural that the niece first encountered the sneakered footprints—the same footprints that had just left a trail through her kitchen beside the cryptic painted message instructing her to "Follow the Murals," signed with a capital letter *O*.

Now the Previous Mayor of San Francisco was at her door. She suspected he hadn't come to Jackson Square to buy antiques.

Her uncle was definitely up to something. Who knew what was coming next.

Sometimes, I wish he'd just pick up the phone, the niece thought in frustration.

Out loud, she said politely, "Hello, Mayor. How can I help you?"

AS THE NIECE greeted the Previous Mayor, she noted his perfectly tailored outfit, classy from head to toe, and suddenly became aware of her own disheveled appearance.

Her sweaty running clothes were spattered with flecks of paint. More than half of her hair had escaped her ponytail holder. Her bare feet stood next to the soggy socks and running shoes she'd slipped off when she returned from the run.

Not exactly the best first impression, she thought ruefully.

But if the PM was offended by her bedraggled state, he didn't show it. His neatly trimmed mustache spread evenly over a pleasant smile.

"Hello, little lady," he said smoothly. "I'm looking for your uncle."

She glanced away, averting eye contact, before responding. "I'm sorry. My uncle passed away almost two years ago."

The PM leaned forward conspiratorially and whispered, "I think we both know that's not true."

The niece opened her mouth as if to protest, but then seemed to think better of it. She shrugged noncommittally.

The PM motioned toward the showroom. "Why don't we step inside," he said, neatly stepping around her. The skilled politician had maneuvered his way through many a half-shut door.

"I've got something to show you."

THE NIECE FOLLOWED the Previous Mayor into the Green Vase showroom. He looked down at the trail of painted paw prints and pumped his eyebrows in an amused fashion, but did not comment. Instead, he reached into his vest pocket and pulled out a folded sheet of paper.

Isabella crossed the room, her tail pointed up inquiringly, the bright red tip waving like a paintbrush. Rupert, who had moved his nap to the recliner, cracked open a single furry eyelid.

The PM laid the paper on the cashier counter and folded it so that the left half was visible. Isabella leaped gracefully onto the space beside the page and leaned over it, closely studying the details of its printed image. After a moment, she issued her report.

"Mrao."

The niece peered over the cat's shoulder, trying to get a line of sight to the paper. Gently, she moved Isabella to the side, revealing a photocopy of a colorful mural—the same one she'd seen earlier at Coit Tower.

She turned her head ever so slightly, trying to catch a glimpse of the Previous Mayor out of the corner of her eye. Did he know where she'd been that morning? And that she had just spent an hour staring at the real-life mural?

Unsure of how to respond, she decided on a cautious approach.

"Hmm," she said, thumping her chin with her finger. "That looks familiar. Where have I seen it before . . ."

"You're a horrible liar," the PM said kindly.

"It's *City Life* from Coit Tower," the niece quickly conceded, clearing her throat uncomfortably. "A Depression-era work, part of a New Deal program to employ artists."

She glanced across the showroom to a row of bookcases. "I think I've got a book on San Francisco painters from that time frame." She added a muttered aside: "I had planned to look for it when I got back from my run."

Isabella dropped lightly from the counter, following her person across the room to one of the bookcases. As the woman began scanning the shelf, Isabella balanced on her back legs, providing guidance by pawing the air with her front paws.

"So, Mayor, what's your interest in this mural?" the niece asked, running her fingers along the spines as she skimmed the titles. "And what's it got to do with my uncle?"

The PM removed his hat and thoughtfully stroked the brim. "You're aware of the recent events at City Hall?"

With a weary sigh, the niece nodded toward the art studio across the street. "Montgomery Carmichael is my neighbor. He's *extremely* excited about becoming the interim mayor. We've heard about nothing else for the past two months."

With her attention focused on the bookcase, she didn't notice the PM's pinched expression.

"It's this one, Issy," she said, pulling a book from the shelf.

The cat issued an agreeing *"Mrao,"* as the woman flipped

through the contents to a two-page spread. Carrying the book, the niece returned to the front of the store.

"Here it is. *City Life* by Victor Arnautoff. This picture is a little clearer than your photocopy."

The PM cleared his throat. "Actually, I was referring to the murder of the City Hall staffer." His voice cracked as he added, "A young man named Spider Jones?"

"Oh yes," the niece sputtered, her face flushing with embarrassment. "You meant *that* event. That was, well, that was tragic . . ."

She stopped, the unwanted suspicions she'd been harboring for the past two months instantly resurfacing. If the PM was about to give her another piece of evidence connecting her uncle's disappearance with the intern's murder, she didn't want to hear it.

Outwardly, she managed an apologetic smile and asked, "Have they figured out who killed him?"

"James Lick is at the top of the suspect list," the PM replied dryly.

The niece tried to gulp down her anxiety as her visitor tapped the folded paper still resting on the cashier counter.

"I found that picture in a box of Spider's research materials. He had been working late at City Hall in the weeks before his death. He told me the project had something to do with the outgoing mayor, but that wasn't the case."

The PM leaned his elbow on the counter. "He had taken up his own private investigation."

Frowning, the niece hugged the reference book to her chest. She walked the last few steps to the counter and glanced down at the picture.

"You think there's a connection between this mural and"—she gulped—"his murder?"

The PM dropped his gloved hand to the photocopied paper. "It's not the mural. It's who's standing next to it."

Unfolding the paper, the PM spread it flat across the cashier counter. As he smoothed the center crease with his palm, the niece drew in her breath.

The other half of the photo showed two men in overalls standing in front of *City Life*.

The first was a loose-jowled man, wrinkled from head to toe and with gaping holes in the fabric that should have been covering his knees. The niece knew him well. Harold Wombler, a jack-of-all-trades, had most recently served as the sous chef for Lick's Homestyle Fried Chicken.

Standing beside Harold was a rounder gentleman, of similar advanced age, whose thinning gray hair had been combed over his balding scalp.

It was her uncle Oscar.

The niece looked up at the Previous Mayor.

"What was Spider Jones doing with a picture of my uncle?"

The PM met her gaze with a solemn stare.

"Maybe he figured out the connection between James Lick and the previous owner of the Green Vase."

He paused and then added, "Perhaps he discovered that your uncle Oscar is still alive."

THROUGHOUT THIS DISCUSSION, a ghostly figure stood just inside the shop's entrance, hovering discreetly near the Previous Mayor's left elbow.

Neither of the two humans noticed Spider's presence during their conversation—or his exit through the showroom door. The paint had worn off his shoes during his race down the stairs.

Only Isabella watched Spider slip through to the sidewalk and cross the street to retrieve the skateboard.

Leaping silently from the counter, the cat circled to the store's front windows. Pressing her furry face against the glass, her blue eyes tracked the skateboard as it wiggled off the sidewalk and rolled up Jackson Street.

City Hall

Chapter 27

THE SILENT STALKER

ANOTHER ROUND OF rain swept over the city as Spider steered the skateboard toward his next destination.

Wheels clicking over the rough pavement, he threaded his way up Market, dodging buses, taxis, streetcars, and the typical flood of midday pedestrians. With the lunch hour in full swing, a mass of downtown office workers, ivory-tower dealmakers, sidewalk vendors, and ragged panhandlers converged on Market's central corridor.

It was a zoo of swagger and grift, one in which Spider felt immediately at home.

Wary of the visual he might receive should he pass through a human being, he took care to avoid contact with any passersby. Using the skateboard, he weaved through the crowd with casual ease, nimbly whizzing around a cluster of umbrella-wielding secretaries. Giving the board an extra push, he scooted through an intersection just before the traffic light released a stream of cabs.

He'd always preferred his bike for intra-city transportation, but the skateboard's maneuverability was quickly winning him over—although he felt increasingly guilty about having stolen it from its rightful owner, who, Spider suspected, must be missing it by now.

As if on cue, a voice yelled out, "Hey, that's my skateboard!"

AFTER DODGING CAPTURE from a mystified man who had never seen an inanimate object take off in such a fashion, Spider hooked a right at the United Nations fountain and headed up a short concrete walkway to the Civic Center Plaza.

He had arrived at a familiar location.

City Hall's elegant gray facade stretched across the plaza's northern flank. A giant gold-topped dome rose from the building's center, the metallic trim gleaming against the backdrop of swirling dark clouds.

Spider stashed the skateboard behind a row of bushes and cautiously approached the front steps. It was his first return to the scene of his murder, and he was unsure how the experience would affect him.

"Suck it up, Spider," he said, pulling on the brim of his baseball cap.

He had business to attend to. He needed to see how Mayor Carmichael was progressing with his latest sketch.

INSIDE CITY HALL'S front doors, Spider breezed through the security area, snatching an unattended donut on his way to the other side of the scanners. The floating donut hovered in the air for a few seconds before dropping back to the counter, a tempting treat that the ghost unfortunately couldn't eat.

The rotunda loomed at the end of a wide hallway. Spider could sense the nearness of the vast space beneath the dome, the draw of the ornate interior—but his sneakered feet stayed firmly rooted to the floor in the shadowed foyer. He wasn't yet ready to revisit the central marble staircase.

Instead, Spider slipped into an elevator carriage and rode

it to the second level. The doors soon opened in front of the mayor's office suite. Spider tiptoed across the hallway and crossed through to the reception area. Remembering the area's layout from his previous eavesdropping exercises, he sneaked into a small supply room and crawled through its window out onto the balcony that fronted the main office.

He positioned himself so that he was standing just under the eaves, avoiding the rain pouring down off the roof. The dampness didn't cause him any discomfort or chill—one of the few benefits, he supposed, of being dead—but he wanted to avoid the telltale disturbance his vaporous body would have created in the pattern of the falling raindrops.

A light inside the main office illuminated the person Spider had traveled to City Hall to see.

Montgomery Carmichael had moved to a chair by the balcony windows, where he sat with the sketchpad propped on his knees. Spider watched as the interim mayor ran his charcoal pencil across the textured paper, tracing out an image of the Green Vase showroom.

Chapter 28
AN INCRIMINATING IMAGE

HOXTON FINN SHUFFLED into City Hall, still mulling his stop at the vacant fried chicken restaurant. His reporter's instincts told him there had to be a link between the murdered intern's piles of discarded takeout containers and the missing proprietor of the North Beach chicken joint—the man seen fleeing City Hall in the minutes after Spider's murder.

Hox frowned with frustration.

He was missing something; he could feel it in his bones—or his left foot, to be precise. He winced as his shoe pinched against the nub of the amputated toe. Bending to adjust his laces, he muttered to himself.

"But why would the fried chicken guy kill one of his best customers?"

AS HOX KNELT over his shoe, Humphrey and the rest of the news crew sped past.

It was a conspicuous group, the cameramen with their

shoulder-mounted cameras and bulky lighting equipment, the producer with her multiple cell phones and clipboard, and the stylist fussing with his travel kit that he'd retrieved from the van when it parked outside City Hall.

Humphrey was a mobile one-man salon. His satchel-ed briefcase was filled with enough makeup, combs, and brushes to accommodate an entire high school cheerleading squad. Strapped around his waist, he wore a tool belt whose hooks and pockets had been modified to accommodate his styling equipment. One of the belt's slots secured a portable hair dryer, allowing Humphrey to holster the hot air gun like a weapon.

The harried producer led the pack. A working mother of four, Constance Grynche ran a tight schedule. Connie, as she was known by most of her friends and colleagues, had recently reentered the workforce after taking several years off to raise her family. She was generally well liked in the newsroom, but being the newest member of the producing team, she had drawn the most difficult assignment: Hoxton Finn. No one wanted to put up with the grumpy veteran reporter.

They'd been working together for just over two months, but during that time, Hox had managed to push every one of the producer's buttons. He'd frayed her last nerve and driven her half-mad—quite an accomplishment, given her extensive childrearing experience.

Connie had quite a few nicknames for Hox, but out loud she generally referred to him as the Demon Spawn.

Hox called her "the Grynch."

HAVING FINISHED ADJUSTING his shoe, Hox caught up to the news team on the far side of the rotunda. He heard Connie speaking into her private cell phone.

"Hon, you're going to have to take the boys to their orthodontist appointments." She shot Hox an accusing stare. "My shoot's going to run a little later than I had planned, and then I have to get it through production for tonight's broadcast."

Ah, it's the husband, Hox thought. Mister Grynch, a green-skinned troll with a penchant for stealing Christmas trees—or at least, that's how the reporter envisioned him.

As Connie clicked off the phone, he sang out in a deep baritone that echoed across the marble-floored rotunda.

"He's a mean one . . ."

"Can it, Hox."

Hox grinned as Connie stomped up the stairs. If he managed to crack the Spider Jones case, she would have a career-making story.

Until then, she would just have to put up with him.

MIDWAY UP THE central marble staircase, Hox slowed his pace and once more lagged behind the rest of the news team. By the time he reached the top of the steps, the group had already rounded the corner for the second-floor corridor leading to the mayor's office suite.

Unconcerned, Hox let them proceed ahead. He stopped instead to stare at the ceremonial rotunda, the site of the murder that had consumed him for the past two months.

The marble floor showed no signs of the carnage that had taken place there. The surrounding columns had been wiped clean. Harvey Milk's bust gleamed a polished bronze.

Hox shook his head. It didn't seem right that so horrifying a scene could be completely erased.

He *thwacked* the file he'd been carrying against his left thigh. Something about that night's sequence of events continued to trouble him, an anomaly or inconsistency that he couldn't put his finger on.

But before he could rehash the scene again, Connie appeared at the edge of the ceremonial rotunda, beckoning sternly for the reporter to get a move on.

Resigning himself to the inevitability of the Monty interview, he plodded toward the hallway.

"Keep your hat on, Grynch. I'm coming!"

MINUTES LATER, HOX followed the news crew through the entrance to the mayor's office suite. He nodded to an elderly woman in a feathered hat sitting at the desk typically reserved for the mayor's administrative assistant.

A temporary hire, Hox surmised, based on the woman's outfit. In addition to the monstrous hat, she wore a blue sweater, green skirt, and matching striped stockings.

With the group's arrival, the woman jumped up from her desk and ushered them toward the inner office space.

After a short knock, she pushed open a heavy wooden door and led them into the main room.

The interim mayor rested on a chair beside the floor-to-ceiling windows that ran along the room's south wall. His back was turned toward the door, and a sketchpad spread across his knees. Hox couldn't see the surface of the sketchpad, but Monty's gaze remained fixed on the paper as he waved a charcoal pencil in the air.

"Make yourselves at home, fellows. Just let me know when you're ready."

The producer and cameraman bustled about, arranging chairs, adjusting the floor rug, and checking the ambient light. A series of expandable metal poles with retractable tripod feet were quickly set up around the perimeter. Supplemental lighting canisters mounted atop each of the temporary stands were arranged with their beams aimed at the seating area.

Hox skirted around all this activity, deftly avoiding Humphrey and his hair dryer, and headed for the window, where Monty had resumed work on his sketch.

The reporter leaned over Monty's shoulder, at first only glancing at the image on the sketchpad. Then, he leaned in for closer scrutiny.

It appeared to be a portrait of sorts, set in a quaint antique-filled shop.

In the middle of the picture, a fluffy cat sprawled across a person's lap. The cat was particularly well done, capturing the essence of its furry personality.

But it wasn't the feline that had caught Hox's attention.

He felt a sudden surge of suspicion as he shifted his gaze from the sketch to the artist.

The figure seated on the chair in the center of the drawing was Spider Jones.

Chapter 29
THE INTERVIEW

SENSING HOX'S PRESENCE, Monty jumped up from his chair. He flipped the top cover over the sketchpad, hiding the drawing from view as he turned to face the reporter.

"Hoxton Finn, it's a pleasure," he said, extending his free hand for a shake.

Still thrown by the sketched image of the murdered staffer, Hox found himself struck by a rare moment of indecision. After a brief hesitation, he clasped Monty's outstretched hand.

"I didn't realize you were a sketch artist, Mayor Carmichael."

Monty's head bobbed with the handshake. "Oh, it's just a hobby. It helps me think." Grinning, he repeated the reporter's salutation. "Mayor Carmichael. Got a nice ring to it, don't you think?"

Hox stifled a snide reply. Pulling his hand free, he motioned toward the area that had been set up for the interview.

"Shall we get started?"

Connie ushered the two men into their seats and attached

tiny microphones to their shirt collars. Humphrey buzzed about Hox's head with his various styling tools, fiddling with the reporter's hair, until he swatted him away. The cameraman hunched behind his rig and, raising his fingers over his head, counted down to the start.

Three, two, one . . .

"Mayor Carmichael," Hox began. The formal title still made him cringe internally. "Thank you for granting us the exclusive for tonight's broadcast. I believe this is your first interview since the appointment."

"It's my pleasure, Hoxton."

"Can you give us an overview of your plans for the abbreviated term? What are your legislative priorities? What initiatives do you plan to tackle?"

"Well, Hox, that's a good question. There are a number of items on my agenda. One of the first things I'd like to address . . ."

Hox flipped open his notebook, preparing to take notes as the interview progressed. But as he glanced down at the top sheet, he noticed a strange marking. Someone had drawn a large looping *O* on the paper.

The combination of the sketch of the murdered intern and the strange symbol in his notes threw the reporter completely off his game. As the dialogue went back and forth, Hox had difficulty keeping his focus on Monty's longwinded responses. Normally, he would have cut in for more cross-examination, but he was too distracted to dissect the interim mayor's answers.

The producer's face grew increasingly concerned as Hox passed up several easy openings for critical follow-up, instead lobbing softball questions, which Monty easily deflected.

"Now, I'd like to bring up the matter of Mountain Lake and the albino alligator," Hox said, glancing once more down at his notepad. "We've all seen the footage of you exiting the water in a wet suit and snorkel mask. What, exactly, were you doing there that evening?"

Monty nodded agreeably to the question, but there was

a noticeable tightening around the corners of his mouth. He sucked in a deep breath and then meted out a response that Dilla had suggested to him before the news crew arrived.

"It's simple, really. A minor misunderstanding that got blown way out of proportion. You see, I was just out for an evening swim."

The producer leaned forward, anticipating a verbal punch as Hox stroked his chin.

"Of course."

Connie threw her hands in the air, letting loose an audible *spfft* of disappointment.

Monty nearly fell off his chair in relief. His face broke into a wide smile, and the tension in his body instantly released.

With the next question, however, his concern returned.

"Let's talk about your other hobbies," Hox suggested, sensing the interview was nearing its end. "I understand you're an amateur sketch artist."

Monty's long fingers began to fidget. He crossed one leg over the other, and then switched the order, nervously shifting his weight. "Uh, yes," he finally replied, drawing out the answer, as if trying to give himself time to think.

Hox leaned forward in his chair, his signature interrogation move for extracting information. "And where do you get the inspiration for your drawings?"

Monty's upper torso weaved back and forth. He glanced up at the ceiling and then down at his feet.

"Well, I suppose I like cats . . ."

Connie shook her head in disgust. None of this would make the cut for the evening broadcast. Twirling a finger in the air, she motioned for Hox to wrap things up.

"What else, Mayor?" he pushed, doggedly pursuing the line of questioning. "What other things do you include in your sketches?"

"We're going to have to cut it off right there," Connie interjected. "Thank you, Mayor, for your time."

As the crew began packing up their gear, she whispered harshly into Hox's ear, "Have you lost your marbles? You pass up the alligator debacle for a cheesy art discussion? What's gotten into you?"

The reporter shrugged her off, giving only a cryptic response.

"Must be something about this office," he said blithely. "Look what it did to the previous guy who worked here."

OUTSIDE ON THE balcony, Spider watched the news crew depart. Unlike the producer, he knew exactly why the reporter had questioned the interim mayor about his artistic abilities.

Sure enough, no sooner had the door shut behind the news team than Monty returned to the sketchpad and started on a fresh sheet, once more outlining the scene in the Green Vase showroom.

Spider stared intently at the paper, sending a focused beam of thought to the charcoal pencil, as his image began to appear at the center of the sketch.

The Lieutenant Governor

Chapter 30

BACTERIA BEAR

EARLIER THAT SAME morning, the Lieutenant Governor steered his fuel-efficient compact down one of Sacramento's straight boulevards as he neared the end of his morning commute. Leafy elms lined the route, transitioning to planted palm trees as he reached the outer boundaries of the State Capitol.

At nine forty-five A.M. sharp, the car pulled into the marked entrance for the underground parking structure. The driver flashed his badge to the posted security guard, who released the red and white barrier bar and waved him through to his designated parking spot.

The Lieutenant Governor had been in his new position for just under a week, but he was quickly learning the routine. With a relaxed smile, he killed the engine and stepped out of his ride.

The termination of his duties as San Francisco's mayor had meant the loss of his personal driver and a cut in his annual salary. His new job provided far fewer perks and benefits, but he wasn't complaining—unlike his wife, who had recently given birth to their first child.

He'd found he rather enjoyed the much lower profile, the flexible hours, and, most important, the Capitol Building's frog-free interior.

THE LIEUTENANT GOVERNOR didn't have any appointments on his calendar that morning (or, for that matter, later that afternoon), so he decided to take a leisurely stroll through the Capitol grounds before checking in at his office.

He set off on a peaceful walk through the multi-acre park. Even in the middle of winter, there was still plenty of colorful foliage to enjoy. A few bright globes of ripening fruit nestled among the orange trees' upper boughs. Several flowering bushes and red-leafed ferns added to the colorful display.

The Lieutenant Governor stopped several times to admire a recently pruned plant or a freshly sprouted patch of bulbs. He even paused to greet Herman, the park's resident box turtle—a slow, nonthreatening, and blessedly nonamphibian creature.

Stretching his arms out over his head, he took in a deep cleansing breath of Sacramento air. He had started to let his hair down, literally. His once shellacked comb-back now flopped about his ears without constraint. After years of daily gel application, his scalp felt crisp and rejuvenated. He was considering letting his hair grow out even longer. Another six months, and he might be able to pull it into a ponytail.

"You look like a hippie," he wife complained almost every morning.

He couldn't disagree. His hair wasn't the only aspect of his personal appearance that he had loosened up.

It had been weeks since he last whitened his teeth, and the enamel had returned to a more natural cream color. The light fuzz of a beard had begun to grow around his chin. He was hoping it would mature into a goatee.

Gone, too, was the stiff formalwear he had donned as mayor. A closet full of dark suits, pointed leather shoes, and narrow blue ties were left hanging in the closet of his San Francisco home. He had transitioned into far more casual khakis, knit shirts, and low-cut hiking boots.

His wife had disapproved of all these changes, but the last clothing item had drawn particularly sharp criticism.

"Why do you need hiking boots?" she'd protested the first day he wore them to work. "You're not climbing any mountains there at the Capitol."

"Sometimes I sneak into the cupola for a look around," he'd replied, only half joking. "There's a great view of the city from up there."

"That's not funny," she'd said through gritted teeth.

GLANCING PROUDLY AT his hiking shoes, the Lieutenant Governor proceeded to the Capitol entrance and queued up for the security line. It took a little more time to get through the scanners, but the comfort was well worth the minor inconvenience.

Once through to the other side, he ambled down the main hallway toward his office. He wasn't in any hurry, so he stopped several times along the way to study the informative plaques that lined the wall.

Eventually, he reached the entrance to the governor's office suite.

The doorway was manned by a state trooper, standing at attention next to a pairing of US and California flags and a life-sized brass statue of a bear.

The bear was configured in a natural stance, similar to the depiction on the state flag, astride all four feet as if prowling through the wilderness. It was a life-sized rendition, spanning about six feet across and four feet high.

The bear's head was noticeably more polished than the rest of his body. Bacteria Bear, as the state troopers called him, received a loving pat from almost every curious child who ventured within arm's reach. With the Capitol being a routine field trip destination for almost every one of the local schools, the bear received several hundred rubs a day.

Giving the bear an obligatory head pat, the Lieutenant Governor stopped for his daily chat with the state trooper. As they exchanged pleasantries, he found himself wondering, not for the first time, what went on behind the heavily barricaded door. He had yet to receive an invitation inside.

Before last November's election, he'd been unable to discern exactly what a lieutenant governor's job duties might entail. As it turned out, the matter was left largely to the discretion of the sitting governor, who had, in this instance, opted for a minimalist approach.

All he was required to do was show up each day and sign in. There were no contentious meetings with the press, no belligerent board of supervisors, and no nefarious frogs plotting to ambush him. He was virtually anonymous within the State Capitol's corridors—it was an experience that he was starting to enjoy.

The Lieutenant Governor turned down a narrow opening in the main hallway to a locked door, painted the same flat white as the walls. It looked as if the door might lead to a storage closet, except that a heavy numerical lock had been mounted around the knob. A small sign posted over the threshold gave his name and title.

Yawning, he punched in the code. With a slight click, the lock released, and he pushed open the door.

"Morning, Mabel," he said with a wide yawn.

Mabel sat at her desk, prim and proper, as always. She wore her typical outfit of a heathered gray skirt and a soft cotton sweater. Her feet were clad in sensible dress shoes fitted with a sturdy round heel, the same style she'd worn throughout her lengthy career as an administrative assistant.

"Good morning, sir," she replied as he crossed the windowless room to the couch positioned against the far wall. "How was your commute?"

"Not too bad," he said with a tired sigh. His wife had refused to move from their San Francisco apartment, so he was driving the ninety-mile distance to and fro each day. "I've started a new book on tape."

The Lieutenant Governor caught a whiff of the lemony-sweet perfume that his assistant sprayed against the sides of her neck. She'd been using the same scent for years. Always predictable, that was his Mabel.

She'd been with him since the very beginning of his political career, going all the way back to when he started out as a lowly supervisor for San Francisco's Marina district. She'd been a steady, reassuring force in his life. He trusted her with the most sensitive and important matters of both his personal and professional career.

Lately, of course, there hadn't been much for Mabel to do, other than handle the mundane details of his new office. As she had during his tenure at San Francisco's City Hall, Mabel took care of his constituent mail, organized his calendar, and managed his interns—the last of which there always seemed to be far more of than was actually needed.

The Lieutenant Governor let loose another yawn as he unfolded a blanket and stretched his tall frame out over the couch. His feet, still in the low-rise hiking shoes, hung off the end.

Interns, he thought as his eyelids began to flutter. The position was a transient one, with low pay and little recognition. They came and went with a high frequency, or so it seemed, often disappearing from one day to the next. It was a relief to be able to rely on Mabel for all that. Such a shame about that boy in San Francisco . . .

"Going to rest my eyes for a bit. The baby kept me up again," he murmured before drifting off into his regular morning nap.

The light drone of a nasal snore filled the office as Mabel took out her knitting.

"As you wish, sir."

Chapter 31

THE ASSAILANTS

MABEL'S KNITTING NEEDLES clicked a steady cadence in the broom closet–converted office, drowning out the Lieutenant Governor's whiffling snores.

She gazed at the sleeping figure on the couch and sighed. She had already completed three afghans, two sweaters, and an assortment of baby booties. She was running out of nieces, nephews, and bare-footed infants upon which to bestow the blankets and booties. Unfortunately—from a knitting perspective—Sacramento tended to have mild winters.

The Lieutenant Governor's first week had been slow, to say the least.

He'd had so much potential when they first started out, she reflected, remembering those early heady days.

He'd risen like a rock star through the ranks of San Francisco's supervisors. His schedule was always full; the city's heavy hitters had all wanted to clock time with the up-and-coming politician. They had elbowed one another for the chance to stand next to him at public events, and they had vied for his endorsement of their projects and initiatives.

His election to mayor was viewed by most as yet another stepping-stone in his inevitable political ascendency. Many thought he was destined for a seat at the statehouse and, quite possibly, the presidency.

No one had predicted this.

It was the frogs that did him in, Mabel reflected bitterly. They had destroyed his credibility as mayor. She nearly dropped a stitch in anger.

Damn those amphibians.

The Lieutenant Governor's childhood phobia might never have come to light had it not been for City Hall's bizarre frog infestation. His was a rare affliction, and in the normal course of business, it wouldn't have been a hindrance to his career. But the sight of all those slimy green creatures swarming the building had sent the poor man into a full-blown mental breakdown.

Shaking her head, Mabel pinned one of the knitting needles into a stitch and reached into her bag for a new skein of yarn. She selected the next color, tied it to the hanging end, and resumed her work.

As the needles knotted the thread into its patterned design, her thoughts drifted to the other major calamity of the Lieutenant Governor's mayoral term, the murder of Spider Jones. While far more serious in nature, at least the intern's death hadn't caused any further damage to her boss's tarnished reputation.

THE TEMPO OF the knitting needles ticked up a notch as Mabel recalled the troublesome intern. Her lips pursed into a small frown of disapproval.

The epitome of discretion, Mabel would never sink to gossip, but in the days before his death, young Spider had been acting rather suspiciously. For one thing, she'd caught him sneaking around City Hall's second floor dressed up in a janitor's uniform and posing with a mop. His rather ineffectual cleaning technique had given him away.

Not wanting to embarrass Spider, Mabel hadn't let on

that she'd recognized her intern beneath the poorly conceived disguise. She'd assumed he'd been co-opted into the ruse by the Previous Mayor. It was just the type of shenanigans the old politician might cook up, and there were rumors the pair had been seen palling around town together.

While concerned, Mabel had seen no reason to call Spider's bluff. She'd merely filed the information away for possible future use—and vowed to keep a closer eye on the impressionable young man.

But after the murder, she had spent a great deal of time wondering exactly what Spider had been up to.

TWO MONTHS AFTER the fact, Mabel was still deeply troubled by Spider's death. It was more than just the loss of someone she knew—she had been the one to find the slain intern's body.

The morbid scene was forever burned in her memory.

Mabel remembered telling her story to the police the night of the murder. Like the rest of City Hall's workforce, she had stayed late in the building awaiting the outcome of the supervisors' meeting. When at last the board completed a successful vote to select the interim mayor, she'd returned to the mayor's office to send a few quick e-mails alerting friends of the results.

Once at her desk, Mabel had found herself distracted by the list of items that needed to be taken care of before her pending move to Sacramento. After spending forty-five minutes reviewing Internet sites for prospective apartment listings, she'd finally closed down her computer and prepared to leave.

She was feeling nostalgic, she'd explained to the police detective, so she had taken the long way out of the building, walking around the second-floor hallway overlooking the rotunda to the central marble staircase.

That's when she'd discovered Spider's body at the top of the stairs.

The knitting needles clacked with adrenaline as Mabel

recalled the horrifying scene. It was such a mess, with blood spattered everywhere . . . so visceral . . . so gory . . . and so disturbingly untidy.

Turning away from the shocking display, she'd immediately run back to the mayor's office to call for help. The battery had run down on the cell phone she carried in her purse, and she'd feared the perpetrator might still be lurking nearby.

"Maybe if I had stayed to help him . . ." she'd told the investigator as her voice trailed off into a single tear.

The detective had nodded sympathetically. She'd reached out and patted Mabel's hand, offering condolence.

Then Mabel delivered the most important piece of information.

Hurrying back along the second-floor walkway, she'd noticed a movement on the rotunda below. Looking over the railing, she'd seen two shadowed figures scurrying across the marble floor toward the exit.

"Did you get a good look at either of them?" the investigator had asked urgently. "Can you describe them in any way?"

Mabel closed her eyes, as if trying to focus. "It was dark," she replied tearfully. "But they both struck me as familiar . . ."

She proceeded to give the details of the two suspects.

The first she identified as Sam Eckles, a husky red-haired janitor who had worked at City Hall until the frog infestation a few years back. He'd been fired for his involvement in the caper—or so she'd heard from reliable sources.

Afterward, Sam had taken up a position as an amphibian consultant, securing jobs with a team of UC Davis wildlife biologists as well as the California Academy of Sciences.

Sam seemed an unlikely candidate for the carnage Mabel had witnessed at the top of the staircase. Despite his penchant for mischief, she had never seen any indication that he was prone to violence. But perhaps, she mused to the investigator, he'd fallen into bad company.

She had fewer reservations, however, about the second shadowed figure.

The elderly round-shouldered gentleman had also done a tour as a City Hall janitor, several decades ago, before opening up an antique shop in Jackson Square.

Mabel had never liked the man, even when he was masquerading as a lowly janitor. Oscar was always meddling in something, he and his group of friends. The Bohemians, the Vigilance Committee—they'd operated under a number of different names. They were a scheming bunch, constantly interfering, causing chaos, up-ending the regular order of business. The frog escapade, she felt certain, had originated with Oscar and his crew.

Recent rumors had confirmed what Mabel had long suspected: that Oscar hadn't died two years ago of a sudden heart attack inside the entrance to his store.

But she knew she'd have a tough time convincing the detective that Oscar had faked his death, so instead of identifying him as the former owner of the Green Vase antique shop, she provided the name of his most recent alias, fried chicken restaurateur James Lick.

"I wish I could be more helpful," Mabel had concluded with a weak smile.

"There, there, miss," the detective had replied. "You've given us a great lead." She flipped shut her notepad and handed Mabel her business card.

"If you think of anything else, please give me a call."

MABEL SET DOWN her knitting. Her hands had begun to sweat from the frantic pace of the needles, and she had started to lose her grip. She glanced at the scarf's top rows. The last several stitches had been strung too tight. She would have to pull them out.

It had been a frustrating couple of months, Mabel thought wearily. Oscar and Sam had gone into hiding the night of Spider's murder, and so far, the police had been unable to locate them.

How could she feel safe with two dangerous criminals on the loose? What if they found out she was the witness who had seen them fleeing City Hall? It had been a relief, in a way, to move out of San Francisco. She'd taken extra precautions when renting her Sacramento apartment, picking a building with state-of-the-art security, ensuring that her address and phone number were unlisted.

Mabel wrung her hands for several minutes before reaching for her purse. She took out the business card given to her by the detective.

Perhaps she should call and ask if the police had made any progress.

Maybe it was time she gave them another clue to Oscar's real identity.

After checking that the Lieutenant Governor was still fast asleep, she picked up the phone and began to dial.

The Green Vase

Chapter 32

CLEAN CATS

OSCAR'S NIECE LOCKED the front door to the Green Vase as she watched the Previous Mayor depart down Jackson Street. He had left behind the photocopied picture of Coit Tower's *City Life* mural—the image that included her uncle and his friend Harold standing in the mural hallway.

Thoughtfully tapping the tulip-shaped doorknob, she stared out at the rain.

She couldn't imagine why Spider Jones had stored this picture in his hidden research files, but she could no longer ignore the link between the young man's death and her uncle's and Sam's disappearances.

Holding up the picture, she studied Oscar's face, the paint brush he held in his hand, and the equipment on the floor at his feet. She could discern nothing unusual about the layout.

Glancing up at the ceiling, she remembered the painted message she'd found on the kitchen floor. Then she returned her gaze to the photocopied picture.

She had better learn everything she could about that mural.

Turning away from the windows, the niece folded the

paper and slid it into the cash register's bottom drawer. She looked at the red footprints that tracked across the storeroom floor, quickly focusing her attention on Rupert and Isabella, both of whom were still covered in red paint.

"First things first," she said briskly. "You two are getting a bath."

Suddenly awaking from his nap on the seat of the leather recliner, Rupert's head jerked up with alarm.

In his vocabulary, the word *bath* was second only to *diet* in terms of its visceral offense.

His eyes opened wide as his person crept slowly toward the recliner. His fluffy tail thumped against the seat cushion.

Isabella called out a warning.

"Mrao!"

The niece made a lunge for the aquaphobic feline, but he eluded her grasp, leaping from the recliner, scrambling across the showroom floor, and sprinting up the stairs.

SEVERAL HOURS LATER, the niece settled into the living room couch. Two damp and almost-paint-free cats rested peacefully on either side. It had taken a great deal of shampoo and much vigorous scrubbing to remove the paint from their coats. A few tiny flecks still remained on the pink padding of their paws, but given the paint-spattered starting point, the woman deemed the bathing operation a success.

Of course, the niece had incurred the regular round of gouges, scrapes, and scratches. She held out her hands, surveying the damage. She'd smeared antibiotic cream over all of her wounds; the worst of them had received a bandage covering. Considering the amount of cat-cleaning done during the baths, she mused, her injuries could have been far worse.

Closing her eyes, the niece leaned back into the couch cushions. Every muscle ached from exhaustion.

Once the bathing operation was concluded, she had started to work on the showroom and kitchen. After a couple of hours spent crawling around on her hands and knees, she had managed to wipe up the bulk of the spilled paint. A solvent had facilitated the paint removal, but even so, the process had required a great deal of elbow grease.

"The house has never been cleaner." She sighed wearily and then looked sideways at Rupert. "That'll last about twenty-four hours."

Stretching his front legs across the couch, Rupert breathed out an agreeing snore.

From the niece's opposite side, Isabella tapped a front paw against her person's knee, as if reminding her to get back to the business of the mural.

"Mrao."

UNDER ISABELLA'S CLOSE supervision, the niece pulled out the reference book she'd retrieved during the Previous Mayor's visit. Flipping through the pages, she found an overview on the city's Depression-era artists and began to read.

Examples of New Deal art, like the murals in Coit Tower, were scattered across San Francisco. The initial public works program had been so successful, additional murals were commissioned in other public spaces, such as the Rincon Post Office and the Beach Chalet at Golden Gate Park.

Many of the artists were inspired by renowned Mexican muralist Diego Rivera, who made several visits to San Francisco, often with his wife, Freida. Rivera himself created three murals for the Bay Area, including one located inside the Pacific Stock Exchange building.

Rotund and charismatic, Rivera dominated the world art scene of the early 1900s, leading an artistic movement called "social realism" that strove to capture the often dismal lives of the working poor. His controversial paintings were infused with left-leaning political themes, an element that frequently caused friction with the benefactors who commissioned his works. Nelson Rockefeller famously destroyed a Rivera mural in New York's Rockefeller Center when the artist refused to remove an image of Vladimir Lenin from its center.

The Coit Tower muralists took up an active defense of their mentor. In retribution for the destruction of Rivera's Rockefeller mural, a Communist sickle and hammer symbol appeared over one of the windows in the tower's circular hallway. It was the only item in the finished project to face censorship and removal.

As the niece reached the end of the article, she honed in on its concluding paragraph with interest.

Given the public scrutiny the artists received for their government-funded works, the New Deal murals were riddled with symbols and secret meanings, some only discernible by a close study of the time frame represented in any particular piece—and some known only to the artists themselves.

CLOSING THE BOOK, the niece pondered the article as she recapped her day.

A flood of images swept through her brain: Monty and his morbid sketch, Dilla winking as she nodded toward the *City Life* mural, the wet footprints appearing in Coit Tower's hallway, the Previous Mayor and his photocopied photo, and, finally, the red painted message on her kitchen floor—accompanied by the same sneakered footprints.

She rubbed her eyes, trying to make sense of it all.

Was the mural another of her uncle's treasure hunt quests? How did the murdered intern fit into the picture? Had Spider uncovered something about Oscar's past? Is that what got him killed? Was her uncle a conspirator in the murder or had he disappeared to escape a similar fate?

Most important, who had left the message painted on her kitchen floor?

There was only one way to find out.

She gently stroked Isabella's head, and the cat pushed against her human's hand, enjoying the massage.

Thinking of the cryptic message, the niece said sleepily, "Tomorrow, we're going to follow the murals."

City Hall

Chapter 33
THE SPARKLING GLOW

SPIDER STOOD ON the balcony outside the mayor's office, watching Monty sketch yet another portrait. He waited until he was sure the image in the center remained the same; then he slowly eased back through the window to the supply room and returned to the hallway by the elevators.

He punched the call button and stared up at the meter above the doors, purposefully avoiding the view down the adjacent corridor that overlooked the rotunda and, at its center, the marble staircase.

Nope, Spider thought to himself. *I'm not ready. It's too soon. Just being this close is giving me the heebies.*

But as the elevator *ding*ed and the carriage opened, a movement caught Spider's attention.

Hoxton Finn strode briskly past, brooding as he thumped a file folder against his left thigh. After the interview with the interim mayor, the reporter had split up from the rest of the news crew. He had made his regular rounds, visiting with his various sources, chatting with whichever supervisors he could find in their offices that afternoon.

Spider knew the reporter's routine. He had tracked Hox through the building back in his intern days, and he recognized the route. Hox had finished his last check-in and was about to circle to the main staircase, descend to the first floor, and out the front doors.

Spider hesitated for several seconds, summoning his courage, before finally straightening his shoulders and turning to face the rotunda.

It was time to push the limits of his ghostly abilities. He had practiced enough with projecting images onto Monty's brain. He was ready to attempt a more challenging communication.

As Hox tromped down the second-floor hallway, the elevator's doors swung shut minus the ghostly rider.

A POTENT MIX of fear and determination pumped through Spider's phantom veins as he followed Hox down the corridor. The prospect of returning to the scene of the slaying terrified him.

It was the first truly intense emotion he'd experienced since his run-in with the delivery truck. Unbeknownst to Spider, the energy from his inner turmoil created a faint mist, a cloudy apparition visible to the building's other occupants.

Intent on his mission, Spider failed to notice the startled gasps as he surged past a suited man carrying a briefcase and threaded through a crowd of photo-snapping tourists. It wasn't until he neared the end of the corridor and spied his reflection in a decorative mirror that he realized what had happened.

Spider paused, awestruck by the sight of his translucent figure, but there was no time to gawk.

Hox had lumbered to the far end of the corridor. The reporter veered right, disappearing around the corner leading to the side entrance of the ceremonial rotunda.

If Spider was going to implement his plan, he had to act now.

Rushing forward, he sped toward the turn, his rubber-soled sneakers squeaking against the marble floor. The next stride would bring the ceremonial rotunda into view. His right foot planted for the pivot—but at the last second, he skidded to a stop.

His figure quickly faded to its invisible form. He couldn't bring himself to take the last step.

Flattening himself against the wall, he closed his eyes, concentrating as he quickly counted to ten.

Holding his hands over his face, he slid his feet forward, feeling his way around the marbled corner. Still blocking his vision, he listened for the reporter. Had he waited too long?

Then he heard Hox's stilted gait approaching the top of the central staircase.

This was it. This was his moment.

Dropping his hands, Spider forced open his eyes. At the sight of the Harvey Milk bust, his figure once more appeared in a sparkling glow.

His body electrified by emotion, Spider envisioned the scene from the night of his murder: the blood-spattered walls, the flat pools of blood on the floor, and there in the middle, his body, sprawled, lifeless.

Chapter 34

THE MISSING MEMORY

HOXTON FINN ENTERED the ceremonial rotunda at full speed, intent on returning to the newspaper's offices. Halfway across, however, he slowed and glanced around the space.

Visions of the crime scene photos ran through his head as he stared at Harvey Milk's bronze bust. The man's cheerful face was frozen in a smile, his flapping tie thrown back against his chest.

Hox turned to look out over the expansive rotunda and once more replayed the moments before the attack.

The vision wasn't difficult to re-create. The rain now pouring down outside had darkened the windows that framed the rotunda's upper walls. The time was nearing five o'clock, so City Hall had begun to empty out. And just like the night of the murder, the air was damp with fog, moisture so dense that you could almost taste it on your tongue.

Lastly, the reporter's foot had begun its end-of-day throb, a reminder of the ache he'd endured the evening after he'd chased the albino alligator all over the city.

Hox ground the aching stub of his foot against the tip of his shoe. He envisioned the young intern crossing the pink marble floor at the bottom of the staircase. The image was blurry, as if distorted by the fog.

Hox squinted, straining to bring the memory into better focus.

Then he shook his head and let out a frustrated sigh. It was no use.

"Time to give up this nonsense," he muttered to himself.

But just as he lifted his left foot off the top step of the staircase, a rush of color swept through his brain. The jolt nearly caused him to lose his balance and fall the length of the stairs. His wild wobble drew a few concerned looks from passing bystanders, but he paid them no heed.

He'd finally received his breakthrough.

Suddenly, he saw the scene with a renewed clarity, a deeper, more enhanced perception that broke with the previous script.

The intern began climbing the steps. His face, at first apprehensive, soon flashed with recognition. Hox nodded an informal greeting as Spider passed alongside him.

The sequence was the same as before, but this time, the reporter noticed something new.

He caught a glimpse of the intern's profile—and the detail that had slipped from his initial recollections.

There was a bulky lump draped over the young man's shoulders.

A whisper soaked through Hox's subconscious: Spider was carrying a backpack.

• • •

MINUTES LATER, SPIDER collapsed on the front steps outside City Hall, spent from the effort of transferring the vision. He felt as if the interaction with Hox had drained every last bit of energy from his ghostly being, but when he looked across the Civic Center's open green space, his dimpled face beamed a satisfied smile.

At the far end of the plaza, he could just make out Hox's

silhouette, hurrying through the rain as fast as his hobbled foot would allow.

• • •

HOX RACED BACK to the newspaper's offices. Soaking wet, he sprinted through the front door and up the stairs, ignoring for once the pain in his left foot.

The paper's managing editor looked up with a frown. He had been briefed on Hox's less-than-stellar interview with the interim mayor. Connie stood beside the editor, her arms crossed over her chest.

Hox waved them off and charged down the hallway to the conference room. Slamming the door behind him, he began rummaging through the Spider Jones files, tossing papers this way and that until he found the stack containing the police report.

Holding his breath, he scanned through the report, searching for every reference to the items that had been found with the victim's body.

After ten minutes of increasingly frantic review, Hox blew out a sigh of relief and collapsed into the chair. There was no mention of a backpack having been found anywhere near the ceremonial rotunda.

Hox drummed his fingers against the table, contemplating.

What did Spider have in his backpack the night of the murder and had it been worth killing for?

The Sonoma Woods

Chapter 35
THE CAMPSITE

THE LAST EMBERS glowed in the fire pit of the Sonoma woods campsite where the burly frog aficionado and the former proprietor of Lick's Homestyle Chicken had been hiding for the past two months.

From his seat on a log at the edge of the camp, Sam looked up at the redwood canopy. He always preferred a natural roof to any man-made contrivance. While his companion had been sleeping on a bunk inside the cabin, Sam had spent every night outside by the fire.

He took in a deep breath, soaking up the surrounding earthy scents. It had been weeks since his last shower; a grimy layer of black dirt covered his skin and clothing. His overgrown beard gave him the look of a Sasquatch.

But he'd never felt as clean as he did right now. The air in his lungs carried the purified oxygen of a thousand-acre forest. The mist drifting down through the trees dampened his face with a refreshing spritz.

He sighed. He wasn't ready to go back to the city.

Regardless, they couldn't stay any longer at their current location. Oscar had heard over his radio that a forest ranger had been sent to check on their campsite. Even though they were camped on private land, it would be best to pack up and leave to avoid potentially awkward questioning.

The nosy ranger was the least of their problems. More concerning was the news that the murdered intern had hidden a stash of documents near his cubicle at City Hall. The bundle would have to be retrieved before the police discovered it—and the sensitive information inside.

Standing to full height, Sam dusted himself off and returned to his duties. He loaded the camping gear and the remaining provisions into the rear of the cargo van. Then he turned to the two domesticated frogs. Opening their carrier, Sam carefully set them inside.

"Don't worry, my friends. You'll be out again soon." He hoped the amphibians didn't detect the anxiety in his voice.

It would be a short visit to the city. He and Oscar couldn't afford to be seen in San Francisco.

INSIDE THE CABIN, Oscar carefully tapped the paint-covered canvas with the tip of his index finger. Happily, no color transferred to his skin.

The painting was finished and, despite the moist air, it had dried sufficiently to cover it for transport.

He stepped back, studying the busy scene depicted on the canvas.

A midday crowd gathered near the San Francisco intersection of Washington and Montgomery. Mismatched landmarks spread across the painting's upper horizon. It was a near-perfect replica of Arnautoff's *City Life*—with two small but important exceptions.

Bending back toward the frame, he looked closely at the anomalies and nodded with approval.

Now it was just a matter of his niece putting the pieces together.

Securing the cover over the canvas, he carried the large frame to the cargo van and handed it inside to Sam.

Grabbing a stitch in his lower back, he turned and gazed

at the empty campsite. Then he returned to the cabin to retrieve one last item.

Slowly, he walked to the far corner of the room. His face shadowed with guilt, he reached down to pick up the blood-stained backpack last worn by Spider Jones.

Following the Murals

Chapter 36

THE PAINTED CORNER

THE MORNING DAWNED clear and bright in San Francisco, a temporary break from the endless stream of clouds lined up across the Pacific. Waterlogged citizens poured into the streets, thankful for the respite, however brief. From the Marina Green to the Ferry Building, the city was alive with movement. Dog walkers, joggers, coffee drinkers, and commuters were all eager to take advantage of the temporary dry spell.

Inside the redbrick building that housed the Green Vase, the niece prepared for her own outing—although of all the excursions being planned that day, she suspected hers was the only one that was mural-inspired.

After digging through a cramped closet, she managed to extract a stroller with green nylon siding.

Hooked to the stroller's side was a triangular yellow tag with a black silhouette icon positioned beneath the words *Cats on Board.*

It took a few minutes of struggling—and several instructional comments from Isabella—before the stroller was unfolded and snapped into its operational configuration.

A gift from their then-aspiring mayor neighbor, the stroller had been used to transport Rupert and Isabella through several Northern California host cities for the Tour of California cycling race.

The niece had been skeptical when Monty first presented her with the "green machine." She hadn't thought she'd be able to convince Isabella to voluntarily climb inside its mesh-covered passenger compartment.

But after a thorough sniffing and inspection, Isabella had reluctantly complied. After a few trips in the stroller, the cat soon got over her concerns about being trapped inside.

If she sat upright in the passenger compartment, she could see out through the top netting. With a clear view of the sidewalk ahead, she had become skilled in communicating directions back to the niece, who steered the contraption by pushing on a waist-high handlebar.

Isabella had eventually given the stroller her stamp of approval. She generally enjoyed her stroller experiences—so long as her commands were understood and dutifully obeyed.

THE NIECE LOADED the reference book, her notes, and the photocopy of the mural into one of the nylon storage compartments built into the stroller's side walls.

Since its bike race debut, the modified carriage had been surprisingly useful in both transporting the cats and sneaking them into areas where they wouldn't ordinarily have been permitted. Given the unexplained events that had transpired within the Green Vase the previous day, the niece didn't like the idea of leaving the cats alone again.

"I think I'd better take you guys with me," she said with a wary glance around the showroom.

She'd puzzled long and hard about what might have gone on in the apartment during her jog to Coit Tower. After a night's fitful pondering, she'd concluded that her uncle must have been responsible for the "Follow the Murals" message painted on the kitchen floor—but she hadn't been able to reconcile that theory with the mysterious sneakered footprints.

Since moving into the apartment above the Green Vase, she'd encountered a lot of strange things. The invisible intruder ranked near the top of the list.

In any event, she didn't want to endure a repeat of the cat-painting disaster.

The niece unzipped the stroller's top cover and folded it to one side so that Isabella could leap into the passenger compartment. Then she scooped up Rupert and gently dropped him in next to his sister.

For his part, Rupert didn't mind the stroller. So long as he could snuggle into the blankets for a nap, he found the rides comfortable enough. From the confines of the stroller's passenger compartment, he had slept through raucous bike races, Mark Twain impersonators, and squawking mother ducks.

Today's outing would offer something a little different.

He had never ridden in the stroller while being trailed by a ghost.

THE NIECE DECIDED that the street sign depicted in *City Life* was her best starting point for trying to interpret the mural message that had been painted on her floor—and for figuring out why the murdered intern had collected the Coit Tower picture of her uncle.

Setting off from the Green Vase, it was a short walk to the intersection of Washington and Montgomery. Propelled by its human-powered engine, the cat stroller arrived within minutes.

Pausing at the near curb, the niece gripped the handlebar as she stared at the familiar landscape.

The bottom tip of Columbus Avenue cut into the cross streets at a diagonal, creating a multipronged juncture—and a snarl for traffic. The interchange formed a meeting point for three distinct neighborhoods: North Beach, Chinatown, and the financial district.

The surrounding businesses reflected the jumbled mix.

An Irish pub with fliers advertising an upcoming European soccer match sat across from a chichi champagne bar frequented by stockbrokers and young lawyers. Across the lopsided intersection, a plastic sign emblazoned with Chinese characters advertised a jointly operated dry cleaners and Szechuan noodle palace.

Towering above it all, in geometric concrete serenity, was the TransAmerica Pyramid building—along with the posted street sign featured in the *City Life* mural.

After waiting for the light, the niece pushed the stroller toward the bottom of the intersection at the pyramid's base.

From the cat compartment, a commanding feline voice issued the charge—one that startled the ghostly spirit hovering near the stroller.

"Merrrr-ow-ow!"

REACHING THE OPPOSITE side of the crosswalk, the niece stopped to look up at the pyramid. The modern-day financial center rested on a spot brimming with San Francisco history.

The pyramid stood at the edge of San Francisco's pre–Gold Rush shoreline. Truckloads of landfill had been used to flatten the space and make it suitable for building. All manner of seaborne relics lurked in the sandy depths below, including the remnants of a wrecked ship embedded in the foundation walls.

While the pyramid's signature shape was now universally associated with the San Francisco skyline, the building was only about forty years old. Back in the thirties when the *City Life* mural was conceived, the lot was occupied by another famous structure.

The Montgomery Block, affectionately known as the "Monkey Block," was a favorite gathering place for many of the city's artists, including the writer Mark Twain.

Upon this last realization, the niece tapped the stroller

handle with confidence. One of her uncle's favorite authors, Twain was also a founding member of the Bohemian Club.

"Issy," she called down to the stroller, "I think we're on the right track."

PULLING OUT THE New Deal art book from the stroller's nylon pocket, the niece opened to the pages with the *City Life* spread. She positioned herself on the corner of Washington and Montgomery with the TransAmerica Pyramid to her back, so that she was in the same orientation as the mural's painted street signs.

In the mural's depiction, the corner of the Pacific Stock Exchange building could be seen in the distance, a few blocks away from the marked intersection. One of the curved stone statues from the building's front entrance protruded into the street, as if summoning the viewer to investigate.

Recalling the details she'd read the previous evening, she flipped to the section of the text that discussed the New Deal artists' influences and jumped to the header on Diego Rivera. One of Rivera's earlier San Francisco works was located inside the Stock Exchange.

The niece thumped her finger against the commission date. Diego's Stock Exchange mural was completed just a few years prior to the WPA murals inside Coit Tower. The master's work would have been foremost in the minds of Arnautoff and his crew.

Holding the book in front of her chest, she shifted her attention to the modern-day perspective and looked up the diagonal offshoot of Columbus Avenue. The Exchange building wasn't visible from this intersection. Too many high-rise office buildings blocked her direct line of sight.

"But even if I could see through concrete and steel," she murmured, "it wouldn't be located at the angle presented in the mural."

After a moment's contemplation, she repeated the painted message from her kitchen floor.

"Follow the murals," she murmured, slowly rotating as she compared the two images. "It's as if the painting is intentionally skewed . . . "

Puzzling, she turned the mural's layout 90 degrees to the left. The Stock Exchange and several other downtown landmarks suddenly fell into their proper alignment.

"Follow the murals," she repeated again, this time awestruck. She slipped the book back into the nylon pouch and pushed the stroller forward. "Let's head to the Stock Exchange."

Rupert let out a snuffling snore as Isabella offered her expert guidance. Nose pushed up against the mesh cover of the passenger compartment, she issued an encouraging command.

"Mrao."

WITH THE NIECE rolling the carriage forward, Isabella shifted her gaze to a passing pedestrian—a transparent young man in high-top canvas sneakers.

The cat winked at her ghostly friend as he jogged around the stroller, nodding her acknowledgment of his silent hand-waving directions.

Chapter 37

A FROLIC IN THE FOUNTAIN

SETTING HER BEARINGS for the Pacific Stock Exchange, the niece rounded the corner of the TransAmerica Pyramid building.

Having worked for several years in one of the financial district's high-rise office buildings, she knew the downtown area well. And in the years since she'd left the accounting job for her uncle's antique business, she had studied countless maps of San Francisco, particularly the streets that encompassed the former Barbary Coast.

Pondering the layout in her head, the niece pushed the stroller past the pyramid's southeast flank.

"If we go about a block toward the water," she said, thinking aloud, "and then turn right, that should put us in front of the Stock Exchange."

Remaining vigilant inside the stroller, Isabella peered out at her surroundings. She piped a consenting *chirp* at the niece's proposed route, but as the stroller reached the gate to the small park located immediately behind the Pyramid, she appeared to change her mind.

"Wrao-ow."

"Let's not get distracted," the niece replied absentmindedly, still focused on navigating toward the Stock Exchange.

The second instruction was more direct.

"Mrao!"

Stopping, the niece strummed her fingers against the stroller handle. Isabella's indignant blue eyes stared up through the passenger compartment's net cover.

"Okay, we can take a short break by the fountain. I think I have a map in the stroller. I can check the route."

Seemingly satisfied, Isabella returned to a forward-facing position.

She'd seen something that her human had missed.

Spider's transparent figure had loped through the park and was beckoning Isabella to come toward the fountain at its center.

MUTTERING UNDER HER breath about taking orders from a cat, the niece pushed the stroller through the open gates of Redwood Park.

Sky-high redwoods ringed the half-acre green space, blocking out most of the adjacent office buildings. Frequented by workers from the downtown's many financial institutions, the park was a popular spot for coffee breaks and sack lunches. For the time being, however, the area was empty.

The niece parked the stroller by a bench positioned near the fountain and began searching the many pockets for the map.

Isabella, meanwhile, focused her intensity on the fountain. Several spigots shot aerated spouts of water up from the center, an imitation of the surrounding redwoods. Around the fountain's edges, a number of metal frogs posed in various leaping positions, their bodies wet from the center spray.

The fountain's frog theme was a tribute to Mark Twain, playing off the subject matter of one of his earliest writing successes, a short story involving a prized jumping frog.

The niece finally pulled the map from a stroller pocket. The laminated folio had seen a great deal of use. Unfolding the worn sheet, she sat down on the bench to study their location.

"I think we're heading in the right direction," the niece said after a brief inspection. "Funny, it puts us right on the track of . . ."

She stopped and looked up as the stroller began to rock back and forth. Isabella stabbed at the net cover, urgently signaling to her person.

Rupert poked his head up through the blankets, stretched his mouth into a sleepy yawn, and turned his gaze toward the fountain—and the object that was causing his sister's tizzy.

His blue eyes opened wide as his furry face registered shocked surprise; then he ducked back down into the stroller's passenger compartment.

Brow furrowed, the niece glanced at the fountain—and sharply drew in her breath.

A human image had formed in the splashing water. It was something less than solid, but dense enough to cause the moving water to divert around its shape.

The niece stared at the figure in the fountain, dumbstruck.

The liquid silhouette was that of the murdered intern.

He was emphatically pointing toward the park entrance—and across the street to the northern terminus of Leidesdorff Alley.

Chapter 38
LEIDESDORFF ALLEY

BEFORE THE NIECE could utter a word, the figure in the fountain disappeared. The water resumed its regular bouncing rhythm, shooting out the spigots in the fountain's center base, rising ten to twelve feet into the air, and then pattering like rain back into the frog-ringed pond.

Stepping tentatively toward the nearest stream of water, the niece reached with her free hand to touch the outer droplets. The moisture that coated her skin was a regular liquid consistency—with no apparent transformative properties.

Crouching to her knees, she squinted at the metal spigots, trying to identify the device that had been used to manipulate the spray.

There was nothing to indicate the application of a special effect, no sign that the fountain had been altered in any way.

Wiping her wet fingers on her pants leg, she struggled to wrap her mind around what she had just seen.

What could have possibly caused the water to form the shape of the murdered City Hall intern? Why had he been pointing toward the park exit?

"And was he wearing rubber-soled sneakers?" she asked,

thinking of the previous day's footprints. She hadn't had time to look at the apparition's feet.

"I must be losing my mind," she said, returning to the stroller.

"But then again," she added with a shrug toward the passenger compartment, "here I am, talking to my cat."

Isabella glared sternly up through the mesh netting and sniffed her offense.

TRYING TO REGROUP, the niece once more focused on the map.

Both the figure in the fountain and the *City Life* mural had directed her toward a path she had studied before—and traveled directly beneath.

A half block off of Montgomery, Leidesdorff Alley had been the subject of the niece's first Oscar-inspired treasure hunt. Below the narrow side street lay a secret tunnel that ran across the financial district. Near Market's busy thoroughfare, the tunnel system branched out, threading through the multi-layered underground BART and Muni systems to the Palace Hotel. On the north side of the financial district, the tunnel's main access point was in Jackson Square—through a hidden door in a basement wall beneath the Green Vase showroom.

The tunnel's path, like Leidesdorff Alley at ground level, traced the edge of San Francisco's original shoreline, a marshy landscape that was filled in during the city's massive Gold Rush–era expansion into the Bay.

The niece had stumbled across the tunnel entrance two years earlier while exploring the Leidesdorff-related treasure her uncle had been researching before his apparent death. Leidesdorff and his tulip-shaped cuff links had been the key to the location of a set of valuable diamond jewels—and an important clue to the sleeping potion used to facilitate her uncle's disappearance.

The caper eventually culminated in a kitschy cat show at the Palace Hotel, where Rupert and Isabella modeled elaborate costumes fashioned out of the diamonds, followed by a race back through the tunnel to the Green Vase basement and a showdown intended to trap her uncle's long-term nemesis.

"Maybe it's just a coincidence," the niece murmured to herself, looking up from the map and through the park gates to the opening of the nondescript alley. But she couldn't dismiss the correlation.

William Leidesdorff marked the beginning of the weird and wonderful journey she'd begun when she and her two cats moved into the apartment above the Green Vase. She'd left behind a secure but tediously predictable career as an accountant and taken on a pursuit of endless mystery.

It was difficult for her to imagine ever going back to her previous life—even with all the hassles she'd had to endure from her crazy neighbor.

No, she thought resolutely. This had to be it. A path down Leidesdorff Alley was just the type of route her uncle would have devised.

Isabella sent up a trill of agreeable cat chatter as the niece slid the map into the side pocket and pushed the stroller across the street.

Chapter 39

THE NOSE KNOWS

THE NIECE ROLLED the cat-filled strolled into Leidesdorff Alley. Raising her hand to block the sun's overhead rays, she peered down its short length. No more than a single car's width, the alley stretched a few short blocks, wiggling from one side to the other as it cut through the downtown financial district.

Other than a sandwich shop that had recently opened at the alley's midway point, there was nothing much of note. To the casual observer, it was just an empty service corridor, flanked by the solid brick-and-concrete walls of the adjacent buildings.

But the niece knew better.

She stopped in front of a nondescript wall near the alley's entrance and studied a historical marker that had been mounted, shoulder height, onto the brickwork.

The square plaque featured a relief-style sculpture of William Leidesdorff's head and shoulders. The metal surface had been stained a dark brown, perhaps in recognition of Leidesdorff's Caribbean roots. The son of a St. Croix sugar plantation owner and a West Indian slave, Leidesdorff had been born with a dusky complexion that allowed him, during a time of racially drawn boundaries, to blend in and mix with different cultures and social classes.

The plaque's center portrait image was surrounded by a series of smaller scenes, each one depicting a seminal event from Leidesdorff's life.

After leaving St. Croix at a young age to work on the shipping vessels that moved goods up and down the East Coast, Leidesdorff eventually established a successful transport business in New Orleans. There, he fell in love with a debutante from a wealthy society family. They were set to be married—until her parents found out about the groom's mulatto ancestry. With the wedding called off, a brokenhearted Leidesdorff sailed up the Pacific coast to the wilds of Upper California, then a Mexican territory.

Along with a Russian maid, who bore a strong resemblance to the New Orleans fiancée, Leidesdorff built a new life for himself in the frontier town of Yerba Buena (the predecessor of San Francisco). This renaissance was unfortunately cut short when Leidesdorff died under suspicious circumstances days before the discovery of gold at Sutter's Mill.

Leidesdorff was buried in San Francisco at the Mission Dolores, a site that the niece, memorably accompanied by Montgomery Carmichael, had visited during her first treasure hunt.

In order to give the niece time to examine the gravesite, Monty had distracted the supervising priest with questions about pursuing a career in the ministry.

"I don't think the father ever recovered from that experience," she said, shaking her head as she recalled the scene.

***"MRAO,"* ISABELLA CALLED** up from the stroller. In her opinion, the niece had spent long enough staring at the plaque. It was time to get moving.

"Onward," the niece replied, grabbing the stroller's handle and giving it a strong push down the alley.

They soon reached the sandwich shop, which was starting to percolate with midmorning customers. Around the corner from several legal and accounting firms, the alley location had proven to be a convenient niche.

A few tables had been spread across a small patio on the alley side of the building. The outdoor eating area was framed by a line of distinctive black posts, each one topped by an iron horse head with a flat nose and a metal ring threaded through the mouth like a bit.

The niece braked the stroller, yielding to a patron who had just exited the sandwich shop carrying a paper bag with an early lunch.

As the door swished open and closed, Rupert's orange ears suddenly perked. Something had awakened his sleeping sonar. From the stroller's cat compartment came a loud snuffling sound, followed by a disbelieving *"Mow?"*

Isabella looked at her brother, puzzled at what he could have possibly sensed that she would have missed.

Rupert snorkeled in another volume of air, seeking confirmation. After the recent switch to diet cat food, his smelling skills were, if anything, amplified by the dissatisfied rumbling in his stomach.

Yes, he thought jubilantly. It was just a sliver of a scent, but he was confident in his nasal analysis. He had expertise in just one area, but on this topic he commanded full feline respect.

Lifting his head, his furry chest puffed out as he made the gleeful pronouncement.

"Mreow!"

Bemused, the niece looked down at the stroller.

"What's got into you?" she asked with a laugh.

"Mreow!" Rupert repeated, this time a forceful statement as he stared with intensity at the sandwich shop.

"Don't be silly," the niece said placatingly. "You don't eat sandwiches. And besides, that takeout bag was marked pastrami, not chicken."

Rupert's face registered panic and confusion as the niece pushed the stroller past the shop. In the stroller compartment beside him, his sister added her voice to the cause, to no avail.

"Don't worry," their person said. "When we get back to the Green Vase, I'll pour you a big bowl of your new diet giblets."

Rupert's sorrowful howl echoed down the alley.

• • •

DISTRACTED BY THE cat commotion inside the stroller, the niece failed to notice a white cargo van parked around the corner from the sandwich shop. The vehicle had received several additional dents and scrapes on its exit from the Sonoma forest, and the windshield now bore a long crack across the passenger's viewing side.

Minutes earlier, two men, grungy from their months of camping in the woods, had retrieved a covered painting from the van's rear cargo area.

The niece and stroller bustled past the sandwich shop just as Sam and Oscar hung the artwork on a wall inside. Having been painted in the cabin near the cooking fire, the canvas had absorbed trace amounts of fried chicken scent.

The painting was a near-perfect replica of Victor Arnautoff's *City Life.*

Chapter 40

THE LETTER *O*

AS SOON AS the niece departed Redwood Park for Leidesdorff Alley, the Previous Mayor stepped from behind a wide trunk about fifteen feet away from the frog fountain.

A few weeks back, he'd hired an off-duty detective to conduct occasional surveillance on the woman who owned the Green Vase antique shop. He'd tracked the woman's daily jogs, her trips to the grocery store, and any other outing from Jackson Square. Nothing had tripped the radar as unusual—until today.

The cat-occupied stroller was a clear indication that this excursion was different. The woman was clearly on the hunt for something.

The Previous Mayor hoped it was her uncle Oscar. He had some serious questions to ask his old friend.

So after receiving the alert from his surveillance man earlier that morning, the PM had rushed down to the financial district. He had intended to follow the woman into Leidesdorff Alley, as his detective had departed for a much-needed coffee break, but he couldn't leave Redwood Park without a closer inspection of the fountain.

THE PREVIOUS MAYOR circled the fountain's perimeter, examining the center spigots and each brass frog, trying to ascertain the trick that had been used to generate the human image in the liquid curtain.

He crouched at the fountain's edge, watching the aerated streams shoot upward, crest at their high point, and then disperse into droplets that sprinkled back to earth. Pulling off his leather gloves, he reached his hands into the spray, at one point nearly falling into the surrounding pool, but he could see no mechanical means for creating the illusion.

Nor did the water spirit reappear.

Puzzled, the PM expanded his search. He tiptoed through the landscaping, checking for a projecting lens or other electronic equipment that might be hidden in one of the massive redwood trunks or beneath the spreading ferns and flowering cyclamen.

But he found nothing.

Finally, he sat down on a bench to think. As he stared at the fountain, puzzling over the hauntingly familiar image that had materialized in the water, a damp spot appeared on the seat next to him.

The imprint was just the right size for the rear end of a skinny young man who had once ridden his bicycle up and down San Francisco's steep hills.

The Previous Mayor was a cynical man—forty years in state and local politics tended to have that effect on a person. But over the course of his long life, he had developed a healthy respect for the spiritual world. He had experienced his share of odd events.

He wasn't beyond believing in a real-life actual ghost, but he still felt silly speaking the name of his dead friend, particularly since he halfway expected an answer.

"Spider?"

The air beside him shimmered, generating the faint outline of a human silhouette.

Startled, the PM jerked away from the image. His hands

shook as he reached for the brim of his bowler. He was no longer trying to come up with a rational explanation for this strange phenomenon. If this was a hoax, he could only applaud the trickster for creating such a spectacular ruse.

Cautiously, he leaned forward.

"Spider, I'm so sorry . . ."

His voice caught with emotion. His chin trembled as he struggled to speak.

He felt a light pressure on his shoulder, a comforting, consoling gesture.

Regaining his composure, the PM voiced the question that had plagued him for the last two months.

"Who did this to you?" After a steadying swallow, he added, "That night at City Hall?"

Spider looked at the ground, his translucent face one of intense concentration. The appearance in the fountain had drained his energy levels. It was taking all of his strength to make himself visible on the bench. With the toe of his sneakered foot, he drew a circle on the pavement.

"What's that?" the PM asked, urgently trying to discern the meaning. "A circle?"

Spider continued to focus on his foot, forcing it to make another swirl.

"An *O*," the PM murmured, watching the ground.

"No," he said as the foot faded from view. He shook his head adamantly. "It can't be."

He shifted his gaze back to the bench, but the apparition had disappeared, leaving him alone and with even more troubling questions than before.

The Lieutenant Governor's Residence

Chapter 41
LIGHTHEADED

HOXTON FINN STRODE briskly up a steep sidewalk in one of San Francisco's most fashionable residential neighborhoods. Traditional apartment buildings intermixed with multistory homes, both of which had been renovated, often several times over, and converted into condos and co-ops.

The architectural design of the older homes along with the close proximity of all the structures, sometimes less than a foot apart, allowed little room for formal parking. Occasionally, a garage would be carved into a once-submerged basement, the narrow, claustrophobic slot accessed by a steep driveway no wider than a compact car's width. Given the technical difficulties of navigating into the cramped subterranean spaces and the few available openings, parked cars lined the street.

The neighborhood's parking inconvenience was more than offset by the scenery. Even at street level, the elevated vantage point of this prime location provided a stunning view of the bay that swept from Alcatraz all the way to the Golden Gate Bridge.

The location's beauty was lost on the gruff reporter striding forcefully up the block.

Hox popped his notebook against his left thigh, thinking about his upcoming meeting with the Lieutenant Governor. He hoped to gain some insight into Spider Jones's intern duties, especially the projects on which he had been working right before he died.

No fan of the frog-phobic former mayor, Hox had given the politician a number of irreverent titles, the most benign being the Light Governor. But if Hox was feeling cheeky or even slightly grumpy, he quickly switched to a more derogatory nickname: Lightheaded.

The meeting would take place at the Lieutenant Governor's penthouse condo. The digs were far too posh for the politician's government salary, but Lightheaded had married into money. It was the wife's fortune that enabled their high standard of living—just another strike against him, as far as Hox was concerned.

Almost as bad as marrying a movie star, he thought with chagrin.

With an irritated sigh, Hox looked back down the hill at the slender man trailing fifteen feet behind. The news station's stylist, carrying his full kit of shears and beautifying tools, had stopped to catch his breath. Face flushed, he stood panting on the sidewalk.

"Come on, Humphrey. Try to keep up!" Hox hollered a belligerent encouragement.

"I still don't understand what I'm doing here," the stylist replied, wiping his brow. "And why I had to bring all of my equipment."

"It was a requirement for the meeting," Hox said as he checked the address written in his notebook against the house number of a pink-painted six-story structure.

"But," Humphrey sputtered as he closed the distance between them, "we're not filming this, are we?"

"It wasn't Lightheaded who requested your presence," Hox replied wryly. He pushed the call button by the building's front entrance.

"It was his wife."

A BUZZER SIGNALED the unlocking of an iron gate, which led through a small garden into the main lobby. As the two men stepped inside, a doorman in an ill-fitting uniform nodded a welcome, motioned toward the elevator, and returned to his newspaper.

Hox squinted at the paper's folded-over top half, pleased to note his byline. Then he turned his gaze from the newspaper to the doorman's workspace. The lobby was vintage San Francisco, with polished wood flooring, decorative crown molding, and high-end art hanging on the walls. The lobby's rear windows looked out onto a well-groomed courtyard and, beyond, a view of the bay that eclipsed the one visible from the street.

Hox was a reporter through and through. The profession might as well have been encoded in his DNA. But in moments like these, even he found himself second-guessing his chosen career. A job in low-vigilance lobby security certainly had its appeal.

"Too late to change course now," the reporter muttered as he squeezed next to Humphrey inside the building's tiny elevator. With a creaking groan, the door slid shut, and the unit began a wobbly climb.

A small landing and a single door greeted the pair at the building's top floor. There was only one residence on this level, the penthouse suite.

Before Hox could ring the knocker, the entrance swung open.

The man standing in the doorway was almost unrecognizable.

His brown hair flopped down around his ears. The shaping was ragged and uneven, as if he had gone far too long since his last haircut. He wore rumpled pants designed for hiking or camping. Pockets of various sizes had been sewn into the canvas fabric, and elastic cords had been fitted at the bottom cuffs. His face bore a couple days' growth of downy facial hair. There were signs of a patchy goatee forming around his chin.

The casual lifestyle appeared to suit the Lieutenant Governor. Hox had never seen the man in such a jovial mood. He greeted the visitors with an enthusiastic, "Welcome!"

"Governor," Hox replied with a bemused grin.

After a quick survey of the politician's disheveled hair, sportsman's T-shirt, and low-rise hiking boots, the stylist unzipped his bag.

"Oh my," Humphrey said with a shudder. "Let's get started."

Chapter 42

THE KNITTED BOOTIES

HUMPHREY DIDN'T WASTE any time. He immediately steered the Lieutenant Governor toward the kitchen sink.

"Let's start with the hair," he said briskly, turning on the water as the wife ran to the bathroom pantry to fetch towels.

Hox waited in the foyer, angling his head to see into the kitchen, hoping for a break in the shampooing action so that he could pose his questions.

Unfortunately, the full-fledged makeover session left no room for bystanders. Hox dodged an errant spray of water from the dishwashing hose mounted onto the sink. A foaming shot of shaving cream narrowly missed his left ear, tagging a glass-fronted print hanging on the foyer wall.

"Make yourself at home, Hox," the Lieutenant Governor called out over the buzz of an electric razor. With difficulty, he lifted a hand to point toward the living room on the opposite side of the condo.

Bending at the waist to avoid further friendly fire, Hox retreated to the seating area. As he scooted out of the foyer, he heard the Lieutenant Governor issue a fruitless caution.

"Watch the goatee, there, Humphrey. It's not fully grown in yet."

There was a brief silence, followed by a resumption of the humming razor.

"My apologies, Governor," Humphrey said after another short pause, with what Hox assumed included a wink to the man's wife. "I seem to have nicked the goatee's left side. I'm afraid you'll have to start over from scratch."

A FEW MINUTES later, Humphrey led the clean-shaven Lieutenant Governor to the living room. The wife had laid out a piece of plastic on the floor and positioned a stool at its center. As the makeover subject settled into the seat, Humphrey wrapped a drape across the politician's chest and snapped it shut at the base of his neck.

With his modified tool belt secured around his waist, Humphrey began combing through the Lieutenant Governor's wet locks. The wife paced a circle around her husband, closely supervising the process.

Hox grabbed a chair from the side of the room and slid it as close as possible to the haircutting operation.

"I need to ask you a few questions about Spider Jones," he said, flipping open his notebook. After a quick glance at the page containing the scrawled letter *O*, he turned to a clean sheet.

The wife shifted her attention to the reporter. "That's the name of the murdered staffer, isn't it?" she asked, sharply interested. "The one who was killed at City Hall last November?"

She walked toward Hox's chair. He squirmed uncomfortably as she peered over his shoulder. He felt himself instinctively trying to hide his notepad, despite the fact that the top sheet was still blank.

"Yes," Hox said, looking up from his notepad to give the woman his sternest stare. The typically effective expression had no effect. She didn't budge from her intrusive position.

Clearing his throat, Hox tried to focus on the Lieutenant

Governor. The man's eyes were closed. His head was tilted back, and his pale face appeared loosely relaxed.

"Sir, I was wondering if you could tell me what Spider was working on in the weeks before his murder."

"Hmm," the Lieutenant Governor mused absentmindedly as Humphrey's scissors whirred around his ears.

"I'm sure he wouldn't know," the wife cut in informatively, stepping around Hox to insert herself between the reporter and her husband. "It's Mabel you want to talk to. She handles all of the interns and any low-level staffers."

She crossed her arms in front of her chest and pointed at Hox's notepad, as if instructing him what to write. "Hires 'em and fires 'em."

The Lieutenant Governor broke free long enough to peek around his wife's torso.

"That's right. Mabel's your gal," he said as Humphrey pulled him back onto the stool. "Lucky for you, she's here watching my son."

The wife gestured down a hallway leading away from the central living area. "She's in the guest room."

As Hox stood from his chair, she poked her finger into his chest.

"Don't wake the baby."

BRUSHING SCATTERED HAIR clippings from his trousers, Hox tiptoed down the hallway to the indicated room.

The baby's quarters were easy to pick out. Decals of dinosaurs and blue balloons decorated the entranceway's trim and facing.

Cautiously, Hox creaked open the door. The Lieutenant Governor's long-serving administrative assistant sat on a rocking chair beside a crib, a basket of yarn at her feet.

Hox knew Mabel from her many years at City Hall, but theirs was not a collegial relationship. She had always viewed him with suspicious disapproval. As a reporter snooping for secrets to reveal in his next column, he was clearly on the opposing team.

He wasn't looking forward to questioning her about Spider Jones.

"Hello, Hoxton," she said with stiff formality as he glanced into the bassinet at the sleeping tot, who wore a pair of hand-knitted booties on his feet.

"Mabel."

Hox had never understood the universal fascination with babies. It had been one of many areas of contention with his ex-wife. The wrinkled, alien-looking creatures made him extremely uncomfortable—and on the concept of diapers, he was particularly squeamish. Best to get this interview over with before the little tyke made any stinky deposits that might require Mabel's attention.

Cringing, Hox took a seat on a wicker hamper next to the rocking chair and flipped to another clean page in his notebook.

"Mabel, I'd like to talk to you about Spider Jones."

Frowning, she picked up a new skein of yarn and looped the end around her needle. The matter was obviously a touchy subject. Hox's questions were unlikely to raise the reporter's standing.

"I understand you were directly involved in supervising Spider's work for the mayor. What sort of research was he working on in the weeks before he died?"

"Just routine assignments mostly: legislative items under consideration by the board of supervisors, a proposed dog-walking ordinance."

The needles began clicking with furious intensity. Mabel's lips pinched together, as if she were carefully considering her next words.

"He stayed late those last couple of weeks, but that research wasn't on a project for the mayor."

Before Hox could press for clarification, there was a disturbance in the hallway.

"Now, let's talk about your wardrobe for tomorrow," Humphrey said as he ushered the Lieutenant Governor toward the master bedroom. "Your wife has laid out several options for you here by your closet."

The baby began to rustle in his crib. Panicked, Hox watched as the tiny hands opened and closed. The mouth yawned as if preparing for a full-throated scream. He had only seconds left before the wife stormed in and terminated the rest of his questioning.

Leaning toward the rocker, Hox prodded anxiously, "What was Spider working on?"

Mabel looked up from her knitting and took a deep breath.

"It had to do with the man who ran that fried chicken restaurant," she said. "That James Lick fellow."

Scribbling madly on his notepad, Hox nearly dropped his pencil as she added, "I think Spider figured out Lick had once owned an antique shop in Jackson Square. Back in those days, everyone called him Oscar."

New Deal Art

Chapter 43
THE STACKPOLE STATUES

THE NIECE REACHED the end of Leidesdorff Alley, pushing a stroller filled with a despondent Rupert and an increasingly frustrated Isabella. Neither cat had forgiven their person for making the grievous error of passing the sandwich shop without stopping, but the niece showed no signs of turning back.

The narrow passage emptied out onto Pine Street, just a block and a half shy of Market, immediately in front of the Pacific Stock Exchange building.

The niece glanced back at Leidesdorff Alley, peering down its wiggling length to the gates of Redwood Park.

"This has to be it, Issy," she said excitedly. "The street signs in the mural and whatever that was in the fountain directed us down Leidesdorff. We're on the right track, I'm sure of it."

Isabella warbled skeptical commentary from the passenger compartment, which the niece chose to ignore. Wedging the reference book beneath her arm, she waited for a break in traffic and then pushed the stroller across the street to the targeted landmark.

An impressive facade of white stone and concrete, the

Exchange stood out amid the surrounding high-rise offices and banks. A wide line of steps led to a portico framed by Doric columns, but the property's signature feature was the towering concrete statues positioned at either corner.

Designed by Ralph Stackpole, a Coit Tower muralist and a prominent member of the Bohemian Club, the sculpted blocks featured a relief-style grouping of human figures. The subjects had slightly swollen bodies, flat noses, and—particularly noticeable from the street level view—enormous toes.

The two statues were grouped by sex, with the male figures accessorized to highlight industrial themes and the female ones dressed to represent agriculture. It was the latter statue that had been poking around the corner in Arnautoff's Coit Tower mural, the niece reflected as she pulled out the reference book and opened it to the two-page spread of *City Life.*

As the niece compared the real-life statue to the one in the book, a man in an expensive suit and tie jogged up the front steps, carrying a workout bag.

With the original stock exchange having evolved into a digital entity that was later subsumed in a merger, the historic building no longer housed market traders. It was now used as an exclusive exercise club for the wealthy and the well connected. Banners advertising fortified bottled water and toned physiques hung from the front eaves.

In addition to the exterior Stackpole statues, the private club had retained the Diego Rivera mural painted on one of the building's second-floor walls. The Mexican master's socialist-themed fresco was locked inside a members-only retreat, an odd contrast of message and materialism.

"Of course, this all begs a bigger question," the niece murmured as she stared up at the female-themed Stackpole statue. "If we're supposed to be following the murals, where do we go next?"

• • •

SPIDER STAGGERED DOWN Leidesdorff Alley, struggling to catch up to the niece and her cat-filled stroller.

He wasn't sure if it was the day's exertions or an indication that his ephemeral existence was nearing its end, but he was rapidly losing strength. The appearances in the fountain and on the bench beside the Previous Mayor had drained his energy reserves.

Despite his fatigue, he couldn't give up.

The niece's mural hunt represented his only chance to bring his murderer to justice, but the process had just gone horribly awry.

She had completely missed the clue in the alley.

She had walked right past the *O*.

• • •

INSIDE THE STROLLER'S passenger compartment, Isabella shook her head in disgust. Over the years, her person had taken countless wrong turns and had misconstrued all manner of obvious directions, but never had the cat seen the woman act so obtuse.

She watched with dismay as the niece climbed the front steps of the Exchange to get a better look at the female-oriented Stackpole statue.

"Maybe I'm supposed to get instructions from one of the stone figures," the niece called out, squinting at the detail. "What is this smaller woman holding? A sunflower?"

• • •

SUMMONING HIS LAST reserves, Spider crossed to the Exchange and mounted the stairs. He slid around the statue, positioning himself between the woman and the concrete block. His face skewed up with concentration, but he couldn't generate the slightest shimmer of a reflection.

The only reaction he triggered was feline. Isabella began clawing at the stroller's net cover. Even Rupert poked his head up to watch.

Meanwhile, the niece continued her observations. She slipped through the narrow space between the sculpted block and the nearest column and stared up at the figure carved into the block's street-facing side.

Spider followed her around the ledge. He reached for her shoulder, tapping it with all his might, but the action had no effect.

"It looks like this one's holding a bundle of wheat," the niece said without much hope. "I feel like this is all wrong." Shaking her head, she started to retrace her steps.

Spider's eyes widened. He hadn't counted on the woman making such a quick retreat. He tried to get out of the way, but she had moved too fast.

Isabella chirped out a warning. Rupert shut his eyes and ducked his head beneath the covers.

The niece plowed right through Spider's vaporous form and out the other side, oblivious to his presence. Spider, on the other hand, took a flashing vision of flesh and bone, before crumpling to the ground as if he'd received a blow to the stomach.

By the time he managed to pick himself up, the niece had returned to the stroller.

"Follow the murals," she said, pondering. "Maybe we should keep going in this same direction. There's another set of New Deal–era murals in the Rincon Center. That's a straight shot from here on the other side of Market."

Spider threw up his hands in frustration.

Isabella offered her condolences. Her person wasn't the easiest creature with which to communicate.

• • •

AN ELDERLY MAN with short rounded shoulders stood at the edge of the alley watching the events transpire in front of the Pacific Stock Exchange.

As the niece set off toward the Rincon Center, accompanied by her stroller-bound felines and an exasperated ghost, Oscar thoughtfully stroked his chin.

Unlike the other observers, he thought the niece was proceeding on exactly the right track.

A Lunch Date

Chapter 44

THE REGULAR PLACE

THE PREVIOUS MAYOR sat on the bench by the frog fountain in Redwood Park, contemplating the great mysteries of the hereafter. He didn't pretend to know how Spider's spirit had managed to cross back into the land of the living, but he felt certain he knew the reason for the ghostly appearance.

A youthful death of such a sudden and unexpected nature demanded resolution. He'd felt that keenly—and he wasn't the crime's hapless victim.

Closing his eyes, he replayed their interaction in his mind. He envisioned Spider's face, partially hidden by the baseball cap jammed down over his forehead.

"Who did this to you?" he had asked, wanting to know and yet fearful of the answer.

Then he saw the transparent image of the sneakered foot making the circular *O* shape on the ground.

The Previous Mayor opened his eyes. Frowning, he bent his head to stare down at the concrete. He must have misinterpreted the meaning.

He had an easier time believing in Spider's ghost than he did in Oscar's guilt for the horrific crime.

THE PREVIOUS MAYOR stood up from the bench, straightening the brim of his bowler as he glanced one last time at the fountain. He was about to leave for Leidesdorff Alley to try to catch up to the niece when his cell phone rang.

"Hoxton Finn," he said after reading the name associated with the number on the phone's digital readout. He brought the receiver to the side of his face. "What can I do for the city's most fashionably coiffed reporter?"

He held the phone away from his ear, grimacing at the predictably terse response. The comment, however, didn't stop him from making a further tease.

"Calling me from the newspaper's salon?"

He nearly dropped the phone at Hox's rude reply. This remark was, however, followed by a more substantive communication.

"You want to meet?" The PM pulled up his sleeve to check his watch. "How about lunch?"

The proposal was apparently met with approval. He nodded his head and closed the conversation.

"I'll see you at my regular place."

A HALF HOUR later, the Previous Mayor strode into one of his preferred lunch spots. Before his recent stretch of self-imposed isolation, he had typically visited the restaurant three or four times a week.

The lunch crowd had packed in, filling all of the available tables and the stools around the bar, but the hostess waived him forward as soon as he walked through the front doors, offering to store his overcoat and bowler on a rack by her station. An empty seat appeared at the corner of the bar, a space that had been held open, just in case he arrived.

The PM cracked a superior smile as he slid around the line of patrons waiting for their name to be called and strolled across the dining room to his seat. Local celebrity had its perks. It was good to be back at his familiar haunt.

As for Hox, he would just have to fight his way in.

The bartender looked up from a rack of wine glasses. "Good afternoon, Mayor," he said in a polite tone that bordered on reverence.

Regardless of whatever nominal changes occurred in the pecking order at City Hall, this was still the only mayor who counted both in terms of prestige and tipping potential. If he approved of the day's service, he would pay his tab with a $100 bill. Waving his hand, he'd then utter the bartender's favorite phrase.

"Keep the change."

Pushing his other orders to the side, the bartender set a wide-mouthed martini glass on the bar next to an iced shaker and began preparing the PM's standing-order mixed drink.

Shifting in his seat, the PM casually surveyed the surrounding patrons. He held up the laminated menu, but he had already decided—back at the frog fountain when he received Hox's call—what he would be eating. It was crab season in the Bay Area, and there was only one dish that would suit his palate.

As the bartender carefully set a martini in front of the PM, he pointed to the daily special section of the menu.

"Crab Louie for me, Leonard," he said, loud enough to be heard over the din.

Nodding smartly, the bartender turned to relay the order to the kitchen.

Sighing with contentment, the PM lifted the glass, filled to the rim with a dry martini. A twisting lemon peel curled through the center of the liquid, spiraling in perfect symmetry.

But just as the drink reached his lips, a rumpled reporter shoved himself into the six-inch space between his stool and the corner of the bar.

"You might have picked a place with a little more privacy," Hox spat crankily.

The PM maneuvered his elbow around the newcomer, narrowly avoiding dribbling the drink down his chin. He straightened his shoulders, bristling with mock affront.

"Hoxton, these people are my friends." He gave a wide wink at the bartender, who smiled impishly as he set the Crab Louie plate on the counter.

The PM picked up his fork and dove into the creamy crab mixture. As he brought the mouthful to his face, Hox leaned in next to the mayor's shoulder.

"I've remembered something from the night of Spider's murder."

The PM stopped with his mouth wide open. Setting down the fork, he pushed back his plate. Then he turned, giving the reporter his full attention.

Hox lowered his voice to a whisper.

"He was carrying a backpack," he said, tapping his shoulder for emphasis. "I've checked the police report. There's no mention of it being found with the body. I just left the Lieutenant Governor's house. His assistant Mabel was there, and she told me Spider was working on some sort of private research project in the weeks before his death . . ."

The PM held up a shushing hand. "Leonard, can we move to the back room?"

A moment later, the pair was ushered through a side door to a smaller dining area with a single table. The PM pulled out a chair for Hox and then seated himself.

Leonard dutifully carried in the martini and the Crab Louie. The PM waited while the bartender set down his tray and then disappeared through the door before propping his elbows on the tablecloth and leaning toward Hox.

"Now, tell me about this backpack."

The Rincon Center

Chapter 45

A HISTORY OF CALIFORNIA

STILL CONFIDENT IN the accuracy of her route, the niece rolled the stroller across Market and headed in a zig-zag fashion toward the shoreline. Two blocks south of the main thoroughfare, she reached the next stop on her mural-projected path of New Deal art, the Rincon Center.

Located near Mission Street's lower end, the area was in much better shape than the neighborhood surrounding the newspaper's offices, about a mile farther up.

Like much of downtown San Francisco, the landscape had changed dramatically following the onset of the Gold Rush. The now relatively flat streets had originally been part of Rincon Hill, an elevated region filled with prestigious homes.

Rincon Hill began to lose its volume (and prestige) in the late 1860s with the implementation of the Second Street Cut, a leveling effort meant to create a flatter route between Market Street and the southeast waterfront. Further leveling occurred in the early 1900s during the construction of the Bay Bridge. The bridge's main downtown access ramps now cut through the old neighborhood.

The architecture transitioned with the changing use. The grand estates of the early years were gradually replaced by warehouses and industrial property. The late 1990s saw another evolution, with a wave of loft conversions and shiny new office buildings.

The former Rincon Post Office was swept up in this latest building trend. The once-small rectangular building was now but a tiny part of a commercial complex that took up an entire block. The facility housed a food court, a dim sum restaurant, several thousand feet of glitzy office space, a pair of apartment towers, and yes, even a post office—although the modern postal facility was located in the building's new addition, not the original structure.

Preserved during the massive addition, the vintage post office now served as a gallery for the extensive set of New Deal murals painted on its walls.

"YOU'LL SEE," THE niece assured the stroller's skeptical feline occupants. "We're on the right course." She muttered a less confident aside. "I can't think of any other way to follow the murals."

Isabella murmured a dubious response. Rupert merely shoved his head, ostrichlike, farther beneath the blankets.

After crossing with the light, the niece bumped the carriage up a few short steps to enter through the building's older north side.

Streamlined Art Deco styling prevailed both outside and in the original post office space. A tile floor of muted green covered the length of the interior. Matching green walls, a combination of textured drywall and tile, rose toward a cream and yellow ceiling. The murals were painted just above eye level, at the intersection of the color change.

On the lookout for any mural-related clues, the niece rolled the stroller past a security desk where a female guard in uniform sat reading a book. The woman looked up only briefly; the feline cargo in the stroller's passenger compartment slid by undetected. The post office was otherwise empty of pedestrian traffic.

Staring up at the walls, the niece piloted the stroller around the circumference of the room. Isabella peered up through the protective netting, quietly making her own observations. Even though the cat doubted the accuracy of her person's intuition, there was much to observe inside the renovated post office.

The building contained twenty-seven murals, each one depicting a different scene from California history. Plaques positioned at regular intervals gave titles and brief descriptions of the works, all of which were painted by the artist Anton Refregier.

Another Russian emigrant, the niece mused, just like the creator of *City Life*.

As she moved from one mural to the next, she was once more struck by the sensation that she was retreading episodes from the past two years. Several of the places she'd visited during her Oscar-inspired treasure hunts were represented in the pictures.

One panel showed the Mission Dolores, where she and Monty had visited the grave of William Leidesdorff, while another depicted the Sonoma Bear Flag Revolt, the pivotal event that led to California's independence from Mexico.

The murals continued a visual map through California history, featuring scenes from the Gold Rush, the Vigilance Committee, the territory's controversial induction into statehood, and the 1906 earthquake.

"It all fits," the niece said. "Everywhere we've been in the last two years, every bit of history we've researched, it's all here."

Isabella clicked out an unconvinced series of chirps.

Meanwhile, the niece couldn't help noticing a second unifying theme across all of the paintings. Each of the human figures was drawn with a sharp, swooping nose, oversized with respect to the rest of the body's features.

As she self-consciously cupped her hand over the center of her face, Rupert burrowed out from beneath the blankets.

His tummy was rumbling again. It was time for his person to return them to the Green Vase—and to dish out a decent serving of non-diet cat food.

He looked crankily up at the niece and then shifted his gaze to the noses in the nearest mural.

"Mao-wow."

Grimacing down at the stroller, the niece's muffled voice replied.

"That's not funny."

Chapter 46

THE FRIED CHICKEN DANCE

THE NIECE REACHED the far end of the Rincon Post Office display area, but after closely studying all of the Refregier murals, she had little to show for her efforts.

Despite the numerous California landmarks she'd identified in the murals, she'd found no clear sign of her uncle or where to search next. Even she was about to concede defeat.

"It had seemed so promising," she said, deflated.

Isabella looked up at her person and emitted a barely audible but clearly sarcastic "*Mrao.*"

With a sigh, the niece turned the stroller, preparing to leave. As she swung the stroller around, she noticed the security guard striding toward them.

The woman had a purposeful look about her, as if she had spotted questionable activity that needed to be investigated.

She's seen the cats, the niece thought, guilt blushing her cheeks.

"Time to go," she whispered, steering the stroller toward the exit.

She was halfway across the room when the guard called out, “Is this yours, ma’am?”

The code violation that had caught the guard’s attention wasn’t the presence of cats in the display area. Frowning with disapproval, the guard pointed to an apparently discarded takeout container sitting on the floor beside a flat bench at the rear of the room.

“No,” the niece replied. But as she gave the stroller another shove toward the front door, there was a rustling inside the passenger compartment. Rupert’s head poked out of the covers, his pink nose prickling at a recently detected scent.

Looking over her shoulder, the niece watched as the guard opened the lid of the container—green with gold printing—and released the distinctive aroma of fried chicken.

She caught only a glimpse of the gold writing on the container’s lid, but a quick look was all she needed to identify the large looping *O* printed on the container’s top. It was her uncle’s handwriting.

“Oh, wait,” the niece called out. She smiled awkwardly. “Actually, that is mine.”

The guard began walking toward the niece, eying her suspiciously as she held out the carton. The woman’s eyes traveled down to the stroller, where Rupert had thrown himself into a full fried chicken frenzy.

The niece stepped in front of the stroller, trying to block the guard’s view into the passenger compartment, but it was impossible to mask the carriage’s spring-squeaking gyrations.

Handing the carton to the niece, the guard peered down into the stroller.

Isabella lifted her head regally while Rupert paused in his fried chicken celebrations long enough to give the guard his most innocent-looking blink. Then his tongue slipped out and licked his lips. *Slurp.*

Putting her hands on her hips, the guard turned back to the niece.

“Are those cats?”

• • •

A FEW YARDS away, a slight glimmer sparkled across the post office's green floor tiles, the ghostly imprint from the rubber soles of a pair of high-top tennis shoes.

Spider had followed the niece through the rounds of the Rincon Post Office murals, all the while puzzling over her interest in the artwork. He could see no relevance to his murder—or the encrypted directions from the *City Life* mural. As far as he was concerned, she had drifted way off track. He gathered that the cats shared his view on the matter.

And so, he was perplexed by the discovery of the takeout carton, particularly the gold printing on its lid.

His ghostly form shuddered with apprehension as he peeked over the niece's shoulder and stared at the letter scrawled across the container, a large looping *O.*

Jackson Square

Chapter 47
CINDERELLA

MONTGOMERY CARMICHAEL STRODE briskly around the corner to Jackson Square, returning from a busy morning at City Hall.

Everything was in place for the next day's inauguration ceremony. The schedule had been finalized, the decorations were going up both inside and outside the building, and rows of temporary seating were being deployed in the rotunda area at the bottom of the central staircase.

He had just one last item to take care of.

Tapping an envelope in his chest pocket, he stopped in front of the Green Vase and knocked on the door.

No answer.

"That's funny," he said. "She should be back from her morning run by now."

Pressing his face against the glass, Monty peered inside the showroom. There was no sign of the niece or her cats.

He looked up toward the second-floor apartment.

"Rupert," he called out. "I've got chicken!"

Still, there was no response.

"Hmm," Monty grunted, curiously scanning the empty

store. There was definitely no one home. He generally kept closer tabs on the goings on inside the Green Vase, but his new position at City Hall was already putting a damper on his snooping activities. "I wonder where they've run off to."

Still puzzling over the whereabouts of the niece and her cats, he crossed the street to his art studio.

As he approached the glass-fronted building, his demeanor began to change. His fingers nervously fiddled with his cuff links, and a light sweat broke out across his forehead.

He cracked open the front door and cautiously poked his head inside. The space appeared to be empty. There was no sign of the—well, he refused to say or even think the word *ghost.* He preferred the term *pesky figment of his imagination.*

With a sigh of relief, he tossed his briefcase on the desk and pulled out his sketchpad. The pad's top sheet was clean. He'd torn off the most recent drawing and thrown it in a bin at City Hall.

There would be no more images of dead people, he told himself firmly as he propped the sketchpad on the easel by his desk.

Monty made a slow circle through the studio, rolling his shoulders as he cleared his head. Other than the niggling appearances by the ghost, he was generally pleased with the week's progress. Yesterday's interview with Hoxton Finn had gone far better than expected, and by this time tomorrow, he would be officially sworn in as mayor.

Flipping on his phonograph, he set a record spinning on the turntable.

As music pumped out of the speakers, Monty began to dance around the studio, sliding his flat-soled dress shoes across the floor's smooth surface in an elegant waltz. He held his arms out, as if they were wrapped around an imaginary partner.

He felt a bit like Cinderella on the night before her big ball. Nothing could spoil this moment. Nothing except . . .

"Nooooo," he groaned as a shimmering image reflected in the studio's wide front windows.

"I don't see you," he whimpered, clamping his hands over his face and squeezing his eyes tightly shut.

Blinded, he pivoted in place. Once he was safely facing the windowless back wall, he carefully lifted his fingers. Furtively scanning the rear studio space, he saw several paintings, a few cabinets filled with supplies, and a couple of easels—but no ghost.

Until the shimmering translucent figure of a young man in blue jeans, T-shirt, and high-top sneakers stepped from behind the nearest easel.

Monty blew out a sigh of frustration.

"Oh, man, you're *killing* me."

Spider crossed his arms over his chest. The toe of his left sneaker tapped a sarcastic response.

"Well, obviously," Monty sputtered, gesturing at Spider's translucent figure, "that was a poor choice of words." His thin lips pursed into a petulant pout.

"But why are you bothering *me*?"

WHILE MONTY WAS whirling around the studio, the niece and the cat-filled stroller arrived back at the Green Vase.

As the niece unpacked the stroller and Rupert finished off the last of the fried chicken, Isabella hopped onto the cashier counter to watch the activities taking place in the art studio across the street.

Between his off-tempo waltzing and his frustration with the intern's ghost, nothing in what she observed changed her dim opinion of their gangly neighbor, who suddenly burst out of the art studio and began marching toward the Green Vase.

She tilted her head, reflecting.

This Spider fellow, however, was starting to grow on her.

Chapter 48

VERY IMPORTANT GUESTS

"SO MUCH FOR your diet," the niece said as she lifted a contented Rupert from the stroller's passenger compartment.

She set him gently on the wooden floor and gave him a slight nudge for momentum. Yawning, he waddled across the Green Vase showroom to the leather recliner, intent on a luxurious, chicken-induced nap.

The niece placed the empty fried chicken carton on the cashier counter. The box had been licked clean by the time they were halfway home from the Rincon Center. Now that the contents had been disposed of, the box was ready for a closer study.

"I'll just put this thing away first," she said, bending to the stroller.

Flicking a lever, she began to collapse the contraption into its folded position. Grunting and groaning, the niece wrangled with the unit until it was nearly flat. As she propped it against the nearest bookcase, she dusted her hands against the legs of her blue jeans.

"Now then," she huffed, straightening her torso. "Let's take a look at that b—"

She cut short the sentence at a familiar noise on the sidewalk. Her shoulders tightened, and her back stiffened.

Isabella issued a sharp *chirp*, but the warning came too late.

The niece shut her eyes, cursing herself for being so careless.

She'd forgotten to lock the door.

The hinges squeaked as the entrance swung open and a whirlwind of meddlesome snooping swept inside. Monty's slick-soled dress shoes slapped against the showroom floor as he commenced his routine inspection.

Cringing, the niece turned to face her nosy neighbor.

"What do you have here?" he asked, scooping up the takeout carton from the front counter. His eyes widened as he lifted the lid and sniffed the greasy interior. Then, with a loud gasp, he slapped his hand over his chest.

"Oh my goodness," he exclaimed. "It's . . ."

Hands on her hips, the niece shook her head. Monty's interference was the last thing her mural project needed.

This was not a good development.

"WHEN DO YOU start the new job?" the niece asked, snatching the takeout container from Monty's grasp.

Raising a suspicious eyebrow, he scrunched his thin lips, leaned inquisitively toward the niece, and tapped the box.

She rolled her eyes and slid the container behind her back.

After a thirty-second stare-down, Monty relented with a "we'll revisit this later" look.

"That's what I came to see you about," he replied, changing tactics as he reached into his coat pocket. "The big inauguration is tomorrow, and I've got special front-row passes for you, Rupert, and Isabella."

From her perch on the cashier counter, Isabella's ears perked with interest.

"No," the niece said, her programmed response to any Monty proposal.

"You should come," he insisted. "There'll be commemorative paper plates, fancy party streamers, hors d'oeuvres—and, of course, me." He finished off the list with a flourishing gesture.

She walked around the cashier counter and slid the take-out container into a drawer.

"Nope."

"I got special permission for you to bring the cats," he added, a wheedling in his voice. "You wouldn't want to deprive them of a once-in-a-lifetime experience like this."

"They can watch it on TV."

Monty tapped his chin, momentarily stymied. "It's really important for me to have my Jackson Square friends present at the ceremony." He moped for a second. Then he tapped the counter as if he'd received a sudden inspiration.

"If you can't be there in person, I'll have to settle for the next best thing. I'll just finish up that portrait." He spread his hands above the counter, illustrating a grand presentation. "Then I can display it on the stage they've set up in front of the central marble staircase. Everyone will see it . . ."

With his left hand, he formed a fist, poking his thumb in the air as if measuring the niece's face. "I hope I can get the nose right this time."

"Okay, okay," she muttered. "We'll be there."

"Great," Monty replied, turning for the door.

"And afterward," he added, nodding toward the drawer behind the cashier counter, "we can discuss your fried chicken friend."

Dilla

Chapter 49
THE VISITORS

BY LATE AFTERNOON, San Francisco once more began to cloud over, the brief spurt of sunshine extinguished by the next storm moving in across the bay.

Dilla Eckles stepped out of a cab stopped on a steep street outside her Nob Hill residence. Having fulfilled her duties as Monty's temporary receptionist, she was happy to be home. It had been an exhausting day, and she was ready for a hot tea and a little nap.

She cradled her feathered hat in her hands as she climbed the rickety stairs to the entrance. The plumes had started the day perky, but at this point, even they needed refreshing.

As she reached the top step, she glanced up at the house. It had been in her family for generations; she'd lived there her entire life.

By size and location, it was a multimillion-dollar property, but the four-story structure was in serious need of maintenance and repair. The hundred-year-old Victorian's front facing featured rotting gables, broken trim, and several cracked windowpanes. From certain angles, the structure appeared to be dangerously leaning to one side.

"I guess we could both use some touching-up," Dilla mused as she unlocked the door. As a matter of habit, her thumb rubbed against the knob's brass surface, which was embossed with a three-petaled tulip, a relic from her numerous escapades with Uncle Oscar and his (now elderly) band of Bohemians.

"It's a delicate process," she thought, smiling to herself. "You don't want the face-lift to damage the underlying character."

STEPPING INSIDE THE house, Dilla set her hat on a narrow side table in the foyer. She stood silently for a moment, listening.

The place was quiet, as expected.

She lived alone. Her son, Sam, had moved out over a year ago, and her current husband, John Wang—the most recent in a long line of husbands—lived with his daughter in a Chinatown apartment. His poor health necessitated their separate living arrangements; he was wheelchair-bound and would have never made it up the front stairs. She suspected the short distance apart had contributed to the longevity of their relationship. His was her most lasting marriage to date.

Dilla crossed into the living room, her gaze skimming over the scattered knickknacks and faded photos that filled the space. The keepsakes held the memories from a life filled with love—*many* loves—and endless adventures.

Such a shame to grow old, she thought with a sigh. Stroking her curly gray hair, she turned to look out a window at the darkening sky above the bay.

As she contemplated the next round of rain, a sound emanated from the rear of the house.

It was the whistling *chop* of a knife.

Startled, she spun toward the kitchen doorway.

The building's layout was typical of its era. Each room was separated and fully walled in. From her position in the living room, Dilla could only see a two-foot wedge inside the galley-style cooking area—but it was enough for her to make out the shadow of the intruder.

Chop.

She shuddered as another loud *whack* thumped against the kitchen counter.

Slowly, Dilla eased around the couch. Her trembling hand gripped its back edge for support. The floor creaked beneath her weight as she neared the kitchen threshold.

Chop.

Taking in a deep breath, she summoned her courage and called out with concern.

"Sam, is that you?"

There was a clattering noise; then a man with a loose wrinkled face stepped into the doorway. A frayed baseball cap covered his greasy black hair. An apron tied around his waist concealed most of his ripped overalls.

Dilla let out a sigh of relief as Harold Wombler wiped his hands on a paper towel. He gummed his dentures, sliding them in and out of his mouth, before replying, "Hello, Dilla."

She brushed past him, her bustling confidence instantly restored.

"I thought you were off camping," she said as she surveyed the scene on her kitchen counter.

A skinned and partially deconstructed chicken lay on the cutting board, next to a mixing bowl filled with flour. On the stove, a cast-iron skillet with a half inch of cooking oil sat waiting for the first battered pieces.

Harold rested a gnarled hand on his hip.

"Do I *look* like I've been camping?" he grunted. "I've been making sandwiches," he grumbled. "Lots and lots of sandwiches . . ."

"Well, then," she replied, frowning at the counter. "Where are the others? Surely you didn't bring them back here."

There was a short cough in the dining room attached to the opposite end of the kitchen's galley.

Dilla scurried to the opening and rushed through.

Sam waved from his seat at the dining room table. At

least, she thought it was Sam. She could hardly see his face behind the wild beard, and he looked as if he hadn't showered in weeks.

"Hi, Mom," he said sheepishly.

She issued a motherly smile and shifted her attention to the elderly man occupying the next seat over. A navy blue button-down shirt covered his short rounded shoulders. A few white strands had been combed over his balding scalp.

On the table in front of him, next to her favorite feathered-bird centerpiece, rested a bloodstained backpack.

Colma

Chapter 50

THE SCENT OF DEATH

SPIDER SHUFFLED DOWN Market Street, weaving in and out of San Francisco's late-afternoon rush, carefully avoiding contact with any of the passing pedestrians.

So many people, he thought, all consumed with their busy lives, all of them marching, inexorably, toward its unknowable end . . . maybe tomorrow, maybe next week, maybe thirty years in the distance.

It was a wonder that the masses approached this terrifying reality with such calm detachment.

Would he have lived his life any differently, he wondered, if he had known how little time he'd been allotted? Could he have altered the course of his life's short trajectory, or had he been destined to die at the top of that marble staircase, a grisly footnote in the history of City Hall?

Sulking at the gross inequity of the scheme, he stared sullenly at the passing faces, flush with life, ripe with possibility.

A jealous rage coursed through Spider's empty figure. He felt robbed, shortchanged, and defrauded.

It was so utterly unfair.

SPIDER'S MOOD CONTINUED to darken as he stomped down the concrete steps leading into the Powell BART station. With an effortless leap, he hopped over the turnstile, an invisible act of rebellion that drew no objections, raised no alarms.

A quick trot down the escalators took him to the cavernous platform area. The blackened concrete walls both amplified and suppressed sound, an odd effect that eerily mimicked his own surreal existence.

A southbound train pulled into the station. The doors slid open, and Spider stepped inside, dodging his fellow passengers, who were oblivious to his presence.

He took a seat as the doors closed and the train scooted out of the station. The electronic connection powering the transport hummed in his ears, dulling the harsh edge of his emotions.

He had logged countless hours in BART trains, particularly in the last year of his life during his daily commute between his family's home in Walnut Creek and San Francisco's City Hall.

It was all so familiar: the rounded walls of the train's bullet-shaped compartment, the multicolored route map mounted by the door, the rows of plastic-framed seating, and the cloth upholstery, stained with the greasy residue from the backsides of hundreds of riders—just as icky in the afterlife as it had been to his living persona.

The train headed south, eventually surfacing from the tunnel to an aboveground rail. The conductor announced each stop along the way, but the weary words were, as always, unintelligible through the intercom. Spider watched the labels for each passing station until the train reached the one for Colma.

This is it, he thought grimly as he exited the train.

Cemetery Central.

My final resting place.

LOCATED ABOUT TEN miles south, just north of the airport, the municipality of Colma served as the main burial site for San Francisco and its environs. There were no active public cemeteries within San Francisco's city limits. With space at such at a premium, even many older burial plots had been transferred down to Colma.

The tiny town boasted far more dead than living residents. The number of the former category had recently been increased by one.

Spider Jones.

SPIDER EXITED THE BART station, crossed the commuter parking lot, and headed toward the iron gates that marked the nearest cemetery entrance.

The traffic from the 101 rumbled in the distance. Otherwise the area was ghostly quiet. He had expected to find other disembodied souls like himself wandering the grounds, but he was alone.

A misty fog settled in around the peninsula hills, obliterating the landscape, leaving only the studded maze of gravestones. The scent of death engulfed him.

Instinctively, Spider walked down the path to his recently covered plot. As he reached the marker, he stared down at the engraving, the block letters of his name, and the dates of his short life span.

His half-life existence was drawing to a close, and a renewed sense of urgency pulsed through his transparent being.

He had little time left to resolve his murder.

Just then, a white cat sauntered out from behind a nearby row of gravestones. It was a female Siamese mix, with flame-point coloring on her ears and tail.

She looked almost identical to the cat he'd encountered in the Green Vase antique shop—except that she shimmered in the same transparent manner as his own ghostly flesh.

• • •

ISABELLA SAT ON the third floor of the Green Vase's redbrick building, staring out the bedroom window at Jackson Square.

Her blue eyes sparkled like jewels as she traveled through her thoughts to the Colma cemetery, walked up to Spider's ghostly feet, and rubbed her shoulder against his calf.

The comfort delivered, her spirit returned to San Francisco.

Padding softly across the wooden floor, she leaped silently onto the bed and curled up beside her brother next to her person's feet.

The Beach Chalet

Chapter 51

FULL CIRCLE

THE FOLLOWING MORNING, the rain returned to full force, beating down on the city as if it were a ship out at sea. Wild whips of water lashed San Francisco's hilly streets, pelting the peninsula with a drenching downpour. Pedestrians perfected their stormy weather sprint, leaping over flooded potholes and gutters as they raced between points of cover.

Outside the Green Vase showroom, an abandoned umbrella scuttled down the sidewalk, its protective cup turned inside out, the waterproof fabric shredded from its round metal frame.

Upstairs in the kitchen, a much warmer—and drier—scene prevailed.

The niece sat at the breakfast table, studying her increasingly worn reference text on San Francisco's New Deal art. Isabella perched on a chair beside her person while Rupert hunkered on the floor beside his diet cat food–filled bowl, protesting.

"I think the Beach Chalet in Golden Gate Park is the next logical place to look," the niece said, raising her voice to be heard over Rupert's mournful howl. "The Chalet's first floor has a series of San Francisco–themed murals that were done by one of the Coit Tower artists."

She glanced over at the empty takeout carton. Other than the distinctive *O* printed on the lid—and the rapidly consumed fried chicken that had been inside—the carton had failed to yield any additional clues.

With a sigh, she buried her head in her hands. She was no closer to sorting out the cryptic message than she had been at the Rincon Center the previous day.

"Follow the murals," she groaned. "What does it mean?"

Isabella shifted her weight, trying not to convey the skeptical thoughts in her head. No need to pile on to an already hopeless situation, she reasoned.

Suddenly, the niece straightened her posture. Her face assumed a resolute expression.

Monty's inauguration ceremony was scheduled for later that afternoon, but they had plenty of time to check out the Beach Chalet before the event at City Hall.

"Who's up for a trip to the ocean?" she asked, flipping the book's cover shut.

Isabella's furry eyebrows crinkled with concern. The weather outside was definitely inhospitable for cats.

After a disbelieving look up at his person, Rupert sprinted to the living room and hid under the couch.

WAVES CRASHED ALONG the wide beach that fronted the Great Highway at the western edge of Golden Gate Park. The ocean raged like an intemperate child, casting fistfuls of sand onto the embankment with each swamping surge of water.

The Beach Chalet's rectangular block faced the ocean monster head on. A Spanish Colonial designed by Willis Polk, the two-story structure had outlasted many a storm. Built in 1924 as a public beach house, the first floor had once provided changing rooms for Ocean Beach's intrepid swimmers. Over the years, the building had been used as a

VFW social hall and, during World War II, as a dormitory for soldiers.

Currently, the Beach Chalet housed two separate restaurants, one in its rear garden area and one on the second floor overlooking the beach and the petulant Pacific.

The main room on the first floor, however, was dedicated to a display of the building's New Deal–era murals.

A TAXI-VAN CARRYING the niece and the cat-filled stroller pulled into the Beach Chalet parking lot and stopped adjacent to the front entrance. After paying the driver, the niece lifted the stroller out of the van's sliding side door.

Battling the wind and rain, she reached into the passenger compartment to fluff up the blankets so that Rupert and Isabella would be less visible. Then she propped open the Chalet door and rolled the stroller through the entrance.

Just inside, a hostess stood behind a counter, taking reservations for tables in the upstairs restaurant. A passage to the ground-floor eating establishment led away from the rear of the room. A small gift shop occupied a narrow space at the north end.

The rest of the lobby was dedicated to the murals.

Avoiding the hostess, the niece pushed the stroller around the room's long circumference, studying the colorful images plastered across the walls.

Her uncle, she thought, would have felt right at home here. From the selection of the artist to the way in which the local scenes were presented, the influence of the Bohemians was readily apparent.

The Chalet's murals were all painted by Lucien Labaudt, a prominent member of the Bohemian Club—and a Coit Tower alumnus.

Quotes from noted Bay Area poets and writers framed the arches of the windows and inner doorways, one for each nautical direction. Bret Harte, George Sterling, Joaquin Miller, and Ina Coolbrith—each author was either a well-known Bohemian or had been closely associated with the group.

"I have a good feeling about this," the niece whispered down toward the stroller. "I know I've said this before, but I think we're on the right track."

Isabella grudgingly concurred. Beside her, Rupert was more interested in the smells emanating from the two restaurants. His nose sniffed into overdrive, hoping to pick up the scent of fried chicken.

The niece stopped near the Chalet's front entrance, her attention drawn to a mural depicting famed architect Arthur Brown Jr. standing in front of his seminal achievement, City Hall.

Brown was shown as a serious-looking businessman in a fedora, red-striped tie, and suit. In his hands, he held the blueprints for another of his noted works, Coit Tower. The scrolled plans had been unfurled just enough to reveal a sketch of the tower and its square base.

In front of the image of City Hall, a fountain shot up a single stream of water, which arced and fell in such a way as to appear that the entire spray was reversed—and coming out of the sketched tower's fluted top end.

Either Labaudt hadn't believed Brown's protestations that the tower's nozzle shape was merely a coincidence or he was poking fun at the stuffy architect, the niece thought with a smile.

Then she paused, struck by the realization that with the Coit Tower reference, her route had just come full circle.

Chapter 52
THE MURAL-ED MESSAGE

STANDING INSIDE THE Beach Chalet, staring at yet another wall of murals, the niece puzzled over the path she and the cats had taken through San Francisco over the last two days.

After receiving a mandate to "Follow the Murals" on the kitchen floor, they had headed to the downtown intersection highlighted in Coit Tower's *City Life* mural. By shifting the mural to fit the real life orientation of the painted landmarks, the trio had been directed down Leidesdorff Alley to the Pacific Stock Exchange (home to one of Diego Rivera's famous works). From there, they had scooted across Market to the Rincon Center Post Office (site of a mural display detailing the history of California), and had now arrived at the Beach Chalet.

Other than a commonality of New Deal art, the niece had little to link the locations, and she was at a loss to explain how any of her mural-gazing could possibly help find her missing uncle Oscar—or have anything to do with the murdered City Hall intern.

She glanced down at her feline assistants inside the

stroller, hoping for some insight or clarification. Isabella gazed wordlessly up at her person, while Rupert, his eyes peeled for another package of fried chicken, merely licked his lips.

With a sigh of dogged determination, the niece continued her review of the Beach Chalet's murals.

A few of the paintings captured urban San Francisco scenes such as Union Square, Chinatown, and the Embarcadero, but most of the wall space focused on outdoor settings. A picnic at Baker Beach took up one swath of the lobby's rear wall. The other half was occupied by people at leisure or play in Golden Gate Park.

It was as she gazed at the second of these outdoor vistas that her spirits lifted.

Just above a couple feeding a squirrel at a park bench, she spied the curiously located Conservatory of Flowers.

She stared for a minute at the juxtaposition of the conservatory vis-à-vis two other structures in the far background, the De Young Museum tower and the gate for the Japanese Tea Gardens, trying to be sure.

Just like the landmarks in the *City Life* mural, this one was geographically out of place—and the building at the center of the mismatch had a close tie to her uncle's most recent alias.

Near the end of his life, the miserly millionaire James Lick had purchased a glass-paneled conservatory for use on his San Jose estate. He died before the conservatory's kit could be constructed; the parts were still wrapped up in shipping crates, unassembled, at his death. The packages were eventually donated to Golden Gate Park and formed the structural basis for one of the park's oldest buildings, the Conservatory of Flowers.

"Follow the murals," the niece said, breathless at the discovery. "Issy, it's the flowers! The Conservatory of Flowers!"

Chapter 53

THE WHITE VAN

EAGER TO MOVE on to what she hoped would be their last destination, the niece parked the stroller in front of the Beach Chalet's front windows and pulled out her cell phone. As she prepared to call the taxi driver who had dropped them off earlier, she glanced out at the parking lot with a shudder.

Beyond the protection of the building's outer colonnade, the water came down in sheets. The expanse of ocean across the street was barely visible.

"Wow, it's raining dogs and . . ."

At Isabella's sharp look, the niece cut short the comment.

"Well, it's really pouring outside."

She checked her watch. She wanted to get to the Conservatory of Flowers as quickly as possible, but there wasn't enough time to make that stop before Monty's inauguration ceremony. They were due at City Hall within the hour.

She gritted her teeth in frustration. She had no desire to watch Monty wallow in his mayoral triumph.

"Maybe he wouldn't notice if we didn't show up," she said, trying to convince herself of this unlikely possibility.

"Mrao," Isabella chirped up from the stroller, a concise rejection of that notion.

"You're right," the niece conceded. "We'd never hear the end of it."

Ruefully, she began punching the taxi driver's number into her phone.

"Hello," she said when he picked up on the other end. "We're ready for you to . . . hold on, wait a minute. I'll have to call you back."

Through the rain, she'd spied the blurry image of a white cargo van at the far end of the parking lot.

There were likely hundreds, if not thousands, of similar vehicles driving around the Bay Area. Other than the occasional logo painted onto their sides, they all pretty much looked the same. There was something about this particular van, however, that struck the niece as familiar.

Despite the number of dents, scratches, and dings, the van looked remarkably similar to the one owned by her nosy neighbor.

She had last seen the van the night of the board of supervisors meeting. Monty had driven the niece and her two cats to Mountain Lake in a futile quest to locate Clive and bring him back to the Academy of Sciences. The rescue mission had been aborted when the alligator discovered a dietary fondness for wet suit–clad interim mayors.

The van had disappeared the next day. Monty claimed it had been stolen, but the niece had always doubted that story.

She suspected it had gone on an extended loan—to the fleeing members of the Bohemian Club.

MINDFUL OF THE downpour they would encounter between the Beach Chalet's front porch and the van's parking space at the far end of the lot, the niece pulled out an extra nylon awning that fit over the stroller's passenger compartment and attached it to the upper framing. The stroller's nylon fabric was water resistant, and the niece had reinforced the cloth surface with a coating of water repellant spray. The combination of these measures, she reasoned, should keep the cats relatively dry.

"At least, you'll be drier than me," she said as she set off from the porch.

Pushing the stroller at top speed, the niece ran through the rain to the far end of the parking lot. The hood to her raincoat fell back as she peeked in through the driver's side window.

A bobblehead figure of the Lieutenant Governor, fashioned during his term as mayor of San Francisco, had been affixed to the dashboard. That confirmed it—this was Monty's van.

Cupping her hands, she pushed her face against the glass, trying to see through the front seating area to the rear cargo compartment.

Isabella *meowed* a warning as a blur of wild red hair suddenly popped into the niece's view, causing her to jump away from the van.

Oblivious to the rain, Sam rolled down the window and cheerfully called out, "Need a ride? I'm on my way to City Hall."

The Inauguration

Chapter 54
FRISKED

"WE'RE ONLY HERE for a few hours," Sam said as he drove the white cargo van through San Francisco's waterlogged streets. Rain drumrolled against the van's metal roof and streamed down the front windshield.

"What's going on?" the niece demanded. "Is Oscar in trouble? The police are looking for both of you."

Sam shifted uncomfortably in his seat before providing an evasive response. "We had to come back to fetch something."

The niece frowned, perplexed by all of the secrecy. "I ran into Dilla at Coit Tower. She seemed to be giving me some sort of clue about Arnautoff's *City Life* painting. When I got home, there was paint all over the kitchen and a message to 'Follow the Murals.' Since then, I've been running all over town looking at New Deal–era murals, trying to find a connection . . ."

Sam tapped the steering wheel, as if endorsing her efforts.

"Sounds like you're on the right track," he said encouragingly.

"For what?" she demanded. "What am I searching for?"

A gap-toothed grin spread across his freckled face.

"You'll know when you find it."

A FEW MINUTES later, Sam pulled to the curb on Van Ness, around the corner from City Hall, and flicked on his hazard lights. Given the inauguration traffic and the blocking local media trucks, this was as close as he could get to drop off the niece and the cats.

Sam was planning to sneak into City Hall on his own after he found a place to park. He still had his security pass from his ten years working as a janitor. He would observe the ceremony from a discreet location—then attend to the item that needed to be retrieved.

"That task should be taken care of by the end of today," he said as the wipers swung back and forth across the windshield. "Then we'll be on our way again."

The niece zipped up her raincoat and glanced outside. The sky was still dumping buckets of rain on the city. The cats would stay mostly dry in their protected stroller, but she was going to get soaked.

"What do I do when I reach the end of this mural trail?" she asked, still frustrated by Sam's response. "How is it going to help you and Oscar? Or are you going to keep running from the police?"

Sam gave her an assuring smile. "Trust me," he said. "You'll know." Then he nodded toward the passenger door. "You'd better get going."

With a quick wave good-bye, the niece jumped out and ran around to the side cargo door. She had no idea when she would see him—or her uncle—again.

She tried to put on a confident front, but internally, she echoed the concerned "*Mrao*" from Rupert as she pulled the hood of her rain jacket up over her head and soldiered off through the downpour.

CITY HALL'S PARTY planners had done their best to festoon the building with inauguration day splendor, but the storm had quickly ravaged the decorations. The wind had ripped the silk streamers from the arches over the front entranceways, and the sparkly bunting that had been strung across the lower eaves hung in sodden rags.

The building looked like a party girl after a wild night on the town, with snagged stockings and mascara running down her cheeks.

At least the interior had retained its dignity, the niece thought as she squeezed the stroller through one of the front doors and stepped out of the rain. Velvet trimming of navy blue and gold adorned the brass fixtures and wrapped around marble columns.

The niece steered the stroller toward the security line for VIPs and registered guests, queuing up behind a number of well-dressed politicians and socialites, all clad in formal attire.

As she stepped up to the scanner, the monitoring guard looked quizzically at her soggy tennis shoes and sopping wet hair. Then he directed his gaze to the two cats sitting in the stroller.

"Ma'am," he said sternly, "we can't let those cats in here."

"Okay," the niece said with a shrug, not the least bit disappointed. She could honestly tell Monty that they had tried to attend.

But as she swung the stroller toward the exit, a voice spoke up from the other side of the security tables.

"Wait a minute," a supervising guard called out. "Are you the cat lady?"

Meekly, the niece nodded as everyone else in the crowded lobby stopped talking and turned to stare.

Her face turned red. She noticed reporter Hoxton Finn standing at the edge of the security area. With her luck, this little episode would make the humor segment on the evening news.

"I have a note on that," the man continued loudly, as if he were enjoying the audience. "Do you have your passes?"

Reluctantly, the niece pulled the packet out of her jacket

pocket and handed it to the guard. He made a show of reviewing the paperwork.

"You're a friend of the interim mayor?" he asked, raising an inquiring eyebrow. He waved his pen at the stroller. "*All* of you are friends of Mayor Carmichael?"

The niece pushed her wet hair from her face and nodded. Over the surrounding whispers and giggles, she heard Hoxton Finn scribbling furiously in his notebook.

"And, uh, this is Rupert *the cat* and Isabella *the cat*?" he asked officiously, emphasizing their species identification.

Deciding to accept her fate, the niece took in a deep breath and straightened her shoulders. Looking the man in the eye, she replied with a terse affirmative.

"Yes, yes, they are," she said forcefully. "Can we just move through the line here?" She paused, pursing her lips, before uttering a phrase she'd never fathomed she would use to her advantage. "Mayor Carmichael is expecting us."

The supervisor backed off his mocking stance.

"I'm sorry. We're just struggling to find the right protocol here, ma'am. We're not used to screening, uh, felines."

He stepped to the side of the stroller and motioned for the junior agent to move in.

"Do you mind if we do a quick search of each cat?" he asked smoothly.

Begrudgingly, the niece hooked a leash into Isabella's harness and helped her out of the stroller's mesh-covered compartment.

The first guard knelt beside the cat, unsure of how to proceed. Isabella growled, ever so slightly, a low menacing warning. The man angled his head, inspecting her from either side, and then held his hands up, capitulating.

"All good on this one," he reported, standing and quickly backing away.

A second guard had scooped up Rupert from the stroller.

"Wow, this one's got a lot of hair!" he said, gently pressing his fingers against Rupert's round stomach. Fluffy white clumps floated up into the room. The supervisor, standing nearby, reached for his handkerchief to smother a sneeze.

Rupert looked up at his person as the guard handed him back to her. His blue eyes crossed in confusion.

What just happened? he thought, shaking his head. *I've been frisked!*

Chapter 55
AN INAUSPICIOUS BEGINNING

A TRIO OF trumpets trilled a salute as the city's new mayor pivoted at the top of the central marble staircase and began a regal descent.

The landing at the foot of the stairs had been set up to serve as the stage for the inauguration ceremonies. Temporary seating spread across the floor of the rotunda for the standing-room-only crowd.

Monty paused as he reached the bottom steps, beaming at the assembled audience.

The first row was taken up by the most important dignitaries, starting with the newly elected Lieutenant Governor, who was accompanied by the obligatory guests of his wife, baby, and administrative assistant. Alongside the Lieutenant Governor's entourage sat the Previous Mayor, his bald head shining in the floodlights. Several government officials, US senators, and representatives filled in the rest of the premium space.

The board of supervisors, most with sheepish expressions on their faces, had been relegated to the second row.

Noted members of the public filled in the rest of the

reserved seating, leaving the journalists and media types to edge into the remaining openings. Hoxton Finn and his ever-present notebook had commandeered a foldout chair on the end of the last row.

And there, a few feet away from the reporter, Monty found his special guests: the niece and her two cats. Isabella, still in her harness, sat politely on the niece's lap, while Rupert rolled over inside the stroller's passenger compartment and yawned sleepily.

Feeling increasingly pleased and confident, Monty gazed up at the balcony overlooking the rotunda. Standing in the shadows, he spied a pair of unlikely janitors, one with thinning white hair and rounded shoulders, the other hulking with a scraggly red beard. Even the Bohemians had sent a delegation, he mused.

Completing his perusal of the crowd, there was one absence Monty was happy to note. As far as he could see, there was no ghost.

It was all he could do to suppress a giggle.

• • •

ISABELLA SCANNED THE audience, conducting her own surveillance of the inauguration area from her seat on her person's lap. Methodically, she filtered through the various humans gathered in the crowd, dismissing them, one by one, until her gaze settled on her target.

The cat's claws extended, reflexively, drawing a muffled wince from her person.

Her eyes had just latched onto Spider's murderer.

Chapter 56

THE BASEMENT

"THAT WAS SOMETHING I never thought I'd see," the niece said as Monty worked the receiving line snaking through City Hall's rotunda.

Isabella murmured in agreement. With the inauguration over, the niece had returned the cat to the stroller's passenger compartment. In the stroller beside his sister, Rupert yawned sleepily. He had slept through most of the ceremony.

The niece shook her head at the implausible scene. Even after witnessing the event firsthand, she still found it hard to believe.

Montgomery Carmichael was now the official mayor of San Francisco.

The man once mocked by all—by some as recently as the start of the inauguration ceremony—stood at the center of political admiration. By coronation, he had been transformed from an object of derision to the focus of those seeking favor. Everyone, it seemed, wanted to be near him: to shake his hand, to share a joke, anything to demonstrate their friendship with San Francisco's newfound wunderkind.

The same supervisors who had whispered disparaging

comments as Monty paraded down the central marble staircase now elbowed one another for the chance to pose next to him in photographs. The newspaper columnists who had derided the day's inauguration as "Mont-apocalypse" each vied for the new mayor's attention, seeking punchy quotes to use in their next byline.

Such was the fickle character of human nature, the niece mused.

She glanced up at the dome, several hundred feet above the rotunda floor, and the arched windows that framed the building's upper walls.

If the dark storm swirling overhead offered any prediction of the future, the adulation would be short-lived.

Monty wrapped an arm around the Lieutenant Governor's shoulders. With his free hand, he raised a triumphant fist as flashbulbs exploded in the air.

"At least he's not letting this go to his head," the niece said with a sigh.

From the stroller, Isabella offered up a concurring *"Mrao."*

HAVING OBSERVED MORE than enough of Monty's moment of glory, the niece turned the stroller toward the front lobby and began making her way out of the rotunda.

She was halfway to the security barriers when the carriage began to shake from a commotion in the passenger compartment. Looking down, she saw that Isabella was stabbing her front paws at the enclosure netting.

Concerned, the woman circled to the side of the stroller and crouched to the ground.

"What seems to be the problem?"

"Wrao," Isabella called out, eying the niece with a stern expression.

"Having issues with Rupert?" she asked, trying to be sympathetic. The orange and white lump curled up beneath the blankets thumped his tail in sleeping rebuke.

"Wrao," Isabella repeated, a sense of frustration in her voice.

Puzzled, the niece glanced around the area where she'd parked the stroller. They were inside the building's front lobby, near the bank of elevators. She studied the labels on the brass fronting. The cars climbed four floors up, stopping along the way at the mayor's office suite—and traveled down one level to the basement.

"Mrao," Isabella remarked, this time encouragingly.

"Not the mayor's office," the niece murmured. "I can't imagine you want to spend any more time with Monty. Plus, I don't need him asking questions about the green takeout box we found at the Rincon Center."

A low growl confirmed that assessment.

"So that leaves the basement," the niece reasoned. "What's in the basement?" she asked—and then answered her own question.

"The office space where the murdered intern used to work," she said softly. "It's not part of our mural quest, but that's where the Previous Mayor found the photo of Oscar standing in front of *City Life*. Maybe we should take a look around, just in case there's anything he missed."

Standing, she grabbed the stroller's handle and steered it toward the elevators.

"Why didn't I think of that?" she muttered to herself.

A predictable response floated up from the stroller.

"Mrao."

MINUTES LATER, THE niece pushed the stroller out of the elevator platform and into City Hall's much quieter basement level. They were stopped only briefly by a patrolling security guard. A flash of the special visitor passes quashed his objection to their wanderings, if not his curious expression.

The niece and the cats had visited City Hall's basement before—although on that occasion, they had been following a trail of frogs. Glancing up and down the empty corridors, the woman couldn't help thinking that she preferred tracking frogs to sleuthing around the murdered intern's workspace.

She wasn't ready to admit she'd seen a ghost in the frog fountain or that a spiritual being had left the footprints at Coit Tower and in her kitchen, but she didn't have a satisfactory alternative explanation for those events either.

Isabella issued her regular navigational instructions as the niece rolled the stroller down the hallway. They passed a long line of locked office doors before reaching an intersection with a narrower passageway.

The niece paused, trying to remember the basement's layout from her previous visit. The walls had been painted since then, and several pieces of new artwork had been hung, making it difficult for her to match the current schematic with the fuzzy one in her memory.

Even Isabella was feeling a little lost. The feline's voice warbled with uncertainty as they rounded yet another corner.

In the end, it was Rupert who alerted them to the unmarked entrance to the area housing the overflow cubicles for the building's lowest-level staffers and interns. His overactive sense of smell apparently picked up on the residual fumes from the endless takeout lunches that had been eaten in the cubicle area.

The niece manned the stroller like a Geiger counter, measuring her progress by gauging the intensity of Rupert's snorkeling sniffs.

"It's a shame we can't patent this technology," she said as she pushed the stroller through the doorway to the cubicle area.

THEY PASSED SEVERAL empty cubicles before they found the one at the far end of the room that had once belonged to Spider.

Set up as a shrine to the fallen intern, it was easy to pick out.

A red bicycle leaned against the cubicle's prefab wall; a matching helmet dangled by its chinstrap from the handlebars. Mementos of the intern's life had been pinned to a pegboard or arrayed on a nearby ledge.

The item that had led Rupert's homing radar through the basement to this location lay on the center of the desk: another grease-stained paper carton that had once held a generous serving of Lick's fried chicken.

Rupert nearly passed out from the rapid intake of air. The niece examined the carton, but found nothing more of note. Its presence was curious, but then, a lot of people had enjoyed the restaurant's fried chicken.

Isabella pushed her head against the netting, trying to see out as the niece explored the rest of the cubicle area.

"I'm sure the police have already been through all this," she murmured as she sifted through an innocuous-looking pile of papers stacked on a shelving unit. The documents appeared to be photocopies of draft legislation from last fall's board meetings. "I don't know what we could possibly find at this point that would be helpful."

Just as she reached the bottom of the stack, Isabella chirped out a warning. Looking up, the woman heard a pair of voices at the room's front entrance.

Instinctively, the niece felt the need to hide. She wasn't doing anything wrong, but the guilt associated with snooping overwhelmed rationality and common sense.

She shoved the stroller into the next empty cubicle and squatted down behind the partition as two men approached Spider's cubicle.

Chapter 57

A SIREN CALL TO THE STOMACH

"I CAN'T BELIEVE you didn't tell the police about this," Hoxton Finn sputtered as the Previous Mayor led him down the open aisle beside the cubicles. "That's cheeky, even for you."

"*You* didn't tell them about the backpack," the PM retorted smoothly. "I'd say we're about even when it comes to *cheek*."

The politician beamed an impish smile. "How's your ex-wife? I hear she's getting hitched again. Did you get an invite?"

"No, I didn't get an invite, but you probably did," Hox sniped as the PM knelt in front of the ventilation shaft. "You'll tell me how it goes, I'm sure."

Snapping his notepad against his left leg, Hox leaned against the cubicle.

"And they're not the same thing—this ventilation closet and the backpack. Not even close. I happened to remember a detail from the night of the murder. You're . . ." Not wanting to characterize the PM's actions in a formal accusation, he merely waved his free hand at the vent.

"Would you like me to call the police right now?" the

Previous Mayor asked indignantly. He leaned away from the vent's grated cover. Sitting on the heels of his wing tips, he reached into his coat pocket for his phone.

He began to press numbers into the display, but Hox wrapped his hand around the phone, blocking the Send button.

"Might as well wait a few more minutes."

"I thought you'd see it that way," the PM said smugly. "Now, help me get this cover off the vent."

As the two men struggled to remove the protective grating, Rupert resumed his snorkeling sounds. The niece unzipped the stroller's passenger compartment and reached inside.

"Shhh," she whispered, stroking his head in an attempt to distract him from the remnant chicken smell from the carton left on Spider's desk.

With a wrenching of metal, the grate fell away from its fittings. The two men looked through the hole at the box of documents in the space beneath the ventilation shaft.

"You think this is related to whatever Spider was carrying in the backpack?" Hox asked, reaching out a hand to page through the file folder tabs. "I wonder if the person who took the backpack knows about this other stash of documents."

The niece thought about the photocopied picture of her uncle she carried in her jacket pocket. If Sam and her uncle had tried to hide something from Spider's research, they might have missed a potentially damaging source of information.

"I looked through this box the other day when the janitor showed it to me," the PM said. "I didn't see anything of interest."

There was a lack of sincerity in the PM's voice that even the niece picked up on. Hox turned his steely gaze away from the ventilation shaft and toward the politician.

But as the pair stared tensely at one another, the niece felt a dreaded tingling inside her nose. The tickle of a sneeze had begun to work its way through her sinuses.

It was a familiar sensation. She experienced regular fits

of sneezing, often several times a day—and always, the release came in a high pitched "Ahh-choo!"

This time was no different.

Wincing, she shut her eyes, afraid to look up over the cubicle partition. The Previous Mayor cleared his throat, a signal that she'd been spotted.

"I'm definitely not cut out for undercover work," she muttered as she stood beside the stroller.

"Hello, Mayor," she said sheepishly.

The reporter scratched his chin, studying her face as if he recognized it. "Aren't you the cat woman from upstairs?"

The Previous Mayor nodded toward Hox and said, "She's Oscar's niece."

The PM froze, realizing his mistake. The words had slipped out of his mouth before he could stop them.

Brow furrowed, Hox quickly made the connection to the name Mabel had given him at the Lieutenant Governor's condo. "Oscar?" he demanded. "Oscar from the antique shop?"

The PM smiled apologetically at the niece.

"We might as well tell him. He'll figure it out anyway."

Turning to Hox, he replied gravely, "I believe you know him as James Lick."

• • •

AS RUPERT WATCHED the interaction between his person, the reporter, and the Previous Mayor, a new smell wafted into the cubicle room, one that instantly triggered his fried chicken sonar.

It was the same scent he'd detected earlier, but from a dish with a far fresher preparation date.

Three days into his involuntary diet, his hunger had grown to ravenous proportions—even after the chicken dish they'd picked up at the Rincon Center.

Rupert knew he shouldn't leave the safety of the stroller's passenger compartment, but the siren call to his stomach was too strong. Without a second thought, he scrambled out of the hole his person had left open in the net cover and scooted at top speed down the hallway toward the door.

Isabella poked her head through the stroller's passenger compartment and considered issuing a warning. Then she spied two familiar figures standing just outside the entrance to the cubicle room.

Silently, she leaped from the stroller and chased after her brother.

Chapter 58

AN AFFINITY FOR CATS

"RUPERT! ISSY!" THE niece exclaimed as soon as she noticed the feline void inside the stroller.

She looked up at Hox and the Previous Mayor.

"Where did they go? Do you see them? They were right here."

The reporter stepped back, seeking to distance himself from the emerging cat crisis. He was allergic to cats—and any form of female panic.

"Hey, don't look at me."

Dropping to her knees, the niece started crawling along the floor, looking inside cubicles and underneath desks and chairs.

The PM watched her for a moment and then began striding up and down the aisle, assisting in the search. Hox stood next to the ventilation shaft, pensively observing.

The PM turned, hands on his hips, and motioned for Hox to help.

"But . . ." the reporter sputtered, visibly uncomfortable. He lowered his voice to ensure the niece wouldn't hear, "I don't even *like* cats."

AFTER HURRIEDLY SEARCHING the cubicle area, the niece rushed out into the hallway. She scanned the empty corridor, trying to keep calm.

"Rupert! Issy!" she hollered as loud as she could. City Hall was a large building in which to lose two cats.

The PM tugged Hox into the hallway.

"Maybe we should split up," he suggested. "They can't have gone far."

Hox looked over the niece's shoulder and pointed.

"What's that over there?"

The niece spun around in time to see Isabella's pink nose peek around the far corner—and then disappear.

She set off at a full sprint down the hallway. The Previous Mayor followed at a quick trot. Hox reluctantly brought up the rear, shaking his head as if he'd rather not be involved in any cat-chasing caper.

The niece reached the end of the corridor, scrambled through the turn, and anxiously peered into the space beyond. Another hallway stretched out before her.

It was empty, save for the same pink nose and orange-tipped ears once more poking around the edge of a distant corner.

"Issy, wait!" the niece called out, to no avail. The cat was gone by the time she reached the second intersection.

The niece was beginning to fear she might never corral her wayward cats, but as she cleared the second corner, she was greeted by a welcome sight. Isabella sat in the middle of the hallway, about twenty yards beyond the turn, placidly tapping the tip of her tail.

This time Isabella waited for her person to catch up. As the niece skidded to a stop beside her, Isabella stood and issued her instructions.

"Mrao," she said, rotating her head toward the opening of a smaller side corridor.

Isabella trotted alongside her person as she hurried the

short distance to where Rupert sat in front of a now-empty paper takeout box. Given the container's strong smell and the fresh smear of grease on the interior walls, the box had, until a few seconds earlier, held a cat-sized serving of fried chicken.

The niece flipped the lid of the green carton over so that she could read the gold text printed on the top.

It was a large looping *O*.

RUPERT BURPED CONTENTEDLY as the niece scooped him up. She returned to the main corridor, kicking the green takeout container to one side before Hox or the Previous Mayor could see it.

"We're over here," she shouted, trying to corral Isabella as she carried Rupert. The cats were too big for her to pick up both of them at the same time.

The niece gave the men a hopeful look. "I need a little help," she said, gesturing that her hands were full.

"I'll go back for the stroller," the PM offered, wisely avoiding the proximity of loose cat hair to his thousand-dollar suit.

"I'll, uh . . ." Hox said, realizing he'd been out maneuvered by the cagy politician.

"Here," the niece said, shoving Rupert at the reporter's chest.

"I'm not really . . . a cat . . . person," he protested as the heavy ball of fur landed in his arms.

Rupert gazed up at the reporter's gruff face, snuggled happily against the front of his jacket, and let out a fried chicken–smelling burp.

"Trust me," the niece replied as she reached down for Isabella, "I've given you the easy one."

Now carrying Isabella, she breezed past him and headed off after the Previous Mayor.

As Hox moved to follow, he caught a sniff of Rupert's fried chicken breath.

Glancing down the side corridor to where the niece had found the cats, the reporter's eyes narrowed at the shadow of the green takeout container, kicked up against the wall.

• • •

WHILE THE NIECE and her cat-chasing assistants were distracted, a man in janitor's coveralls with an overgrown beard and matching red hair wheeled a dolly through the cubicle room toward the open ventilation shaft on the far wall. After swiftly lifting out Spider's banker's box of notes and files, Sam Eckles secured a protective plastic sheeting over the box and strapped it to the dolly's base.

Whistling to himself, Sam rolled the cart out of the room, down a side hallway, and through a service door to the loading dock behind City Hall. A second janitorial imposter waited behind the wheel of the white cargo van, which was backed up to the door, its engine running. The box was quickly loaded into the rear cargo space, along with the dolly, and the van drove off, disappearing into the pouring rain.

THE PREVIOUS MAYOR returned to the cubicle room in time to catch a glimpse of Sam and the box turning for the exit. He stroked his chin for several seconds, thoughtfully considering this development, before fetching the cat stroller.

The Conservatory of Flowers

Chapter 59
THE STAKEOUT

THE TRIO OF the Previous Mayor, Hoxton Finn, and the niece stared at the empty ventilation shaft next to Spider's cubicle.

"*Now* there's no reason to call the police," Hox said sarcastically.

The Previous Mayor attempted to look surprised as the niece tapped her fingers against the stroller handle, silently pondering.

Isabella, of course, knew where the box had gone. She lifted her head proudly as she sat inside the stroller. She had played her part well—in her modest opinion. Although, she reflected, her brother could have shared a bite or two of that tasty snack.

For his part, Rupert lay sprawled across the stroller's passenger compartment, spreading his body as wide as possible in the restricted space. He cared nothing about the missing file box or its contents. He was happily immersed in dreams of fried chicken.

"DO YOU NEED a ride?" Hox asked the niece as the group disbanded.

"Oh, I can catch a cab," she replied, perplexed. The reporter was suddenly far more pleasant than he'd been throughout their entire interaction. "Unless it's stopped raining. Then we'll just walk."

"No," he said. "I insist. It's no problem. The news van will be stopping by to pick me up. Where are you headed?"

"Home to Jackson Square." She glanced down at the stroller. "I'm afraid Rupert is going to need a litter box break before too long."

"Give me a minute to make the arrangements."

Hox stepped into the hallway with his cell phone. He punched the quick dial button and waited impatiently for Humphrey to pick up on the other end of the line.

"I need you to drive the news van over to City Hall," he said as soon as he heard the stylist answer.

"Didn't they have one there to cover the inauguration?" There was a pause as Humphrey walked to the nearest window. "Oh, I see it pulling into the parking spot outside our building right now."

"Great," Hox said brusquely. "Run down there, grab the keys from the afternoon crew, and drive the van back over here."

Humphrey appeared unconvinced.

"Why? Are you afraid you might get your hair wet on the walk back to the office?"

Hox clenched his fist. "Just . . . bring it over here, ASAP. I need you to pick up me and a, uh, friend."

Humphrey's interest was immediately piqued.

"A friend?" he gushed. "What kind of friend? Should I call the paper's gossip columnist?"

"Not if you value your life," Hox spat back. "And it's not that kind of friend." He paused, contemplating his next course of action. "Tell the station we may need the van for a couple of hours."

"But . . ."

"Just do it!"

A HALF HOUR later, Humphrey pulled the news van to a stop outside City Hall's front steps and honked the horn.

"Took you long enough," Hox griped as he ushered the niece to the side cargo door and helped her lift the stroller into the rear seating area. She climbed in next to the cats while Hox slid through the front passenger door.

"Jackson Square," he said sternly to the stylist. "The corner of Jackson and Montgomery."

"I'll be expecting a tip," Humphrey muttered. Then he jumped, startled, as a feline voice piped up from the backseat.

"Mrao."

"YOU CAN STOP here on the right," the niece called up to Humphrey as the news van reached Jackson Street. "I'm the redbrick building in the middle of the block."

Humphrey slowed the van outside the Green Vase antique shop, and Hox hopped out to help lift the cat stroller from the cargo area to the sidewalk.

"Well, uh . . . " the niece said awkwardly. "Thanks again."

"My pleasure," Hox replied with his trademark frown.

"Okay." She wasn't sure what to make of the gruff reporter.

Hox watched as the woman rolled the stroller to the store's front door. She gave him a bewildered wave before disappearing inside.

"Now what?" Humphrey asked as Hox returned to his seat.

"Drive around the corner," Hox instructed tersely.

"And?" Humphrey prodded.

"And we wait."

Humphrey stared out the front windshield.

"Are we on a stakeout?"

Hox thumped the side of his nose, a mocking indicator that Humphrey had guessed correctly. Then he growled out his order, "Well come on then. Don't just sit there. Drive!"

Humphrey shifted the gears and pressed on the gas pedal.

"Sometimes it's hard for me to believe that you're divorced."

Chapter 60

THE SURVEILLANCE VEHICLE

HOX AND HUMPHREY waited for more than an hour in the news van for signs of activity inside the Green Vase antique shop. All the while, the rain continued its nonstop drizzle.

From their parking space in an alley down the street, the pair had an angled view of the store's front entrance. Even after the niece's return, the "Closed" sign remained hanging from the inner side of the glass-paned door.

Despite Hox's persistent stare, the door's decorative iron frame hadn't moved an inch.

"Maybe she's not going anywhere else today," Humphrey suggested with a yawn.

"No," Hox replied curtly. "She's definitely going out. The chicken takeout box was a coded message from her uncle, I'm sure of it. Who else would have stolen the file box while we were running around the basement?" He whacked the dashboard, still irritated at having been duped. "But he wouldn't chance showing up here. She'll have to meet him somewhere else."

"Tell me the story again." Humphrey laughed. "Especially the part where you and the Previous Mayor were chasing a couple of cats through City Hall."

The stylist dodged a head slap from the reporter.

"So this James Lick fried chicken fellow is her uncle Oscar," Humphrey mused. "That's who you think she's meeting?"

"Yes."

"And this Oscar guy is Spider's murderer?"

Hox's steely gaze refused to budge from the Green Vase.

"I'm almost certain of it."

SUDDENLY, A TAXI van swung into Jackson Square and stopped outside the antique shop's redbrick building. The door to the Green Vase opened and the niece pushed the cat stroller onto the sidewalk.

Hox craned forward in his seat, trying to see into the net-covered passenger compartment before the woman hefted the stroller through the van's side door and followed it inside. As the taxi drove off, he leaned back in his chair, confused.

"Why is she taking the cats?"

Humphrey stuck the key into the ignition and started the engine.

"I always bring a feline or two along when I'm meeting hardened criminals. Helps to lighten the mood."

Hox popped his notebook against his left thigh.

"Just drive, Humphrey."

THE NEWS VAN rolled out a safe distance behind the taxi, which was quickly picking up speed. The convoy was soon passing through North Beach, headed toward the Broadway Tunnel.

Hox pressed forward against his seatbelt, urgently feeding information to Humphrey as he navigated through traffic.

"They're turning left up ahead. Get into the other lane."

"No, I was wrong. Her cab was just squeezing around a double-parked vehicle. Shift back to the right."

Gritting his teeth, Humphrey struggled to clear traffic through the van's side mirrors.

"You know, I failed detective driving class at hairdressing school."

Hox's cell phone began to buzz before he could respond.

He glanced at the caller ID and groaned. It was his producer, no doubt wondering why he had absconded with both Humphrey and the news van and when he would be returning both to the office.

After weighing the pros and cons of answering, he punched the transmission button.

"This is Hox."

He winced at the subsequent tirade that poured out of the receiver.

"Let me explain . . ."

The attempt only triggered a more vociferous diatribe from the woman on the other end of the line. Hox grimaced at the producer's foul language. He wouldn't have thought the mother of four had it in her.

Humphrey stole a quick glance over at the passenger seat. He could hardly contain his giggles.

Hox glared at the stylist while he waited for the producer to finish venting. When she finally paused to catch her breath, he spoke as calmly as possible into the phone.

"I understand, Connie, really, I do. But trust me, I'm on a hot lead." He frowned at his own daring before adding, "I'm closing in on Spider's murderer."

The tone of the female voice on the other end of the line slowly transitioned from irate to capitulating. A moment later, Hox hung up and announced with relief, "She's agreed to cover for us."

Humphrey snorted his response. "What do you mean by *us*? You act as if I'm a willing accomplice in this harebrained mission."

"Don't lose the cab," Hox replied curtly.

As they turned onto Van Ness, the news van passed the

wide windows of a car dealership. Humphrey noted the van's reflected image as they drove by—and the bold logo emblazoned on its side.

He shook his head.

"You could have picked a less obvious surveillance vehicle."

• • •

UNBEKNOWNST TO THE van's interior passengers, a third party had hitched a ride on the vehicle by grabbing onto the bumper and the rear door handle.

Balancing his feet on the skateboard, Spider was enjoying the ride of his ghostly life, maneuvering over unexpected bumps and potholes. At one point, he narrowly avoided being squashed by a tailgating Muni bus.

His vaporous figure wasn't visible in the rearview mirror—or any mirror, for that matter. The only indication of his presence was the skateboard, rolling along between the van's rear tires.

Chapter 61

TICKETS FOR TWO CHILDREN

THE TAXI VAN dropped off the niece and her two cats inside Golden Gate Park, as close as the driver could get to the Conservatory of Flowers. The street running in front of the building had been closed to vehicular traffic, so he had to take an alternate route.

After paying the fare, the niece climbed out of the taxi and fished the stroller through the sliding side door.

The rain had once more lessened to a thick mist. The niece snapped shut the front of her jacket, all that she needed to keep herself warm from the dampness.

She adjusted the nylon cover over the stroller's passenger compartment, ensuring her furry companions would stay dry. Rupert burrowed beneath the blankets, not taking any chances with the weather, while Isabella nudged her way to the front, eager to monitor where they were going.

As the niece set off down a side path through the trees, she noticed a news van parked around the corner from where the taxi had stopped. The bright colored logo stood out even through the gloomy weather and her mist-blurred glasses.

She wondered what news story had drawn the van to this

location, but soon dismissed all thought of it. They were probably covering one of the many cultural events that went on in the park, she reasoned. On any given day, the area hosted numerous activities.

The niece pressed on, leaving the protection of the trees for the turnoff to the open yard in front of the conservatory.

A wide tunnel ran beneath the road where she stood. Beyond the tunnel entrance, a landscaped lawn rose to a small hill. A series of flower beds surrounded a wide staircase of stone steps that led up the gentle slope to the conservatory's front entrance.

"Here we go," the niece said, bumping the carriage up the slick stair-step incline. Isabella thrust her head against the net cover, offering concerned guidance and critique. Even Rupert poked his head out of the blankets to make sure they weren't about to tip over.

After a few scary wobbles, the stroller cleared the top step.

"There, we made it," the niece said, masking her relief. "I can't believe you ever doubted me."

She opted to ignore Isabella's reply.

The woman guided the stroller across a paved area with a snack kiosk on one side and a ticket booth on the other. Shushing her two feline passengers, she approached the ticket booth and peered through the grating at the attendant reading a book inside.

"One adult," she said, fishing a twenty-dollar bill through the slot. "And, uh, two children."

Without the slightest glance over the wooden counter to the stroller, the attendant reached a gloved hand into the ticket box and counted out three printed passes.

"Enjoy," she said, sliding the tickets and the change through the window.

The niece turned the stroller toward the conservatory entrance.

"I'm amazed every time this works," she whispered.

From the front of the stroller, Isabella concurred with her own surprise.

"Mrao."

• • •

HOX AND HUMPHREY stood inside the tunnel beneath the main road, watching the niece maneuver the stroller up the concrete stairs.

"What's she doing?" Hox muttered as the woman rolled her charges to the ticket booth.

Humphrey pulled up his coat collar to shield his neck from the water dripping from the tunnel's roof. "Surely they don't allow animals inside."

As the niece rolled the cats into the glass-walled building, Hox stepped out from under the tunnel's cover and began striding toward the steps.

"Come on, Humphrey," he called out. "Don't say I never take you anywhere nice."

Humphrey scampered after the reporter, following him toward the conservatory entrance—leaving behind an empty tunnel save for a skateboard, propped up against one of the moss-covered walls.

Chapter 62

THE GLASS HOUSE

AS THEY LEFT the ticket booth and approached the conservatory entrance, the niece folded up the stroller's nylon covering and slid it underneath the buggy so that Isabella could see out unimpeded.

Together, they looked up at the sixty-foot-high onion-shaped dome that formed the centerpiece of the long rectangular building. A skeleton of wood framing supported the structure's innumerable glass panes. Many of the panels had been frosted with a translucent white paint, presumably to help moderate the inside temperature.

Water dripped down both sides of the glass-paned conservatory: on the outside from the rain, on the inside from the building's artificially generated humidity.

"Try not to be conspicuous," the niece cautioned as she pushed the stroller into the front lobby. Despite the woman's best efforts, Isabella insisted on pushing her head against the passenger compartment's top netting. There was too much to see and smell.

The niece handed over the tickets to another distracted volunteer and slipped the stroller through the doors leading into the central domed area—where they were immediately hit with a wall of humidity.

Isabella murmured in wonder at the sudden atmospheric change. Rupert dug himself out of the blankets, which had become far too warm.

They had entered a man-made rain forest. A jungled mixture of bamboo and other tropical trees grew in the center, their leafy limbs reaching up toward the dome's frosted skylights. At ground level, various forms of moss and lichen covered the sides of moist boulders and many of the rougher tree trunks.

Additional glass-enclosed rooms were attached to either end of the domed center. The niece rolled the stroller down the guided walkway toward the door for the next transition. She noticed a gauge mounted to the side wall, measuring each room's temperature and humidity. Squinting at the dial, she was unable to interpret the readings, but the fog-streaked blur on the opposite side of the glass provided a visual predictor for the conditions in the area labeled "Aquatic Plants."

As the niece propped open the door and pushed the stroller through, an even denser humidity filled in around them. Dew formed on the stroller's nylon sides; moisture condensed on her glasses.

"I feel like we've just stepped into the equator," she murmured.

"Mrao," Isabella concurred.

Rupert shook his body, trying without success to release the wetness from his fur.

• • •

HOXTON FINN GREW increasingly agitated as he watched the niece and her cat-filled stroller enter the conservatory. With Humphrey in tow, he hurried over to the ticket booth.

The attendant looked up from her book as Hox scanned the admission prices.

"How much for just a quick look around?" he asked hopefully.

"Five dollars," she replied dryly. "Each."

Hox pulled out his wallet, thumbed through the bills, and pulled out a single fare. Handing the money through the grate, he said, "One ticket for my friend here. I'll just watch from the outside."

The woman raised a skeptical eyebrow, but didn't comment. She tore off a ticket and slid it through the opening.

Hox handed the paper to the stylist. "You go in and check things out. There's less chance the niece will recognize you."

"That's right," Humphrey said wryly. "I'm not a famous newspaper reporter."

Hox tapped the jacket pocket where he kept his cell phone. "Call me the second you see this James Lick character."

Humphrey gave the reporter a sarcastic grin. "And what does Lick look like, exactly?"

"You'll know him when you see him," Hox replied. He turned the stylist toward the conservatory entrance and gave him a push.

HOX HUDDLED BENEATH the awning of the snack food kiosk as Humphrey proceeded through the front foyer and into the conservatory's main building.

Wiping his forehead, the stylist immediately began unbuttoning his jacket and loosening his collar. He'd had no idea that the building would be so muggy.

Before he could locate the niece and the cat stroller, his cell phone began to ring.

Puzzled, he yanked it from his pocket and held it up to his ear. Hox's voice growled through the speaker.

"What—are you performing a strip tease in there?"

Muttering under his breath, Humphrey terminated the connection.

HOX SOON LEFT the protection of the kiosk's eaves. It was too far away from the conservatory's glass walls for him to monitor the movements inside.

The reporter ambled casually through the falling mist as he positioned himself closer to the main entrance. He tried at first to appear nonchalant, but that effort lasted only a few seconds. There was too much at stake. He had to know what was going on. Cupping his hands over his brow, he stared at the blurry images circulating behind the frosted glass.

With relief, he picked out Humphrey's fogged figure. He watched the stylist make his way through the center domed room toward the doorway leading to the structure's eastern terminus.

The conditions in the next section must have been even more oppressive than the first. Humphrey reacted to the second slap of humidity by removing more layers of clothing. He took off his jacket and folded it over his arm. Unbuttoning his cuffs, he rolled up his shirtsleeves.

Hox spied the niece, standing by the stroller next to a lily pond. Hoping for an update, he dialed the stylist's number again.

Thinking Hox was calling with more mocking commentary, Humphrey raised his phone in the air and pointedly set the ringer to mute.

Cursing, Hox pulled out his wallet and stomped over to the ticket booth.

Chapter 63

BEHIND THE LIME TREE

THE NIECE SCANNED the conservatory's Aquatic Plants room, searching for any sign of her next clue. Her uncle had sent her here for a reason; Sam had confirmed as much in the van ride earlier that day.

Somewhere amid all these plants and flowers, she hoped to find the end of the mural trail—along with information that would explain why her uncle's photograph had been found in the murdered intern's research files, why Oscar and Sam had been seen fleeing the scene of the crime, and, most important, how she could clear them both as suspects.

"Right now, I just don't see it," she said, pivoting in place. She shook her head at the endless rows of greenery and sighed. "Maybe Oscar wants me to take up gardening."

Isabella warbled a dubious response as the niece gazed out over the room, taking a brief inventory of the plant collection.

A lily pond occupied the bulk of the floor space in this wing. It was the anchor for much of the surrounding plant life. Elephant ears, several varieties of ferns, and a tuberous tree bent over the murky water.

Carnivorous pitcher-shaped plants dangled from an artificial canopy suspended from the ceiling. The elaborate ruby-red vessels were rimmed with menacing spines, ready to trap and consume any flies—or fingers—that drifted too close.

Rounding out the mix were a number of exotic orchids. Each plant produced a delicate frill of velvety petals, which surrounded a protruding stamen. The niece was fascinated by the complex color schemes and intricate designs, but she hadn't traveled to the conservatory to stare at flowers.

So far, nothing she'd come across shed any light on her uncle or where she was to proceed next. It was time to explore the rest of the building.

Maybe she'd have better luck in the other wing.

RUPERT HEAVED A sigh of relief as the trio reentered the conservatory's center domed room.

He was not a fan of equator-strength heat and humidity—or, for that matter, extended searches for Uncle Oscar's hidden clues, particularly those that involved riding around all day in the cat stroller.

As the niece steered the carriage through the rear portion of the main room, Rupert joined his sister, pressing his nose against the stroller's net cover. From his feline perspective, the surrounding trees and foliage looked like a fabulously designed litter box . . .

Hold on, Rupert thought. *Who's that?*

He pushed his head as far up as the netting would allow, trying to be sure. Yes, there on the other side of the trees was the man from City Hall who had held him after his fried chicken snack.

Rupert nudged his sister, who had also noticed the spy.

Isabella's blue eyes narrowed with concern.

Why is Hoxton Finn hiding behind a lime tree?

UNAWARE SHE WAS being followed by the reporter and the stylist, the niece continued her search into the conservatory's west wing.

She glanced worriedly at a map she'd picked up at the front entrance. So far, she'd covered over half of the collection, but other than the obvious Lick connection to the overall structure, nothing had stood out as a clue or provided her with further directions. The Labaudt mural at the Beach Chalet had seemed like a clear signal to head to this location, but there were no murals at the conservatory, no New Deal paintings to observe.

"A less persistent person would have given up on this by now," she mused as she pushed the stroller through yet another moist room populated by dense foliage.

She listened for cat commentary from the carriage, but Isabella appeared distracted by something in the building's domed center.

After a quick glance over her shoulder, the niece returned her gaze forward. The dull roar of children's voices sounded from the next room over.

She soon reached a gift shop filled with plastic trinkets and toys, all of them related in some way to flowers, the environment, or conservation. Several children had gathered inside the store to inspect the merchandise, but a far greater number were amassed in the adjoining space, the conservatory's last glass section.

The area contained temporary displays that rotated every four or five months. The current theme featured the Barbary Coast, the San Francisco neighborhood once popular with the wild and raucous Forty-Niners—and a region that encompassed modern-day Jackson Square.

A miniature train circled through the landscaped room, passing by several dollhouse-style buildings fashioned after Gold Rush–era landmarks.

The niece guided the stroller around a pack of excited children, surveying the display. Suddenly, she knew they had found the right place.

"Issy," she said, nearly breathless with excitement. "This is it."

Chapter 64

THE BARBARY COAST

THE NIECE MOVED from station to station along the toy train's route, nudging the stroller through the crowd of boisterous children.

Isabella stretched her head upward, trying to see the displays. She would have been noticed by the surrounding youngsters—had they not been so enthralled with the train and an artificial keg of dynamite that ignited with a massive *boom* every two to three minutes.

Meanwhile, Rupert was nowhere to be seen. After the first fake explosion, he dove beneath the blankets and stayed hidden for the duration of the stroller's tour of the train room.

The niece ignored all of these distractions. She was too focused on the Barbary Coast exhibit to be diverted.

At every turn in the tracks, she found mementos from the past two years. Just like her experiences in Leidesdorff Alley and again at the Rincon Center Post Office, she felt as if she were walking through a timeline, revisiting all of the historical places and events she had investigated since moving into her uncle's antique shop.

She found a miniature replica of San Francisco's Mission

Dolores and, a few feet away, the Palace Hotel. Yet another scale model represented the Montgomery Building, aka Mark Twain's Monkey Block.

Amazed at the intricate details, the niece moved to the next Barbary Coast–themed train station. In the middle of a block of redbrick structures reminiscent of Jackson Square stood a miniature of the one that housed the Green Vase. The resemblance was unmistakable, too specific to be a coincidence. Crenellated iron columns framed a line of tiny windows, each one imprinted with the image of a slender green vase. Peeking through the second-story blinds were two tiny white faces with orange-tipped ears and tails.

"Look, Isabella," the niece whispered. "It's you and Rupert!"

The noise level in the room had gradually subsided during the niece's tour. The majority of the children had filed out, summoned by their parents for the next stop in the day's educational outing.

As the area emptied, Isabella called out a sharp *"Mrao,"* seeking to draw her person's attention to a freestanding structure in the middle of the room.

Fake brick siding surrounded a photo-booth-sized jail cell. Fronting each corner of the little square building was a hitching post with a black-iron horse head mounted to its top.

"I've seen those before," the niece murmured as Isabella let loose a stream of feline chatter. The cat made the connection seconds before her person.

"Leidesdorff Alley," the woman exclaimed as the recollection hit her. "The horse heads are identical to the ones in Leidesdorff Alley . . ." She sighed with exhaustion. "Outside the sandwich shop where Rupert wanted to stop for fried chicken."

Wearily, she grabbed the stroller handle and headed for the exit.

Chapter 65

THE LANGUAGE OF CATS

HUMPHREY TRACKED THE niece through the conservatory to the toy store, trying to look like any other flower-appreciating visitor inside the glass-walled building that day.

So far, the stylist had little to show for his efforts. He feared the tirade that would erupt if he had nothing to report, but he wasn't altogether convinced of Hox's theory. The fried chicken aficionado as assassin idea seemed a bit far-fetched.

Humphrey paused at a rack of flower-themed refrigerator magnets.

"Maybe I'll buy Hox one of these as a peace offering."

Glancing over the rack, he saw the brown-haired woman move into the next room, but he held off an immediate pursuit.

I'd stick out like a sore thumb in the middle of all those kids, he reasoned.

The next fake *boom* from the powder keg, along with the commensurate shrieking of the surrounding children, convinced him he'd made the right decision.

Humphrey waited until the parents began siphoning their

offspring back through the toy store; then he slipped inside the Gold Rush exhibit. Pretending to be as interested in the miniature train setup as the niece and carefully keeping his distance from the stroller, he gradually made his way around the circumference of the room.

After watching the niece stop beside the jailhouse photo booth, Humphrey dropped to his knees and crawled across the floor. Assisted by yet another *boom*, he crept inside the little structure and peeked out its grated window.

The female cat chirped up at her person, releasing a stream of feline commentary. The woman appeared to find the cryptic cat language informative, although for the life of him, he couldn't figure out how.

The chug of the passing toy train masked whatever comment the niece made in response, but the cat seemed to have understood the message—the cat, in fact, seemed to understand English far better than any other animal Humphrey had ever encountered. The knowledgeable feline ducked down into the carriage, bracing for sudden movement as the niece grabbed the stroller handle and barreled toward the door.

Humphrey quickly climbed out of the photo booth. He regained his footing and looked through the glass walls to the center room beyond the toy store—just in time to see Hox dive behind a banana leaf.

Oblivious to the fallen reporter, the woman sped through the central domed area and headed for the exit.

"WHERE'S SHE GOING?" Hox demanded as soon as he pulled himself out of the foliage.

"Don't know." Humphrey shrugged. He reached up to Hox's head and removed a stray fern leaf.

Hox staggered down the walkway, trying to keep the woman in sight. "What did she see in there?"

"Don't know," Humphrey replied, trotting to keep up as he slipped his arms through the sleeves of his jacket.

Hox threw his hands up in exasperation. "Did you get *any* useful information?"

"How about a flower magnet for your refrigerator?" Humphrey said hopefully, offering his purchase.

Hox turned to glare at the stylist. "I don't know why I even brought you along."

Humphrey grinned impishly.

"To keep that dashing hairstyle in place."

• • •

SPIDER LEFT THE reporter and his hapless sidekick to bicker their way back to the news van. They would have to scramble, but he suspected they would figure out a way to follow the niece to her next destination.

He retrieved his skateboard from the tunnel and set off down the park's curving main road. Now that the niece was headed toward her final destination, he had another stop to make.

Unlike the stylist, he had understood every word of the conversation between the woman and the cat.

He knew exactly where they were going.

The sandwich shop in Leidesdorff Alley—it was the place he'd been hoping she would find all along—and the location of the looping letter *O*.

The Murderer

Chapter 66

MAYOR MONTY

WITH THE POST-INAUGURATION meet-and-greet finally winding down, Monty climbed City Hall's central marble staircase to the second floor.

He turned at the top of the steps and gave one last wave to the few bystanders below: a huddle of Japanese tourists who had arrived for the late-afternoon docent tour and the janitorial crew who had begun packing up the folding chairs, the navy and gold bunting, and the decorative rugs.

Neither group returned Monty's wave, but he didn't appear to notice. He paraded along the second-floor hallway that looked out over the rotunda, proudly surveying his new domain. Then he swept into the mayor's office suite, aglow from the platitudes and applause of the swearing-in ceremony.

He strode a preening circle around the plush red-carpeted office, admiring the furnishings. A few pieces of his new furniture had already been delivered. He would have the place completely decorated within a week.

He'd been in the room dozens of times before, both as the last mayor's life coach and more recently for his pre-inauguration interview. Still, the office felt altogether different now that he was actually mayor.

"Who would've thunk it?" he asked, stopping in front of a mirror mounted on the wall beside the massive wooden desk. "Me—the mayor?"

But his glorious expression froze at the ghostly image lurking behind his in the reflection.

"No!" he said sternly. "No, no, no." Spinning around, he shook a bony finger at the apparition. "I forbid you from this office. You're banished. I'm the mayor now. It's all official—they swore me in downstairs today. That should mean something." He leaned forward sternly. "Don't you ghosts have a code of conduct?"

Spider watched with bemusement, a half smile on his translucent face. Then he moved closer to Monty so that their noses were nearly touching and silently mouthed the word *Boo.*

Letting loose a high-pitched shriek, Monty raced across the room. He dove for the door, but Spider nimbly cut him off.

"Ahhhh!" Monty hollered, his panic increasing. His storklike legs goose-stepped over a short coffee table and carried him to the balcony. His fingers rattled the handle to the glass door, trying to release it.

Spider sidled up beside him and threaded his head between Monty and the glass.

"Ahhhh!" Monty screeched again, stumbling over the thick carpet as he scrambled away from the window.

There was only one escape left, one sheltered location. Spider smiled as Monty dove beneath the desk's center console and pulled the chair behind him, an effort to keep the ghost from following.

The apparition faded as Monty's muffled voice sounded through the desk's wood paneling.

"Hey, what's this?"

Monty peered up at the interior facing. A package had been taped to the underside of the desk. With effort, he pried it off. Sitting cross-legged on the floor, he studied the package's outer layer, a plastic shopping bag printed with the label of an unknown grocery store.

"What's this doing in here?" he said with disgust.

For environmental reasons, plastic bags had been banned from the city for several years. Eventually, the associated social stigma had become a more effective deterrent than the prohibiting legislation. No self-respecting San Franciscan would be caught carrying his groceries in a Bay-polluting, sea lion–choking, disposable plastic bag.

But curiosity soon overwhelmed disdain. Opening the bag, Monty removed an inner package: a cloth-wrapped bundle secured with strapping tape.

He retrieved a pair of scissors from the middle desk drawer and used them to cut through the tape.

Setting the scissors on the floor, Monty gingerly lifted the top layer of sheeting—to reveal a sharp bloody object.

"Jiminy jumping Jehosaphat!"

Chapter 67

THE MURDER WEAPON

IT TOOK THE police detective and her crew less than twenty minutes to arrive at Monty's office to retrieve the murder weapon.

"I didn't touch a thing," Monty said, his hands shaking as he held out the rewrapped package. "I mean, not after I realized what it was."

"Why don't you just walk me through this," the detective replied as Monty handed the package to a gloved technician. Another man moved in to take samples from Monty's hands and fingernails. Several others hovered about the office, clicking photographs and swabbing every available surface. "How did you come to find the item strapped beneath your desk?"

Monty sucked in a deep breath and slowly blew it out. "I came back up here after the inauguration."

"Can anyone verify this?" the woman asked sharply. "Was there anyone else in the room with you?"

"Well, yes," he replied after a moment's hesitation. "The ghost."

"The what?"

"The ghost of the murdered intern. Spider's ghost. He's been bugging me for days. Every time I think he's finally left me alone, *bam*, there he is again." He shuddered. "I tell you, it's made me a nervous wreck."

"Why would the intern's ghost be following *you*?" she asked suspiciously.

The technician who had taken the package from Monty called out from the other side of the room. After spreading a plastic sheeting over a side table by the balcony windows, he had carefully removed the package's outer layers.

"Ma'am, you ought to see this."

The detective crossed to the table. Reaching into her jacket pocket, she pulled out a pair of gloves and slipped them over her hands.

With her fingertips, she lifted a long curved item and held it up to the light. Bloodstains covered the weapon's sharp, pronged end.

"This explains why the forensic team has had such a difficult time giving us an accurate sketch of the knife," she said as she examined the detailing. "I don't think I've ever seen a murder weapon quite like this one."

Chapter 68

RETURN TO LEIDESDORFF ALLEY

NIGHT WAS FALLING as a taxi van pulled up at a curb near the entrance to Leidesdorff Alley. A dwindling light filtered through the mist, drifting down into the narrow gaps between the high-rise office buildings in San Francisco's financial district.

Redwood Park framed the opposite side of the street. Past the park's iron gates, the ring of brass frogs frolicked in their fountain, their wet bodies shining in the spotlights trained on the surging water.

The niece pushed open the van's sliding side door and stepped out onto the shadowed pavement. A moment later, she had removed the cat stroller from the rear seating area and paid the driver.

"Let's hope this is the last stop," she said, ruefully thumbing through the few remaining bills in her wallet. "After all of these taxi rides, we're about to run out of cash."

Isabella warbled a weary concurrence.

Her brother, on the other hand, popped his head up from the blankets, perking with more enthusiasm than he'd shown in hours. Loud snorkeling noises immediately began emanating from the carriage.

More fried chicken, Rupert thought with hungry elation—*just in time for dinner!*

As the taxi drove off, the niece steered the stroller into the alley. The unlit passageway blackened as it ran between the buildings, escaping the meager reach of the street lamps, but the lights were still on inside the sandwich shop about a block away.

Gripping the stroller's rear handle, the niece approached the shop's exterior. A row of metal posts marked the edge of the sidewalk. Each one was topped with an iron-forged horse head. She leaned in for a closer inspection, running her hand over the nearest nose. It was exactly the same as the posts she'd seen in the Gold Rush display at Lick's conservatory, replicated right down to the horses' flat nose and the metal ring threaded through the teeth like a bridle.

Then she angled her head to look up at the sign posted above the shop's front entrance, positioned to face the intersecting cross street. She'd missed it when she'd passed by during the daylight hours. The sign's lighting was far more visible in the dusk. The lettering read:

Welcome to O's

"Good grief," the woman muttered. "I must be blind."

"*Wrao,*" Isabella agreed. The cat hadn't forgotten how her person had rudely ignored her alley instructions three days earlier.

For Rupert, however, all was forgiven. He sucked in a deep breath, detecting the faint but unmistakable aroma of his favorite dish. His anticipation growing, he made an optimistic smacking sound with his mouth.

A CUSTOMER WALKED out of the sandwich shop and held the door open for the niece to enter with the stroller. She took a few steps inside and stopped to look around.

A few people ate at the inside tables, but no one manned the front counter. The shop would be closing soon. She suspected the staff members were in the kitchen, cleaning their stations in preparation for the end of day shutdown.

The menu boards mounted to the wall behind the register listed an array of healthy sandwich combinations. It was a complicated ordering process. Each meal was prepared to the customer's exact specifications.

First, patrons chose the bread layer. The shop offered homemade loaves in a range of fiber concentrations. There was the regular array of sourdough, potato, whole wheat, and rye, as well as more esoteric artisan formulations with pumpkin puree, pistachios, and bulgur wheat.

After clearing the bread hurdle, the hungry diner faced an even more daunting selection. The extensive listing of vegetarian and meat fillers dwarfed the number of bread options.

The niece glanced down from the menu board to the stroller. Isabella was trying, without much success, to avoid her brother's frantic movements inside the passenger compartment. Even her offended hiss, which had been used to cow dogs three times her size, had no effect.

"Rupert," the niece said, puzzled as she bent to the stroller. "I don't know what you're going on about. There's no fried chicken in here."

But as she tried to calm Rupert's fried chicken frenzy, an image on the far wall at the rear of the dining area caught her attention. She almost fell over when she saw the portrait hanging there.

Standing, she grabbed the stroller's handle and rolled it toward the picture. Rupert's snorkeling gyrations reached near volcanic proportions as she approached.

It was the painting, she realized, that contained the fried chicken scent that had set off Rupert's bloodhound nose.

The familiar scene was a two-by-six replica of Arnautoff's *City Life* mural.

The niece dropped her gaze to the artist's signature, scrawled in the bottom corner. The writing was obscured, save for the start of the first name.

It was a large looping letter *O*.

Stepping back, she scanned the crowded images painted across the canvas. She recognized the street characters she'd studied while standing in the mural room at Coit Tower, a wide range of busy San Franciscans going about their daily life. She found the street sign marking the intersection of Washington and Montgomery and located the fire truck for squadron number five. Across the upper horizon stretched the mismatched landmarks, the clue that had started her mural-themed odyssey—and originally led her to Leidesdorff Alley.

And suddenly it hit her.

"It's a map," she said excitedly. "It's a map to the location of the tunnel."

The orientation of the landmarks had been intentionally skewed, she realized, to create a map to Leidesdorff Alley—or, more specifically, to the secret tunnel that ran beneath.

As a Bohemian, Arnautoff must have known about the underground passageway that followed the city's original shoreline. The clandestine group had likely used the tunnel to sneak around downtown San Francisco. The road map had been hidden in plain sight, the path revealed as soon as one shifted the street corner's orientation to match that of the landmarks.

The niece paused, reflecting. Who knew how many artistic geniuses had passed through the tunnel entrance in the basement beneath the Green Vase over the years?

Her thoughts turned to the murdered intern. Had Spider realized the painting's significance and its connection to the Green Vase? Had he found the tunnel? Is that why he had collected the picture of her uncle in front of the Coit Tower mural?

Most important, she pondered, how had all of this led to his murder?

She pulled out the photocopy of the original *City Life* mural that the Previous Mayor had given her at the start of her three-day journey. Holding the paper up to the wall, she stared at her uncle's wizened face, and then shifted her attention back to the painting.

It was a near-exact replica—but for two distinct discrepancies.

The first difference was a white blob, tucked amid the pack of pedestrians standing by the newspaper stand and the caricature of Victor Arnautoff.

The blob belonged to an albino alligator, who grinned toothily while being walked on a leash. A collar around the gator's neck gave his name as "Clive."

Clive's white nose pointed toward the painting's second discrepancy, located on the opposite side of the newsstand.

Where the original painting had shown an armed robber holding up a suited businessman, the copy depicted a different crime.

The thief had been replaced by a female figure—a middle-aged woman in a demure blue cardigan, charcoal gray skirt, and sensible-heeled dress shoes.

"She looks familiar," the niece murmured down to Isabella. "Where have I seen her before?"

Just then, Hoxton Finn staggered through the shop's front door. He had left Humphrey the task of finding a parking space for the van and chased the niece down the alley on foot.

He was rumpled from the run, dampened with a mixture of sweat and rain. His left foot throbbed with pain, but he ignored it, pushing through to the far wall, where the niece stood looking up at the painting.

He followed her gaze—and nearly choked at the image.

"It's Mabel," he gasped. "The Lieutenant Governor's assistant."

Together the niece and the reporter stared up at the painting and its visual indictment.

Mabel had reached around her victim, a young dark-skinned intern, to stab him in the chest.

Instead of the robber's gun, she held a blood-soaked knitting needle.

Before either one of them could say another word, Hox's cell phone began to ring.

The news from City Hall was about to break.

• • •

A GHOSTLY FIGURE stood at the entrance to the sandwich shop, surveying the scene with satisfaction. With a last glance at the looping *O* on the painting's bottom corner, Spider returned to the alley.

From the stroller, Isabella watched as his spirit slowly faded, leaving just a whisper in the mist.

Chapter 69

THE NIGHT OF THE MURDER

ABOUT A HUNDRED miles to the east, the State Capitol building was shutting down for the day. Government employees, lobbyists, and politicians packed up their briefcases, readying for their return home.

In the modified closet that served as the Lieutenant Governor's office, a lone figure sat at her desk, tidying a small stack of paperwork.

After the interim mayor's inauguration ceremony earlier that day, the Lieutenant Governor had waved a cheerful good-bye to his trusty assistant. Mabel had returned to Sacramento to squeeze in a few hours of work—and to type out her resignation letter.

She glanced around the tiny bare office, scanning the worn carpeting and the ragged couch pushed against the far wall, giving the room a silent farewell.

The time had come for her departure. A source at City Hall had phoned minutes earlier, relaying the news that the police had swarmed the mayor's office suite. Rumors were circulating throughout the building that there'd been a case-breaking development in the Spider Jones murder.

Mabel reached for her purse and carefully tucked her knitting inside. She knew what the police had found in the office.

As she zipped the bag closed, she recalled the night she discovered Spider Jones slain at the top of the central marble staircase—or rather, she recalled the night she murdered him.

AS SHE'D TOLD the police, Mabel had stopped by her office after the board of supervisors meeting and logged on to her computer. She'd sent a few e-mails about the interim mayor results and had checked on a couple of apartment websites for her upcoming move to Sacramento.

But there were a few details about that evening that she had withheld from the investigators.

She was about to close up for the night when she'd noticed one of her file drawers slightly ajar. Puzzled, she'd pulled it open and scanned the contents. Several personnel files were missing. She quickly compiled a list—each missing file belonged to one of the mayor's previous interns.

Spider, she'd thought suspiciously, *what have you gotten into?*

Leaving her computer turned on and logged in to the Internet, she'd taken the elevator downstairs to the basement.

Quietly entering the cubicle room, she'd crept toward Spider's desk. As expected, she found him bent over yet another secretive pile of documents. It was an activity that had been troubling her for the past few weeks.

The intern's preoccupation with the Coit Tower mural and its road map to the Leidesdorff tunnel had been a relatively harmless pursuit—although she imagined Oscar would have preferred not to have that secret revealed to the general public.

But recently, she'd sensed Spider had switched his investigative efforts to a different topic. He'd started to look at her a little differently. There was a wary caution in his eyes. The missing files from her desk had confirmed her hunch.

Hiding behind the row of cubicles, Mabel heard Spider's cell phone ring. She eavesdropped on his conversation with the Previous Mayor, listening with increasing panic as he promised to share the results of his latest research with the seasoned politician.

She believed Spider's new project, the one he was about to divulge to his mentor, concerned a rash of disappearances among the outgoing mayor's former interns.

That was when she knew he would become her next victim.

HURRYING BACK TO the main hallway, Mabel found a janitor and asked him to deliver a note to the young man in the basement cubicle. Hastily scrawled but designed to read as if it were from the Previous Mayor, the message summoned Spider to a meeting in the ceremonial rotunda at the top of the central marble staircase.

Mabel then raced back to the mayor's office suite and grabbed her knitting needles from her purse.

She'd found the unique weaponry in an antique shop in Jackson Square. Fashioned during the Gold Rush days, the hidden knifepoint was concealed within the needle's rounded tip. Meant to provide its owner with a sense of security on the rough-and-rowdy streets of the Barbary Coast, the knifed needle had become her instrument of choice, and she'd purchased several pair. The rounded metal rods were easy to hold and provided the perfect leverage for reaching around a victim and stabbing him in the chest—that is, if you were into that sort of thing.

Needles in hand, Mabel strode silently to the ceremonial rotunda. She knelt behind the Harvey Milk bust and hid just before Hoxton Finn strode past.

Then she waited for the intern.

She heard Spider's rubber-soled tennis shoes squeak against the marble steps, watched as his tall shadow summited the stairs, and prepared to make her move.

Perhaps sensing the danger, Spider glanced apprehensively around the ceremonial rotunda, but he was no match for the stealth attack of the skilled assassin.

With a few jabs of her blade, Mabel silenced the inquisitive intern forever.

Chapter 70

A PECULIAR HOBBY

IT WAS A new experience for Mabel, killing out in the open in such a public space. There was an operatic quality to the act, a drama that she hadn't expected.

Over the years, she had disposed of many an intern, but never in so brazen a manner. She typically chose quiet, out-of-the-way locations, places where the bodies could discreetly decay without discovery. No one had ever questioned the disappearance of her victims. The interns were a disposable lot, their sudden absence readily explained away.

It was a hobby of sorts, like knitting.

But this time was different. Killing out of necessity, spontaneously and without her regular meticulous planning, had been both terrifying and invigorating.

Never had she taken so many risks or left so many loose ends dangling.

First, there was the matter of witnesses.

No sooner had Spider sputtered his last breath than Mabel heard a sound from the far side of the ceremonial rotunda.

Scampering into the darkness, she'd watched from the

shadows as Sam and Oscar rushed up to the dead body. Oscar pressed two fingers against the young man's neck, but the expression on his face indicated he didn't find a pulse.

Then he turned to the backpack. Carefully stepping around the pools of blood, he crouched over the pack, unzipped its main compartment, and thumbed through the contents. With a nod to Sam, he picked up the pack and the two disappeared into a side hallway. Moments later, Mabel saw them race out the front lobby.

The pair vanished the next day, leaving town, or so she'd heard, for a remote campsite in the Sonoma woods. It was maddening, her frustration at being unable to eliminate these potentially incriminating bystanders.

She should have taken care of them that night in the rotunda, she'd told herself over and over since the event. She'd been thrown by their sudden appearance and hadn't had time to think.

The janitor who'd given Spider the note to meet in the ceremonial rotunda had been simple enough to negate, but Oscar and Sam had proved far more elusive targets.

She smiled down at her purse. She would hunt them down. They were still on her list.

MABEL'S NEXT PRESSING issue was the murder weapon.

She'd only meant to hide the sharp-edged knitting needles under the mayor's desk for a short while, but the movers had shown up for his belongings early the next day. With so many people milling about, there'd been no opportunity for her to sneak in unobserved.

She'd hoped the desk would be transported to the new office in Sacramento, but unfortunately, it was part of the room's permanent furniture.

The package with the bloody knitting needles had remained taped beneath the mayor's desk, waiting for a moment of safe retrieval—one that never came.

For the last two months, Mabel had been a nervous

wreck. Any day now, someone might stumble across the package. Or it might never be discovered. There was no way for her to know.

In a way, the phone call alerting her to the police presence in the mayor's office suite had been a relief. The wait was over. She'd had plenty of time to prepare her backup plan. All that was left was the implementation.

Sirens wailed in the background as Mabel stood from her desk, slipped her purse over her arm, turned off the light, and locked the door.

Her sensible-heeled shoes tapped smartly across the pavement as she walked out of the Capitol Building and disappeared into the misty Sacramento night.

It would be her last sighting for several months.

Chapter 71

A LONG TIME COMING

BACK IN SAN FRANCISCO, a beat-up van rumbled onto the Golden Gate Bridge, heading west toward Sausalito. The lone human occupant was the van's driver, redheaded Sam Eckles. In the passenger seat sat two domesticated frogs, both admiring the scenic view.

After a careful perusal and purging of any Oscar- or tunnel-related documents, the box from the ventilation shaft and its remaining contents had been dropped off with an anonymous letter at the police department. The submitted files related to a number of Bay Area residents who had gone missing over a ten-year period—each one had once worked as an intern for the present Lieutenant Governor.

As the van reached the end of the bridge, Sam glanced over his shoulder at the rear cargo area.

There on the metal floor rode several paper bags filled with the shredded remains of the purged documents as well as the contents of Spider's backpack.

The documents Spider had planned to share with the Previous Mayor had related solely to the man who had once run the Green Vase antique shop, the secret tunnel entrance beneath that building, and the curious map the intern had discovered in one of Coit Tower's New Deal–era murals.

Spider's missing persons project had been a work in progress, no more than a passing curiosity. He hadn't been able to determine if the past interns were missing or just un-locatable.

He certainly hadn't suspected Mabel of being a murderess.

• • •

AFTER SEVERAL HOURS covering the chaotic scene at City Hall, Hoxton Finn returned to the third-floor conference room inside the newspaper's Mission Street office.

With a wide sweeping motion, he cleared all of the files and documents off the table. He was ready to reorganize and restart his investigation from scratch.

This time, his analytical skills would be keenly focused on the Lieutenant Governor's fleeing administrative assistant, the mysterious Uncle Oscar (aka James Lick), and the brown-haired woman now running the Green Vase antique shop.

• • •

INSIDE A RUN-DOWN Victorian in San Francisco's Nob Hill neighborhood, a motley group gathered in a galley-style kitchen, discussing how best to cope with their leader's unforeseen illness.

The hushed whispers carried through to the living room, where the invalid lay on the couch, pale and fragile, his breathing labored.

"He needs to see a doctor," Dilla insisted, wringing her hands.

"But not one in San Francisco," Harold cautioned. "They'd have to report him."

No longer the prime suspects in the intern's murder, Oscar and Sam were both still wanted for questioning. The Bohemians had reached a general consensus that a police interview might expose too many sensitive lines of inquiry.

Sam was en route to a Sausalito houseboat, where he could hole up for several weeks, but Oscar was unfit for travel.

A grizzled voice spoke from the couch.

"I'm not going anywhere. Not to a doctor. Not to the police station. And not out of town."

Turning toward the doorway, the kitchen crowd squeezed through to the living room as the invalid propped himself up on the couch cushions.

"This"—he said with a cough—"has been a long time coming."

Dilla rushed around to plump up the pillows. "Don't you think we should get you to a hospital?" she urged in a motherly voice.

"I'm done with doctors, Dilla," he replied, resolution in his feeble voice. "And I'm done running. San Francisco is my home. I won't be leaving it again."

Oscar placed his hands on his chest, indicating that the matter was settled.

He rested his head back on the cushions, reflecting on the niece and her mural journey through the images from their past adventures. It had been a pleasant way to reminisce, despite the grim matter of revealing Spider's murderer.

Then he gathered his breath.

"Whatever time I have left, I'll spend it here in the city." He gummed his dentures, thoughtfully sliding them around in his mouth before adding, "I think this is where we'll find Mabel."

Chapter 72

UNBURDENED

THE NEXT DAY, the Previous Mayor climbed aboard the BART train in San Francisco and rode the main line about ten miles south. He sat silently on the bench seat, wearing his very best suit and tie paired with his favorite two-toned leather wing tips. He wanted to look his best, as a sign of respect for his departed friend.

He carried with him a simple arrangement of flowers, a spring mix, the pastel colors a sign of hope and renewal.

Exiting the train at the Colma station, the PM slowly walked through the commuter parking lot toward the acres of the surrounding cemetery.

The sun glinted off the polished headstones, row upon row of engraved names, dates, and endearments.

Checking a map he'd found online, the PM followed an asphalt path into the maze of graves until he located the one he'd come to visit. Standing at the foot of the plot, he removed his hat and placed the flowers in front of a grave labeled:

Spider Jones, beloved son and brother

As he stared down at the fresh grass, the PM felt an overwhelming sense of peace. He smiled with the knowledge that Spider had finally handed over the worries of this world and departed, unburdened, for the next.

Then he spied an object resting beneath a nearby tree, next to the edge of the main path.

Curious, the PM crossed to the trunk and bent to find a discarded skateboard. He picked it up, his smile deepening with warmth.

Setting the wheels on the asphalt, he placed one wing tip on top of the board and tentatively shifted his weight onto the rolling platform.

Balancing precariously, he began wobbling slowly toward the parking lot.

Chapter 73

HOW TO PAINT A CAT

A WEEK TO the day after her first portrait-posing experience, the niece found herself back in the Green Vase showroom, seated once more on the leather dentist recliner, staring at the rear side of an easel. Rupert dozed happily on her lap as the charcoal pencil scraped against the textured paper.

"What do you think, Issy?" Monty asked, stepping back from the easel and tapping the tip of the charcoal stick against his chin.

The cat studied the image, tilting her head first one way and then another. After a careful analysis, she waved a paw in the air and issued her assessment.

"Mrao."

"I agree," Monty replied. "It's time for you to get into the picture."

Hopping down from the stool beside the easel, Isabella joined her person and brother on the recliner.

She assumed her pose, her piercing blue eyes staring at the artist as he began, once more, to scribble on the sketchpad.

"So, I've got an opening at City Hall," Monty said, his

face hidden behind the easel. "I need to find a receptionist for the mayor's office."

"How about Dilla?" the niece replied. She inched to one side, trying not to crowd Isabella off the recliner's seat.

"Not available," Monty said. "She's gone up to Sacramento to fill in at the Lieutenant Governor's office. Mabel gave notice the other day." He made a dismissive gesture with the pencil. "Walked out just like that."

The niece stroked Rupert's furry chest, reflecting. Mabel had vanished shortly after the discovery of the bloody knitting needles in the package taped beneath the mayor's desk. She'd last been seen leaving the Capitol Building in Sacramento, but at this point, the niece reasoned, she could be anywhere.

"I have another candidate in mind." Monty popped his head over the top of the easel and pumped his eyebrows at the niece. "I thought *you* might be interested."

"No." The niece meted out her reflexive response.

With an exaggerated shrug, Monty returned to the sketch.

"Whatever you say." Then he looked up with a wink. "But according to Dilla, your uncle suggested you would be an excellent candidate."

Cringing, the niece tried to imagine herself at Monty's beck and call, all the while sitting at the desk once used by Spider's murderer.

"I think I might be sick," she murmured to herself.

But then she reconsidered.

What better way to figure out where Mabel might be hiding than to study the place where the woman had spent the last several years? Perhaps a few short weeks might be worthwhile, so long as Monty was given strict guidelines as to the limits of her participation.

She wondered how many days she could serve as the interim mayor's assistant before herself turning to homicide.

Monty resumed his charcoal scraping.

"You know, one of my very first art lessons was how to paint a cat . . ."

When is a white alligator a red herring?

From *New York Times* Bestselling Author

REBECCA M. HALE

HOW TO TAIL A CAT

A Cats and Curios Mystery

An albino alligator on the loose in San Francisco is pretty darn exciting, but my cats and I are investigating the mysterious Steinhart brothers, the 1900s-era benefactors who provided the original funding for Clive the alligator's aquarium.

In the media circus surrounding Clive, one clown—our own aspiring mayor, Montgomery Carmichael—gets a little too close to the renegade alligator. We'd hate to see Monty meet an undignified end, but we're on a hunt of our own—for Uncle Oscar's latest treasure. Assuming, of course, that the whole thing isn't a crock…

PRAISE FOR THE CATS AND CURIOS MYSTERIES

"Will delight mystery readers and elicit a purr from those who obey cats."

—Carolyn Hart, author of *Ghost Gone Wild*

"This exciting road trip goes from danger to humor and back." ***—Genre Go Round Reviews***

howtowashacat.com
facebook.com/Rebecca.M.Hale.author
facebook.com/TheCrimeSceneBooks
penguin.com

M1386T0913

"[A] wild, refreshing over-the-top-of-Nob-Hill thriller."

—The Best Reviews

THE *NEW YORK TIMES* BESTSELLING SERIES FROM

· Rebecca M. Hale ·

HOW TO MOON A CAT

A Cats and Curios Mystery

When Rupert the cat sniffs out a dusty green vase with a toy bear inside, his owner has no doubt this is another of her Uncle Oscar's infamous clues to one of his valuable hidden treasures. Eager to put together the pieces of the puzzle, she's soon heading to Nevada City with her two cats, having no idea that this road trip will put her life in danger.

facebook.com/TheCrimeSceneBooks
penguin.com
howtowashacat.com

M978T0911

FROM *NEW YORK TIMES* BESTSELLING AUTHOR

·Rebecca M. Hale·

NINE LIVES LAST FOREVER

"Follow the frogs . . ."

My cats, Rupert and Isabella, didn't need a note telling *them* to follow the frogs. When the green intruders first began appearing in the antiques shop I had inherited from my Uncle Oscar, my feline friends instantly gave chase. But why were frogs also turning up in San Francisco's City Hall building? And what did my late uncle's mysterious note to follow them mean?

Before long I was caught up in the chase myself, along with a crazy crew of my uncle's oddball friends—as well as his oldest enemy, a master of disguise. With rumors of hidden gold, political conspiracies, faked deaths, and cold-blooded betrayal in the air, I had to try hard not to leap to any conclusions until my kitties and I uncovered the truth, warts and all . . .

penguin.com

M841T0211